One

Evening

in

Paris

ALSO BY NICOLAS BARREAU

The Ingredients of Love

One

Evening

in

Paris

································

Nicolas Barreau

TRANSLATED BY BILL McCANN

St. Martin's Griffin
New York

ONE EVENING IN PARIS. Copyright © 2012 by Nicolas Barreau. English translation copyright © 2014 by Bill McCann. All rights reserved. Printed in the United States of America. For information, address St. Martin's Press, 175 Fifth Avenue, New York, N.Y. 10010.

www.stmartins.com

Library of Congress Cataloging-in-Publication Data

Barreau, Nicolas, 1980–
    [Abends in Paris. English]
    One evening in Paris / Nicolas Barreau.—First U.S. Edition.
      p. cm.
    First published in Germany by Thiele Verlag under the tittle Eines Abends in Paris—T.p. verso
    ISBN 978-1-250-04312-2 (trade paperback)
    ISBN 978-1-4668-4122-2 (e-book)
    1. Theaters—France—Paris—Fiction.   2. Man-woman relationships—Fiction.   3. Dinners and dining—Fiction.   4. Missing persons—Fiction.
I. Title.
PT2702.A757A2413 2014
833'.92—dc23

                                 2014000137

St. Martin's Griffin books may be purchased for educational, business, or promotional use. For information on bulk purchases, please contact Macmillan Corporate and Premium Sales Department at 1-800-221-7945, extension 5442, or write specialmarkets@macmillan.com.

First published as *Eines Abends in Paris* by Thiele Verlag in Germany

First U.S. Edition: July 2014

10 9 8 7 6 5 4 3 2

Whatever you end up doing, love it.

—FROM *CINEMA PARADISO*

One

....

One evening in Paris—it was about a year after the Cinéma Paradis had reopened and exactly two days after I had kissed the girl in the red coat for the first time and was on tenterhooks in expectation of our next meeting—something incredible happened. Something that was to turn my whole life upside down and turn my little cinema into a magic place—a place where yearnings and memories came together, where dreams could suddenly come true.

From one moment to the next, I became part of a story more beautiful than any film could invent. I, Alain Bonnard, was dragged out of my workaday rut and catapulted into the greatest adventure of my life.

"You're periphery, man, an observer who prefers to stand on the sidelines watching what's going on," Robert said to me once. "But don't worry about it."

Robert is, first, my friend. And second, he's an astrophysicist and gets on everyone's nerves by applying the laws of astrophysics to everyday life.

But all at once I was no longer an observer; I was caught up in the middle of this turbulent, unexpected, confusing series of events that took my breath—and occasionally my senses—away. Fate had offered me a gift; overwhelmed, I had accepted it, and in so doing almost lost the woman I loved.

That evening, however, when I stepped out after the last showing into the dim reflected light of a lantern on the rain-drenched street, I had no inkling of all that was to happen. And I was also unaware that the Cinéma Paradis held the key to a mystery on which my whole happiness depended.

I lowered the shutters to lock up, stretched, and breathed in deeply. The rain had stopped—just a brief shower. The air was soft and springlike. I turned up the collar of my jacket and turned to leave. It was only then that I noticed the weedy little man in the trench coat standing there in the semidarkness with his blond companion, inspecting the cinema with interest.

"Hi," he said in an unmistakably American accent. "Are you the owner of this cinema? Great film, by the way." He pointed to the showcase, his gaze lingering on the black-and-white poster for *The Artist,* whose old-fashioned lack of sound had been completely mind-blowing, especially for the inhabitants of the modern world.

I gave a curt nod and was convinced that he was going to thrust a camera into my hand and ask me to take a picture of him and his wife in front of my cinema, which, though admittedly not the oldest in Paris, is nevertheless one of those little old plush-seated cinemas that are today threatened with extinction. Then the little man took a step closer and gave me a friendly look through his horn-rimmed glasses. Right away, I got the feeling that I knew him, but I could not have said where from.

"We'd like to have a chat with you, Monsieur . . ."

"Bonnard," I said. "Alain Bonnard."

He reached out his hand to me, and I shook it in a state of some confusion.

"Have we met?"

"No, no, I don't think so."

"Anyway . . . nice to meet you, Monsieur Bonnard. I'm—"

"You're not related to *the* Bonnard are you? The painter?" The blonde had come forward out of the shadow and was looking at me with amusement in her blue eyes. I had definitely seen that face before. Many, many times. It took a couple of seconds until I caught on. And even before the American in the beige trench coat had finished his sentence, I knew who was standing before me.

No one could hold it against me for opening my eyes wide and letting the bunch of keys fall from my hand. The whole scene was—in the words of the shy bookseller from *Notting Hill*—"surreal but nice." Only the sound of the keys rattling as they hit the sidewalk convinced me that all this was really happening. No matter how unlikely it actually was.

Two

....

Even as a child, the nicest afternoons were those I spent with Uncle Bernard. While my schoolmates were arranging soccer games, listening to music, or pulling the braids of pretty little girls, I ran down the rue Bonaparte until I was within sight of the Seine, turned two corners, and saw the little street in front of me where stood the house of my dreams: the Cinéma Paradis.

Uncle Bernard was something like the black sheep of the Bonnard family, as nearly everyone else worked in legal or administrative jobs. He was the proprietor of a cinéma d'art, a little picture house, and did nothing but watch films and show them to the public, even though the family all knew films were good for nothing but putting silly ideas into people's heads.

No, that was hardly respectable! My parents found my friendship with my unconventional uncle—who was not married and had taken part together with rioting students and famous filmmakers like François Truffaut in the demonstrations during the Paris spring of 1968 against the closure of the Cinématèque française by the minister of culture and sometimes even spent the night on the battered old sofa in the projection room—somewhat disconcerting. But since I was good at school and caused no problems in any other way, they let me go my own way. They were probably hoping that my "cinematic craze" would come to an end of its own accord.

I had no such hopes. Just above the Paradis's old-fashioned ticket booth hung a poster with the heads of all the great directors, and underneath it was the slogan *Le rêve est réalité*, "The dream is reality." I really liked that. And the fact that the inventor of film was a Frenchman named Louis Lumière delighted me.

"Gosh, Uncle Bernard!" I shouted, clapping my hands in childish enthusiasm, "The man brought the light to the screen and that's his name—Lumière—that's just great!"

Uncle Bernard laughed and carefully loaded one of the big reels of film that they still used in every cinema at that time, and which linked thousands of individual moments into a great big wonderful whole as they ran through the projector. In my eyes, that was pure magic.

I was really deeply grateful to Monsieur Lumière for the invention of cinematography, and I believe I was the only one in my class who knew that the very first film—only a few seconds long—shows a train arriving in the station at La Ciotat, and that French cinema was in the depths of its soul a truly impressionist cinema, as Uncle Bernard assured me. I had no idea what *impressionist* meant, but I was sure it must be something wonderful.

A little later, when Madame Baland, the art teacher, took our class to the Jeu de Paume, where the Impressionist paintings were still exhibited before they were moved to the old train station at the quai d'Orsay, I found among the delicately dotted, light-flooded landscapes a picture of a black locomotive puffing out white steam as it drew into a station. I looked at that painting for a long time, and believed that I now knew why French cinema was called "impressionist": It had something to do with the arrival of trains.

Uncle Bernard raised his eyebrows in amusement as I explained my theory to him, but he was too good-natured to correct me. Instead, he taught me how to work the film projector, and that you also have to be hellish careful that the celluloid strip doesn't stick over the lamp for too long.

Once, when we watched the movie *Cinema Paradiso* together, I began to understand why this Italian classic was one of my uncle's favorite films—perhaps he had even named his cinema after it, even though it wasn't a French film with an impressionist soul. "Not bad for an Italian movie, is it? *Pas mal, hein?*" he growled in his grumpy patriotic manner, even though he could hardly hide the fact that he was moved. "Yes, you have to admit that even the Italians are quite capable."

I nodded, though I was still completely shattered by the tragic fate of the old projectionist who is blinded by a fire in his cinema. Of course, I saw myself in young Toto, even if my mother never hit me because I'd spent my money on going to the movies. And I didn't have to, either, because I was able to watch the greatest films for nothing, even those that were not quite suitable for an eleven-year-old boy.

Uncle Bernard didn't care about age restrictions, as long as it was a "good" film. And a good film was a film that had an idea; a film that moved people; a film that worked with them in the difficult task of "being"; a film that gave them a dream to take with them, a dream they could hold on to in this life, which is not always so easy.

Cocteau, Truffaut, Godard, Sautet, Chabrol, Malle—for me, they were just like the people next door.

I crossed my fingers for the small-time crook in *Breathless;* like Orphée, I put on fine gloves and parted mirrors so that I could step through them to rescue Euridice from the underworld; I marveled at the unearthly beauty of Belle in *Beauty and the Beast* as she climbed the stairs with her waist-length blond hair and the flickering five-armed candelabrum, followed by the despondent monster; and I shared the fear of the Jewish theater director Lucas Steiner in *The Last Métro* as he hid in a cellar beneath his theater, forced to listen to his wife falling in love with a fellow actor on the stage above him. I yelled with the boys in *War of the Buttons* as they beat one another up. I suffered with the distraught Baptiste in *Children of Paradise* as he lost his beloved Garance forever in the crowd; was deeply shocked when Fanny Ardant shot first her lover and then herself in the head at the end of *The Woman Next Door;* found Zazie in *Zazie in the Métro* rather weird with her big eyes and that wide gap between her front teeth; and laughed at the Marx Brothers in the opera and all the snappy repartee of the quarrelsome couples in comedies by Billy Wilder, Ernst Lubitsch, and Preston Sturgis, whom Uncle Bernard simply called *"les Américains."* Preston Sturgis, Uncle Bernard once explained to me, had even defined the golden rules of film comedy: A chase is better than a conversation, a bedroom is better than a living room, and an arrival is better than a departure. I still remember those rules of comedy.

Les Américains were not, of course, as impressionistic as "we French," but they were extremely funny and their dialogue was very witty—unlike that in French films, where you often felt like someone eavesdropping on long-winded debates taking place on the street, in a café, at the seaside, or in bed.

You could say that at thirteen I already knew a great deal about life, even if I hadn't had a great deal of personal experience of it. All my friends had already kissed a girl—I dreamed about the lovely Eva Marie Saint, whom I'd just seen in a Hitchcock thriller. Or about the girl from *Forbidden Games,* with her aura of light as she creates a private world in the midst of the horrors of World War II with her friend Michel and puts up crosses for dead animals in a secret cemetery.

Marie-Claire, a girl from our school, reminded me of the little heroine of *Forbidden Games,* and one day I invited her to an afternoon performance in my uncle's cinema. I've actually forgotten what was showing that day, but I know that we held sweaty hands throughout the whole film, and I didn't let go even when my nose began to itch intolerably.

As the titles flickered over the screen, she pressed her cherry red lips firmly to mine, and in all our childish innocence we became a couple—until the end of the school year came and she moved with her parents to another town, one which by grown-up standards wasn't far from Paris but, for a boy of my age, seemed like the end of the world, and therefore unreachable. After a few weeks of deepest grief, I decided that I would later honor our tragic history by making a film of it.

Of course, I wanted to become a famous director one day. And, of course, I didn't. I gave in to pressure from my father, studied business, because with that "you can always make something of yourself," and worked for some years in a big firm in Lyon that specialized in exporting luxury bathtubs and expensive bathroom fittings. Although I was young, I earned a lot of money. My parents were proud that their unworldly son had turned out well after all. I bought an old Citroën with an open roof and had real girlfriends. After a while, they all left me, disappointed that I turned out not to be the go-getter they'd obviously thought I was at first.

I wasn't unhappy, and I wasn't happy, but when I got a letter from Uncle Bernard one hot, humid summer afternoon, I knew at once that everything was going to change, and that deep down inside I was still the dreamer who had sat with throbbing heart in the darkness of a small cinema, immersing myself in new worlds.

Something had happened that no one would have thought possible. Uncle Bernard, who was by now seventy-three, had met the woman of his dreams and wanted to go and live with her on the Côte d'Azur, where it is warm all year round and the landscape is soaked in a very special light. I felt a little stab in my heart as I read that he intended to give up the Cinéma Paradis. In his clumsy handwriting, it said:

> *Since I got to know Claudine, I've had the feeling that a film projector has been standing between me and real life.*
> *So for the years that are left to me I want to play the starring role myself. Still, it does make me unhappy to think that the place where we spent so many wonderful afternoons together will probably be turned into a restaurant or one of those newfangled clubs.*

My stomach turned over at the thought that the old cinema might be altered like that. And when, at the end of his letter,

Uncle Bernard asked me if I could possibly find it in myself to come back to Paris and take over the Cinéma Paradis, I sighed almost with relief.

Even if you're leading a completely new life now, my boy, you're the only one I could imagine as my successor. Even as a child, you had a mania for the cinema and an excellent nose for a good film.

I had to smile when I thought of Uncle Bernard's emphatic lectures in the old days, and then I scanned the final lines of his letter. Long after I had read them, I stared at the paper, which had begun to tremble in my hands and then seemed to open with a rent like Orphée's mirror.

Do you remember, Alain, asking me why you loved films more than anything? I'll tell you now: The shortest path leads from the eye to the heart. Never forget that, my boy.

Six months later, I was standing on the platform in the Gare de Lyon in Paris, where all the trains to the south depart, waving good-bye to Uncle Bernard as he disappeared in the distance with his sweetheart, a delightful little lady with loads of laughter lines. I waved until I could only just make out his white handkerchief fluttering adventurously in the wind. Then I took a taxi back to the most important place of my childhood, the Cinéma Paradis, which now belonged to me.

Three

....

In times like these, it's not easy to run a small art-house cinema—I mean one that tries to survive on the quality of its films and not from advertising revenue, huge buckets of popcorn, and Coca-Cola. Most people have lost the ability to watch carefully; to just abandon themselves for two hours to the important things of life, be they serious or amusing; to let themselves go without eating, drinking, chewing, and slurping through giant straws.

After my return to Paris, I once went to one of the big multiplex cinemas on the Champs-Elysées. There it became clear to me that my idea of the cinema and the need to show it a certain degree of respect was possibly a bit anachronistic. I remember that although I had only just turned thirty-nine, I felt totally outdated and out of place among all the babble and rustling around me. It's no wonder that films today are getting ever louder and faster: All those big Hollywood blockbusters and action films, which have to attract millions in Europe as well, need to drown out all the noise in that kind of cinema, and counteract the increasing lack of concentration in the audience by continually providing new attractions.

"You don't have popcorn here?" is a question that is repeatedly asked in my cinema. Only last week, a chubby little boy dangled from the hand of his mother, whining because the idea of spending a couple of hours in a seat watching *Little Nicky* without having anything to stuff in his mouth was obviously totally unheard of. *"No popcorn?"* he repeated in desperation, twisting his neck in search of the counter where it would be sold.

I shook my head. "No, we only have films here." Even if this answer always gives me a little glow of triumph, I sometimes worry about my cinema's future.

After my return from Lyon, I'd invested a little money in restoring the Cinéma Paradis. The crumbling facade had been repaired and repainted, the old carpet renewed, the burgundy velvet of the seats cleaned, and the technical side of things brought up to scratch, at least enough for me to show digital films as well as the old celluloid reels. I had aspirations where the choice of films for my program was concerned; it didn't always coincide with the tastes of the masses. François, a student at the film academy, helped me with the showings, and Madame Clément, an elderly lady who had earlier worked in the Printemps department store, worked in the box office in the evenings—if I wasn't selling the tickets myself, that is.

When I reopened the Cinéma Paradis, a lot of people who had known it in the past came again. And a lot of people who were curious also came, because the reopening had seemed worth a couple of column inches to the press. The first few months were good, and then came the times when the auditorium was only half-full, if that. When Madame Clément showed me in sign language how many were in the audience some evenings, ten fingers were often more than enough.

Not that I'd believed that a small cinema was a gold mine anyway, but my savings were melting away and I needed an idea. What came to me was the idea of having an extra late-night performance on a Wednesday, showing the old films that had so inspired me. The special thing about this concept was that the films changed every week, and that they were all films about love, in the broadest sense. I called the whole thing *Les Amours au Paradis* and was pleased to see the late Wednesday performances beginning to fill up.

And when, on those evenings, I opened the doors after the titles had run and saw the loving couples leaving the auditorium arm in arm with glistening eyes, a businessman who for sheer elation had forgotten his briefcase under his seat, or an old lady who came up to me and shook my hand, saying, with longing in her eyes, that the film reminded her of the days of her youth, I knew that I had the most wonderful job in the world. On these evenings a very special enchantment lay over the Cinéma Paradis. It was my cinema that gave people the gift of dreams, just as Uncle Bernard had always said.

But after the young woman in the red coat began coming to the late performances and, every time she came to the box office, gave me a shy smile, it was I who began to dream.

Four

....

"What do you mean, you haven't asked her yet? How long has she been coming to your cinema?"

My friend Robert rocked impatiently on his chair. We were sitting outside the Café de la Mairie, a little place to the left of the church of Saint-Sulpice, and although it was only March and the weather in recent weeks had been quite rainy, the sun was blazing in our faces.

When we meet at lunchtime, Robert always wants to go to the Café de la Mairie, because they're supposed to have the best vinaigrette for his beloved *salade paysanne*—there are little bottles full of it on every table.

"Well," I said as I watched him empty the whole bottle over his salad in one go, "I'd say it's been going on since December."

My friend looked at me in amazement. "'It'? What do you mean by that? Are you two an item or not?"

I shook my head and sighed. For Robert, the first and only important question is whether a man and a woman are "an item." None of the rest interests him. He's a scientist, and profoundly unromantic. Subtleties are totally alien to him, and the delight of stolen glances leaves him cold. If he fancies a woman, then something happens—usually on the very first evening. No idea how he does it. Of course, he can be very charming and funny. And he approaches women with a disarming openness, which most of them seem unable to resist.

I leaned back, took a sip of wine and blinked into the sun, because I didn't have my sunglasses with me. "No, nothing's going on, at least not in the way you would understand it." I told him the whole truth. "But she's been coming to the late-night show since December, and I just have the feeling that . . . Oh, I just don't know."

Robert speared a cube of cheese dripping with golden-yellow vinaigrette, counting off the months with his other hand. "December, January, February, March." He looked at me sternly. "You mean to tell me that this girl you fancy so much has been coming to the cinema for four months and you still haven't even spoken to her?"

"But she only comes once a week, always on Wednesday, when I run that series of old films—you know, *Les Amours au Paradis*—and of course I've spoken to her. The sort of things you say. 'Did you like the film?' 'Terrible weather today, don't you think?' 'Would you like to leave your umbrella here?' That sort of thing."

"Does she have a guy with her?"

I shook my head. "No, she always comes alone. But that doesn't necessarily mean anything." I tapped the edge of my glass. "At first, I thought she was married, because she wears a gold ring. But then I looked very carefully and saw that it wasn't a wedding ring—at least not a normal one. It has little red-gold roses on—"

"And she's really cute?" my friend asked, interrupting me. "Nice teeth, good figure, and all that?"

I nodded again and thought back to the time the girl with the red coat had first appeared at the box office. I always called her "the girl," but in fact she was a young woman, somewhere around twenty-five to twenty-eight, with shoulder-length caramel hair, which she parted at the side, a delicate heart-shaped face with a scattering of freckles, and shining dark eyes. To me, she always seemed a little lost—in her thoughts, or in the world—and had a habit of nervously tucking her hair behind her ear with her right hand as she waited for me to tear a ticket off for her. But when she smiled, the whole place seemed to fill with light, and her expression became a bit roguish. And yes, she had a lovely mouth and wonderful teeth.

"She's a bit like Mélanie Laurent, you know."

"Mélanie Laurent? Never heard of her. Who on earth is she?"

"The actress from *Beginners*."

Robert stuffed the cube of cheese in his mouth and chewed thoughtfully. "Not a clue. I only know Angelina Jolie. She's fabulous. Great body."

"Okay, okay. You might come to my cinema a little more often, and then you might have some idea of what I'm talking about. I'd let you in for free anyway."

"For God's sake! I'd fall asleep in there!"

My friend likes action films and Mafia films, and so we would never—seen purely theoretically—have to fight for the last ticket for the same film.

"Like the girl in *Inglourious Basterds*," I said, trying to broaden our points of contact. "The one who sets fire to the cinema so that all the Nazis burn to death."

Robert stopped chewing for a moment, then as he realized who I meant, he raised his eyebrows in recognition and waved his forefinger in circles in front of my face.

"You mean the pretty chick who's on the run from the Nazis. *That's* Mélanie Laurent? And your girl looks like Mélanie Laurent, you say?"

"A bit," I replied.

Robert fell back in the bistro chair with a crash—it wasn't made for a man his size—and then shook his head.

"Boy oh boy, I just don't understand it. You can be such a dope sometimes," he said in the refreshingly direct manner I value so much in him. I let his reproaches wash over me—after all, I wanted his advice. But when he began by saying, "That's exactly like . . ." and then let rip with a load of astrophysical formulae that by some miracle culminated in a Hubble Constant I'd never heard of, I got completely lost and my thoughts wandered.

Have I told you that I'm more the reserved type? I should add straightaway that that doesn't mean boring. Quite the contrary: I have a very rich interior life and a vivid imagination. Just because a man doesn't take every woman he fancies straight to bed, he isn't necessarily a total wimp. Unlike all those showoffs, I see a great deal. I don't mean in the prophetic sense, of course. Perhaps I've just seen too many films in my lifetime, but since I've been running the Cinéma Paradis, I've noticed that I get great pleasure from observing people very closely and drawing my conclusions about them. And without my really wanting it, their stories run to me just like puppies run to other people.

Some customers come only once; others are here in the

Cinéma Paradis quite regularly, and I feel I almost know them. I may not talk a great deal, but I see a lot. I sell them the tickets and see their faces, their stories, their secrets.

There's the tall man in the light brown corduroy suit, his few remaining hairs carelessly combed back, who never misses a film by Bunuel, Saura, or Sautet. I imagine that in his youth he was taken with the ideals of communism and later became a professor. His eyes, which sparkle beneath his bushy silver eyebrows, are bright and full of intelligence. He always wears bright blue shirts under his old corduroy jacket with its threadbare lapels, and I am certain that he is a widower. He is one of the few men of his generation who have outlived their wives, and I'm certain that he loved his. His face is open and friendly. And whenever he leaves the cinema, he always stops for a moment, as if he were waiting for someone, and then continues with an air of surprise.

Then there's the woman with the luxuriant black curls and her little daughter. She's probably in her late thirties, and they both come regularly to the children's show on the weekend. "Papa will be home late today," she once said to the child as she hopped along beside her and held her hand, and her face was pale and sad and tired above her bright scarf. Her mouth suddenly pursed in a bitter smile. She never comes late—she's more likely to be too early. She has a lot of time, and sometimes, as she stands in the foyer waiting to be let in, she twists her wedding ring absentmindedly on her finger. I guess her husband is unfaithful to her, and she knows it. But she doesn't know if she should actually leave him or not.

The tubby man with the steel-rimmed glasses, who mostly watches comedies and likes to laugh a lot, has been left by his girlfriend. Since then, his belly has gotten a little rounder and he has an air of uncertainty. He works a lot these days, there are shadows under his eyes, and when he arrives, it's always just before the show starts—sometimes he's still carrying his briefcase. Nevertheless, I think things are better for him this way. His girlfriend was a peevish little redheaded witch who constantly criticized him—it was never quite clear for what. The guy wouldn't harm a fly.

And so I sit in my cinema evening after evening and indulge in my little speculations. But the customer who puzzles me the most, whose story interests me the most, who always comes on her own and whom I wait for with my heart palpitating every Wednesday, is someone else.

The woman in the red coat always sits in row seventeen, and I wonder what her secret is. I'd really like to find out about her story, and yet at the same time I'm afraid that it might ultimately not fit in with my own story. I feel like Parsifal, who is forbidden to ask questions, and I already sense that this woman's story is very special. She's so very enchanting, and this evening I'm finally going to talk to her and ask her out to dinner.

A large hand grabbed my sleeve and shook me, and so I returned to the place Saint-Sulpice, where I was sitting in the sun outside the little café with my friend.

"Hey, Alain, are you actually listening to me?" Robert's voice sounded reproachful. He looked at me with those piercing bright blue eyes. Behind his shock of blond hair, the sunlit church with its strange angular towers rose in the sky like a gigantic spaceship that had just landed. Robert had obviously just finished giving me a long lecture about Hubble and his constants.

"I said you ought to speak to her this evening and ask her if she'll go out to dinner with you! Otherwise, you'll continue drifting apart like bodies in space."

I bit my lower lip and suppressed a smile. "Yes," I said. "That's exactly what I was thinking."

Five

....

I got to the cinema far too early that Wednesday. After lunching with Robert, I'd rushed off as if I had an appointment. Of course I hadn't, but as you know, the happiest moments are those that you wait for. So I crossed the boulevard Saint-Germain as it basked in the noonday sun and wove my way between the cars waiting at a red light. I lit a cigarette, and a few minutes later was walking along the shady rue Mazarin.

When I unlocked the door of the Cinéma Paradis, the familiar smell of wood and plush seating wafted toward me, and I calmed down a little and began to refill the showcases.

This was the day that Eric Rohmer's *The Green Ray* was showing in the *Les Amours au Paradis* series. I put out new leaflets. I checked that there was enough change in the box office. I glanced in at the projection booth and set the reels of film out. Then I went into the auditorium and tried out several seats in row seventeen, trying to see what was special about it, but I didn't actually notice anything different. It wasn't even the back row, which is very popular with lovers because they can kiss undisturbed in the darkness.

I killed time doing some things that were useful, and a few that weren't, all the time keeping my eye on the hands of the clock in the foyer.

François arrived and disappeared into the projection booth. Madame Clément arrived, bringing homemade raspberry tarts. And when the audience for the six o'clock performance had taken their seats to follow the fate of an inventive pensioners' collective in *All Together,* I opened the door to the projection booth and signaled to François that I was going out for a coffee. François sat hunched over a pile of books and papers. While the films were running, he had enough time to cram for his exams.

"I'll be right back," I said, and he nodded. "And . . . François? Would you mind locking up this evening? I have something to do after the late show."

It was only when I was drinking my *café crème* in the nearby bistro that I realized that my plan wasn't exactly brilliant. The late show finished at quarter past eleven. Who on earth would want to go out to dinner then? Perhaps it would be wiser to ask the woman in the red coat out to dinner on the weekend. If she was prepared to let me ask her out at all, that is, and if she actually came to the cinema that evening.

Suddenly, I went cold with fear. What if she didn't come? Or never came again? I stirred my coffee nervously, although the sugar had long since dissolved.

But she's always come before, I said to myself. Don't be silly, Alain. She'll come. And anyway, she seems to like you. She always smiles when she sees you.

But perhaps that's just perfectly normal friendliness?

No, no, there's more to it than that. I bet she's just waiting for you to get around to speaking to her. You should have done it long ago, you coward. Long ago!

I heard a low rustling sound beside me and looked up. The professor with the corduroy jacket was sitting at the next table and nodded to me from behind his newspaper. His eyes shone with amusement.

Heavens! I hadn't been talking out loud, had I? Was I one of those people who had no control over what they said? Or could the old gentleman read minds?

So I nodded back in confusion, and drank my coffee down in a single gulp.

"I saw that you're showing *The Green Ray* today," said the professor. "A good film—I'll definitely come and see it." A thin smile played around the corner of his mouth. "And don't worry: The young lady will definitely come!"

I blushed as I stood up and reached for my jacket. "Yes, well then, see you later."

"See you later," he replied. And I really hoped that he was right about the young lady.

She was the last in the line standing at the box office, and as she held out a bill to pay for her ticket, I seized the opportunity by the forelock.

"You come to our late show quite often, mademoiselle. Do you like my little film series?" I asked eagerly as I gave her the ticket and her change.

She tucked a lock of hair behind her ear and smiled shyly. "Oh, yes. A lot, actually."

"And I'm very pleased that you come so often," I blurted, and stared in fascination at her perfectly formed little ear, which was now beginning to turn red.

She kept smiling but didn't say a word as she put the coins in her purse. What should she have replied to such a stupid remark?

I could hear Robert's voice. *Don't beat about the bush. Get to the point, man. Get to the point.*

"Well . . . ha-ha . . . I should actually give you a discount since you come here so often," I said in an attempt to be witty. "Like those loyalty points they have in the big stores, you know?"

She took her ticket, and for a second she looked me straight in the eye. Then she smiled again, and I smiled back, as if hypnotized.

"No need for that, monsieur. The films are worth every cent."

The cinema door was pulled open and a gust of wind blew through the foyer. Two students came in, giggling, and headed for the box office. I needed to hurry.

The woman in the red coat turned to go.

"Just a moment," I shouted, and she turned back to me. "You . . . you've forgotten something. . . ."

She stared at me in amazement.

"That is, *I* . . . I've forgotten something," I went on, in a desperate attempt not to lose her attention.

"Well?"

"In fact, I forgot to ask something." I looked at her. "After the show . . . would you like to go out to dinner . . . or for a drink, perhaps? Then . . . we could discuss the film . . . if you like. I'd . . . er . . . I'd really like to invite you, I mean, since you don't want any loyalty points."

Oh good grief, I was talking such nonsense!

"Oh good grief, what nonsense I'm talking," I said, shaking my head. "Please excuse me. Forget all that stuff about loyalty points. Will you accept my invitation? Please say yes!"

My heart was hammering to the staccato rhythm of my idiotic outburst.

The woman in the red coat raised her eyebrows, bit her lower lip, bowed her head a little, and smiled broadly. Her cheeks were fiery red. Then she finally said something.

She said yes!

Six

....

Almost automatically, we landed in La Palette. The people around us were laughing, talking, and drinking, but I didn't notice them. I had eyes only for the woman at my table, and even an earthquake couldn't have torn me away from her spell.

Never in my life had I longed for the end of a film as much as I did that evening. Again and again, I had peered through the little window into the auditorium to see what stage the film was at—I'd seen it so often that I could almost recite the words along with it. And after kooky Delphine had finally seen the green glow, that strangely propitious phenomenon that can be seen only for a few seconds—and then not every time—as the sun sinks into the sea, and was ready to dare the adventure of love, I pulled open the auditorium doors to release the audience back into their own lives.

She was one of the first out of the door, and stepped aside to let the other members of the audience past her as they slowly and dreamily came into the foyer, blinking in the sudden light, before returning to reality and heading for the exit, chatting and laughing.

"Just one moment. I'll be ready right away," I said, and she strolled along the foyer wall, studying the posters intently.

"Is there really such a thing as that green glow?" I heard a student ask. Her boyfriend shrugged his shoulders. "I don't know, but we should try to find out," he replied, putting his arm tenderly around her.

I saw the professor coming out. He was leaning on his walking stick and looked at me questioningly from under his silver eyebrows. I nodded, and glanced unobtrusively to the part of the foyer where the woman in the red coat was still looking at the posters. A look of benevolence and—was I imagining it?—a kind of joyful recognition crossed the old man's face as he winked at me and went out into the street.

Then we were alone at last. Madame Clément was bustling about in the auditorium—she was going up and down the rows to check if anyone had left anything behind.

"*Bonne nuit,*" I shouted to François as he stuck his head out of the projection booth for a moment. Then I put on my jacket, said "Shall we?" and accompanied the woman in the red coat to the exit.

We smiled at each other and walked a few steps in silence along the dark street. It was a strangely intimate moment—this sudden closeness, the silence of the street, the quiet tapping of her heels on the old cobbles. I walked along beside her, not wanting to spoil the moment by speaking—but of course I was going to have to say something to her sometime. I was just racking my brains for something suitable to say, when she looked up at me and tucked her hair behind her ear.

"You have really enchanting ears," I heard myself say, and cursed myself at the same moment. What was I? An ear fetishist? "I mean . . . everything about you is enchanting," I added. "I can't tell you how glad I am that you've accepted my invitation. You know, you caught my attention quite a while ago."

She smiled. "And you caught mine, too," she said. "By the way, my name is Mélanie."

"Mélanie—what a lovely name," I said, and it seemed to me that this was a nod from the Fates. Hadn't I said to Robert that very lunchtime that she reminded me of Mélanie Laurent, the actress?

"And you look a bit like Mélanie Laurent."

"Do you think so?" It seemed to please her.

"Yes, yes . . . absolutely." The spell was broken, and I got a bit reckless. "But your eyes are definitely lovelier."

She gave a flattered laugh. "And you?" she asked. To be honest, the attractiveness of my eyes had never crossed my mind. They were brown and quite passable, I thought.

"My eyes are neither here nor there," I said.

"I meant what's *your* name?"

"Oh. I see. Alain."

"Alain. That suits you." She tilted her head to one side and gave me a searching look. "And you look a bit like Alain Delon."

"That's the nicest lie I've ever heard," I said, and stopped outside La Palette, a rather pleasant bistro that is quite close to my apartment. Without my really thinking about it, my internal navigational system had led me to the rue de Seine, as it had on so many other evenings when I went there for a snack after the show. I opened the door, and we went in.

Seven

....

"Whenever I'm looking for love, I go to the Cinéma Paradis." Mélanie took a sip from her glass of red wine, then held it in the palms of both hands as her gaze became lost in a mysterious distance that lay somewhere beyond the windows of La Palette, and to which I had no access. Her eyes shone and she had a thoughtful smile on her lips.

That was probably the moment I fell in love with her. Her words moved me deeply, and I immediately felt my heart take flight. That one sentence, and the strange little smile that accompanied it. When I think back to it today, I remember that even then something about her words struck me as being unusual, even though I could not have said what it actually was.

A few weeks later, when I was desperately looking for the woman in the red coat, those strange words were to come back to me. They were the key to everything, but I didn't know it then as, in a spontaneous gesture, I put my hands around Mélanie's. It was the first time we'd touched, and it couldn't have been any other way.

"Oh, Mélanie, that's beautiful. You're a poet!"

She looked at me, and once more her smile was for me. Her hands stayed in mine, and she was still holding the wineglass. We both sat there holding it as if it were a kind of happiness that, like a wild bird, you have to hold gently and carefully so that it doesn't fly away.

"No, no, there's no way I'm a poet. I'm just a bit nostalgic, that's all."

Nostalgic was a word I hadn't heard for a long time, and it delighted me. "But that's wonderful!" I leaned forward toward her and the red wine swayed in its round-bellied glass. "Where would we be in this soulless universe if there weren't a few people who hold on to memories, their hearts yearning for long-lost feelings?"

She laughed. "Who's the poet now?" she said. Then she put the wineglass down carefully on the table, and I regretfully let go of her hands. "That's the thing about memories," she said, and was silent for a moment. "They can sometimes make you sad, even if they're good memories. You like thinking back to them; they're the greatest treasure we have, and yet it always makes you a little sad because something is irretrievably past." She rested her cheek on her right hand and painted little circles on the table-top with her left.

"*Tempi passati*," I said—quite the philosopher—and wondered whether I dared to try holding her hand again. "That's why I love films. Everything comes back to life in them, even if it's only for a couple of hours. And you can return to your lost paradise." I reached for her hand, and she didn't take it away.

"Is that why your cinema's called Cinéma Paradis?"

"No . . . Yes . . . Maybe." We both laughed. "To be honest, I don't really know. I'd have to ask my uncle—he used to own the cinema, but unfortunately he's no longer alive."

I raised my hands regretfully. Good old Uncle Bernard! His wonderful time in the south had come to a sudden but peaceful end late the previous fall. "This is a really good wine," he had said to Claudine as he sat one evening in his cane chair on the terrace, holding the glass up to the low setting sun. "Could you get us another bottle, my love?" When Claudine came back, Uncle Bernard was sitting with his eyes half-open, leaning back in his cane chair as if he were looking up at the tall old pines whose smell he so loved in the summer. But he was dead.

The funeral was a very quiet one. In fact, there were only Claudine, a married couple from the village whom they'd become friends with, his oldest friend, Bruno, and me. My parents, who were traveling in New Zealand, sent a wreath and a letter of condolence to Claudine. Still, it was a good and dignified funeral, no matter how sad it was. Instead of a flower, I threw an old reel of *Cinema Paradiso* into Bernard's grave. I sighed as I thought about it, and gazed into Melanie's big brown eyes, which were looking at me with sympathy. "At least he died happy," I said. "I liked him a lot, old Uncle Bernard. In the past, I always thought he'd named the cinema after that Italian film . . ."

"*Cinema Paradiso,*" Mélanie said, and I nodded.

"Yes, that's right, *Cinema Paradiso*. It was one of his favorite films. But the cinema was in existence long before the film."

"It must be great to own a little dream factory like that."

"Great and difficult at the same time," I said. "It's not going to make me rich. Everyone in my family was quite annoyed when I gave up my well-paid job in a big firm in Lyon that exported bathtubs and washbasins to Abu Dhabi just to take on an old art-house cinema."

Oh, man, what are you saying? Do you want to show her that you're a complete klutz? Robert's voice sounded so real that I involuntarily looked up. But of course there was no one there except a waiter rushing busily past us to serve the people at the next table.

"Goodness gracious! Bathtubs and washbasins!" Mélanie said, putting her hand over her mouth. "Well, no matter what your family says, I, at least, am glad you're not doing that anymore. It doesn't suit you. And you should always be true to yourself. Or have you ever regretted your decision, Alain?"

"No, never!" I replied, and listened in my head to the echo of her voice pronouncing my name for the first time. I leaned forward and brushed a strand of hair off her face. "It was exactly the right decision." My heart began to thump and I fell head over heels into her glistening eyes. "Most of all because otherwise I would never have met you."

Mélanie had lowered her gaze, and then suddenly she took my hand, which was hovering near her ear, and held it against her cheek.

Oh, I could have gone on playing this game forever, the game fingers and hands, which intertwine with each other, clasp around each other, the two people aware only of this one moment, which is oblivious of all time and presages complete happiness. Don't all love stories begin like this?

"I'm also very glad that the Cinéma Paradis is there," said Mélanie quietly.

I held her hand, and felt the ring she was wearing, stroking the gleaming reddish band of gold with my fingers.

"In the beginning I didn't dare to speak to you. . . . I thought you were married."

She shook her head. "No, no, I'm not married, and never have been. This ring is a memento of my mother—her engagement ring. Maman didn't wear any other jewelry, you know, and when she died, I took the ring so that I would always have something of her with me to remind me. Since then, I have never ever taken it off." She twisted the ring pensively from side to side, then looked at me. "I live completely alone."

I found the solemnity with which she said that very moving.

"Oh . . . I'm very sorry about that," I said, and began to stammer. "I mean, about your mother." I wasn't the slightest bit sorry that Mélanie lived alone—even completely alone. Quite the contrary: I was very glad about it, even if I thought that that "completely alone" had sounded rather sad. "Don't you have anyone here in Paris?"

She shook her head.

"No family? No brother? No sister? No boyfriend? No dog? Not even a canary?"

She kept on shaking her head, but in the end she couldn't help laughing. "You're very inquisitive, Alain, do you know that? No, not even a canary, if you put it that way. The only member of my family who's left is my aunt Lucie, my mother's older sister, but she lives in Brittany. I visit her there now and again. In fact, by pure coincidence, I'm going there this very weekend. It's lovely there by the sea. And otherwise . . ." She hesitated a moment, then put the wineglass to her lips, drank a little sip, and put it down firmly. She obviously didn't want to talk about it, but it wasn't hard to guess that she'd just been thinking about a man.

"*Ça y est*. Things are as they are," she went on. "But that's okay. I have good friends, a wonderful boss, friendly neighbors, and I like living here in Paris."

"I can't believe that a charming woman like you doesn't have a boyfriend," I said, probing further. I admit this wasn't very original, but I wanted to be certain. Perhaps that wonderful boss was the man in her life. Perhaps she was one of those women who seem to live alone but in reality carry on an affair with a married man for years, someone no one is supposed to know about.

Mélanie smiled. "And yet it's true. My last boyfriend cheated on me with a workmate for a whole year. Then I found a green jade earring in his bed, and we split up." She sighed in comic despair. "I have a talent for falling in love with the wrong men. In the end, there's always another woman."

"Not possible," I said. "They must all be complete idiots."

Eight

....

We stayed on at La Palette for a long time. And we would probably have sat there until the early hours of the morning, drinking wine, holding hands, joking, chatting, smiling, and being silent, if the waiters hadn't begun to express a certain degree of displeasure. They straightened the empty wooden chairs beside the empty table. They clattered glasses together. They leaned on the bar, looked over at us, yawned, and waited. They really showed very little understanding for a man and a woman who were in the process of forgetting that there was anything or anyone else in the world except the two of them. Who was it who wrote that love is egotism for two?

But eventually one of the waiters came to the table and coughed. "*Pardon, monsieur.* We'd like to close now."

We looked up in surprise. Only then did we realize that we were the last customers in the place.

"My goodness, it's half past one," said Mélanie.

She smiled apologetically at the waiter, took her hand out of mine, and reached for her red coat, which she'd laid carefully over the back of her chair. I stood up to help her into her coat; then I took out my wallet and paid.

"Thanks a lot for taking me out. It's been a lovely evening," said Mélanie as the waiter locked the door behind us. She looked at me and then busily buttoned her coat. It was only then that I noticed how old-fashioned the cut was, and how well it suited her.

"Yes, a particularly lovely evening," I repeated. "And over far too soon."

It was the middle of the night, I wasn't at all tired, and the last thing I wanted was for the evening to end—if it had been up to me, it could have gone on and on, as it did for the main characters in *Before Sunrise,* the two students who wander around Vienná for a whole day and night, unable to part from each other. But I could hardly ask Mélanie to stroll over to the Tuileries with me and lie there romantically in my arms until dawn. It was definitely too cold for that.

At that moment, I wished I had a bit more of Robert's "your place or mine" mentality. On the other hand, I wasn't sure if this girl in her old-fashioned coat was the kind of woman you could win over with that kind of approach. And anyway, this was the beginning of something very special, not just any old story. I could definitely sense that.

In the still of the night, words seemed to weigh more heavily than they had inside the snug bistro, where we had just sat at the dark wooden table and chatted, our hands continually touching. Now we were standing beside each other on the street, and I didn't want to say good-bye, all of a sudden becoming as shy as a schoolboy.

I was thinking about inviting Mélanie to see a film the next evening—not a very original idea for a cinema owner. I dug my hands deep in my pockets and tried to think of something brilliant to say.

"Well then . . ." said Mélanie, shrugging her shoulders with a shiver. "I have to go in this direction." She pointed to the boulevard Saint-Germain. "And you?"

My apartment was only a few minutes away from La Palette, in the rue de l'Université, which was in exactly the opposite direction, but I wasn't going to let that bother me.

"Well, what do you know. Me, too." I said, lying, and saw how Mélanie smiled with pleasure. "Yeah, well . . . I have to go exactly the same way. So I can walk you some of the way if you like."

She did like the idea. She took my arm and we walked unhurriedly up the rue de Seine to the boulevard Saint-Germain, which even at this late hour was still very lively, passed the crêpe stand—closed at this hour—which nestled at the side of the garden of the old church of Saint-Germain-des-Prés, though in the daytime there was always a line of people tempted by the smell to buy a chestnut-cream crêpe or a chocolate waffle.

Outside the Brasserie Lipp, which was still brightly lit, a couple of taxis were waiting for late customers. We crossed over and went farther up the boulevard Saint-Germain then crossed the boulevard Raspail, turning a little bit later into the rue de Grenelle, quiet and dark with its tall old city houses.

"Is this really still on your way?" Mélanie asked every time we entered a new street, and I nodded, said yes, and asked her to go on telling me about her friend who worked in the bar of a grand hotel and was never free on a Wednesday evening to go to the late show in the Cinéma Paradis with her; about her boss, the overweight, cigar-smoking Monsieur Papin, who was at that moment in the hospital with pneumonia, so that she and her colleague were running his little antiques shop, where they sold old furniture and Belle Epoque lamps, Art Nouveau jewelry, and bathing belles in hand-painted porcelain.

"You work in an antiques shop?" I said. "How charming. It kind of suits you."

I imagined Mélanie in an enchanted place full of precious objects, and was just about to ask her the name of the shop, when she said, "My friend keeps asking me what I find in all that old junk." She laughed. "But I just like all those old things. They exude peace and warmth. And every object has its own story. . . ."

Mélanie seemed to be in high spirits and in the mood to tell stories. I walked beside her, listened to her melodic voice, looked at her raspberry lips, and thought that this must be what happiness feels like.

When we finally reached the rue de Bourgogne and were standing outside a tall old building with several floors opposite a little stationer's whose window was still lit, Mélanie looked at me quizzically. "Here it is," she said, pointing to the big dark green entrance gate, beside which there was a lock with a keypad. "Are you sure you're still going the right way?"

"Absolutely sure," I said.

She raised her eyebrows, and her eyes shone with amusement. "Where do you really have to go, Alain? Do you actually live here, too? In the rue de Bourgogne?"

I shook my head and gave an embarrassed grin. "I live in the rue de l'Université," I said. "Very near La Palette, to be honest. But that was definitely the loveliest detour of my life."

"Oh," she said, and blushed. "To be honest, I'd kind of hoped that." She smiled and quickly tucked a strand of hair behind her ear. I knew at that moment that I was going to love that little gesture of hers.

"And I'd hoped you'd hope so, too," I replied softly, and my heart began to hammer again. The night embraced us as if we were the only people in Paris. And at that moment, we were. Mélanie's bright face gleamed in the darkness. I looked at her raspberry mouth and thought that this would be the moment to kiss her.

Then we were startled by a noise. On the other side of the road, an elderly man in slippers was shuffling along the sidewalk. He looked in the window of the stationer's shop and shook his head in disgust. "They're mad, all mad," he hissed. Then he looked over at us and waved his finger in the air. "Look at the lovers!" he crowed, and laughed eerily as he slouched away.

We waited until the old man had disappeared in the darkness; then we looked at each other and laughed. And then we just looked at each other. I can't say if it was for minutes or for hours. A bell rang out somewhere. The air began to vibrate. I'm sure Robert could have explained what electrically charged particles were streaming between us like a shower of sparks.

"Might this be the moment?" asked Mélanie. Her voice was quivering ever so slightly as she said it, but I noticed it just the same.

"What moment?" I asked gruffly, and took her in my arms, and to my heart, which was hammering with the wild beat of a conductor gone crazy.

Finally we kissed, and it was just as I had imagined it would be—only far, far better.

Nine

....

I don't think anyone has ever walked along the rue Bonaparte
as happy as I was that night. I strode along in high spirits, my
hands in my pockets. It was three in the morning, but I didn't
feel at all tired. The street was empty of people and my heart
full of anticipation of everything that was going to happen. Life
was beautiful, and Fortuna had just poured her cornucopia out
over me.

Anyone who has ever been in love knows what I mean. I
very nearly tap-danced along the gutter like Gene Kelly in *Sin-
gin' in the Rain*. Unfortunately, I am anything but a gifted dancer,
and so I just sang a few lines of the title song and kicked a Coke
can off the sidewalk.

A drunk lurched toward me from the rue Jacob, reached out
his hand, then turned it over and looked at me in amazement.
It wasn't raining, of course, but I would have welcomed any
drop of rain as if it were a shower of gold. My elation reached
up to the skies. I felt invincible. I was the darling of the gods.

Isn't it simply incredible that, after all the millennia this world has been turning on its axis, love is still the most wonderful thing that can happen to two people? Again and again it's that feeling that enables us to start anew in expectation of great things.

Love—it's the first green shoots of spring, a bird that chirrups its little song, a pebble that you boldly bounce out over the water, a blue sky with white clouds, a winding path that runs beside a sweet-smelling gorse hedge, a warm wind wafting over a hill, a hand that clasps another.

Love is the great promise of our lives. At the beginning of everything, there is always a man and a woman. And that night their names were Mélanie and Alain.

As I unlocked the door to my apartment, I could already hear excited mewing. I went in and bent down to Orphée, who was rolling voluptuously on the Berber carpet in the hallway. "So, what's my little tiger princess up to?" I said, and fondled her gray-and-white-striped fur a couple of times.

Orphée had come to me. One morning, I'd found her sitting outside my door, mewing pitifully. She was still quite small, very thin, and at the time I'd asked everyone in the building if they'd lost a cat—and, in that way, gotten to know all my neighbors. But no one was missing a little tiger cat. In complete ignorance of the biological facts, I thought at first that she was a male and called her Orphée. Then Clarisse, who cleaned the place for me once a week, came to me, put her hands on her hips, and shook her head energetically. "*Mais non,* Monsieur Bonnard! What have you done? She's a girl; that's obvious at first sight."

Well, if you looked closely enough, it was obvious. But in spite of that, Orphée kept her name, and I think she liked it, even if she never responded to it.

"You'll never believe what's happened to me today, little one. You'd be amazed." I tickled her light-colored belly and Orphée rolled happily on her side. No matter what had happened to me, as long as I stroked her, everything was fine.

After our little greeting ritual, I went into the kitchen to get a glass of water. All at once, I felt very thirsty. Orphée followed me, jumped boldly up on the sink, and thrust her hard little skull demandingly against my arm.

"All right, all right." I sighed, and turned on the faucet a little. "But you could just get used to drinking your water from your bowl. That would be the normal thing, you know."

Orphée didn't listen to a word I said. Like all cats, she had her own idea of what was "normal." And clearly it was much more interesting to drink water from a running tap than from a proper cat bowl. I watched her as she stuck her little pink tongue into the fine stream and contentedly lapped up the water.

"Your cat's name is Orphée?" Mélanie had laughed out loud when I told her that the only woman in my life at the moment was a capricious lady cat who had accidentally been given a male name. "Does she play the lyre, as well?"

"Well, not really. But she does like to drink water straight from the faucet."

"How sweet," Mélanie had said. "My friend's cat will only drink out of flower vases."

"Mélanie thinks you're very sweet," I said to Orphée.

"Meow," said Orphée. She stopped lapping for a moment, then carried on.

"Aren't you interested to know who Mélanie is?" I threw my jacket on the kitchen chair, walked over the creaky parquet flooring into the living room, switched on the floor lamp, and fell onto the sofa. Seconds later, I head a soft padding noise. Orphée had jumped down from the sink and was approaching the sofa with sinuous steps. A moment later, she was lying on my stomach, purring. I stretched out, ran my fingers through her silken fur, and stared absentmindedly at the light shining gently through the milky white fabric shade of the lamp. Mélanie's face seemed to be hovering directly above me. Her lips curved into a smile. I stared into the lamp and thought back to the kisses outside the dark green gate in the rue de Bourgogne, kisses that never wanted to end, but which did end when Mélanie finally freed herself from my embrace.

"I must go up now," she said softly, and I saw the hesitation in her eyes. For a moment, I hoped that she'd ask me to go with her, but she decided otherwise. "Good night, Alain," she said, touching her finger gently to my lips before turning to enter the code for the lock. The gate swung open with a soft hum, revealing the inner courtyard, where an old chestnut tree spread its foliage.

"Oh, I don't want to let you go," I said, and drew her back into my arms. "Just one more kiss!"

Mélanie smiled and closed her eyes as our lips met once again.

After that kiss, there had been another last kiss, and then a very last, very passionate kiss under the old chestnut tree.

"When will I see you again?" I asked. "Tomorrow?"

Mélanie thought for a moment. "Next Wednesday?"

"What—not till next Wednesday?" A week seemed an unimaginably long time to me.

"I'm afraid it won't be possible before then," she said. "I'm leaving tomorrow to spend a week with my aunt in Le Pouldu. But we won't lose each other."

And then I finally had to let Mélanie go, with the promise that we'd see each other again on the dot of eight next Wednesday in the Cinéma Paradis.

She waved to me once more, then disappeared in the entrance on the far side of the courtyard. I stood there spellbound for a while longer, watching the light go on in one of the windows on the upper floor and then go out a little later.

This is where the woman I love lives, I thought. And then I, too, set off for home.

Ten

....

The phone rang just as I was drinking my coffee the next
morning. I was still quite shattered after my night on the sofa,
where I'd contentedly nodded off sometime in the early hours
of the morning. I got up from my chair with a groan and looked
for the handset, which, as always, wasn't where it should have
been. I finally found it under a pile of newspapers beside the bed
I hadn't slept in.

It was Robert, who had already, as he did every morning
before his first lecture, jogged through the Bois de Boulogne
and was now obviously taking a break in his office at the university. As usual, he came straight to the point.

"So, how was it? Did the supernova explode?" he yelled into
the phone in his good-natured way. He was so alarmingly awake
that it made me flinch. His voice seemed even louder than usual.

"Good grief, Robert, do you always have to shout into the
phone like that? I'm not deaf!" I went back into the kitchen and
sat down at the little table. "I've only had two hours' sleep, but

it was . . ." Words like *magic, enchanting,* and *romantic* came to mind—all words that would mean nothing to my friend. "It was great," I said. "It was crazy. I'm over the moon. This is the woman I've been waiting for all my life."

Robert clicked his tongue happily. "Well, well," he said. "Once you get going, there's no holding you, is there? I hope I'm not intruding. Is the chick still there with you?"

"No, of course not."

"What do you mean, 'of course not.' Did you spend the night at her place? Not bad."

I had to laugh. "No one spent the night at anyone's place," I explained to my perplexed friend. "But that doesn't matter."

Thinking fleetingly of the hesitant look in Mélanie's eyes as we stood outside the green gate, I sighed.

"Well . . . not that I'd have turned down an invitation: I did walk her home, you see. But she's not the kind of woman who jumps into bed with a man on the very first date."

"Pity." Robert seemed a little disappointed, but then his pragmatism once more gained the upper hand. "Then you'll just have to stick at it," he said. "*Stick at it,* d'you hear?"

"Robert, I'm not an idiot." I peevishly cut a slice of goat cheese from the roll and put it on my baguette.

"Okay, okay," he began, and then broke off for a moment. He seemed to be thinking it over. "I just hope she's not one of the complicated ones. They're no fun at all."

"No worries. I've already had a great deal of fun with her," I replied. "The evening was lovely, and our story is only just beginning. . . ." I thought back to the old man who'd croaked "Lovers" at us, to the way Mélanie would sometimes simply burst out with her refreshing laugh. I did so love hearing it.

"We laughed a lot and talked a lot. . . . You know, everything fits so well. She likes old things—just as I do. She even
works in an antiques shop with old furniture and lamps and
porcelain figurines. She likes cats and her favorite film is *Cyrano
de Bergerac*. That's one of my favorite films, too. . . . Isn't that
just *great*?"

Robert didn't seem very impressed. He brushed off all the
wonderful things that I thought we shared with a brusque
"Good, good." Then he added, "Still, I hope you two didn't just
talk?"

"Good God, no!" I smiled as I remembered the kisses under
the old chestnut tree. "Oh, Robert, what can I say? I'm immensely happy. Everything just feels so right. I can hardly wait to
see her again. . . . She's the most enchanting girl I've ever met.
And she hasn't got a boyfriend, thank God! The Eiffel Tower
always makes her happy, she says. Oh, and she loves bridges," I
continued with the euphoria of all those who've freshly fallen in
love and are sent into paroxysms of delight by every aspect of the
new beloved. "Especially the pont Alexandre—because of the
Belle Epoque lamps, of course."

"Do you know how lovely it is to walk over the pont Alexandre when the reflection of the city lights starts sparkling in the
water and the sky turns lavender?" Mélanie had said. "I sometimes stop under those old lamps for a moment and look at the
river and the city, and every time I think, How wonderful!"

"She says that every time she walks over that bridge she always has to stop for a moment. And that Paris is wonderful."
I sighed happily.

"You sound like a damn tourist guide, Alain. Are you sure
the chick really lives here? I haven't heard such tourist-brochure

kitsch for a long time. I've also walked over the pont Alexandre, but I've certainly never stopped to breathe in the wonder of Paris—at least not when I was alone. My God, so much fuss about a couple of old lamps!"

"But bridges *do* have a magic all of their own," I said.

Robert laughed, obviously amused by my ravings. If he found something good about a girl, it certainly wasn't a predilection for old bridges and Belle Epoque lamps.

"*Très bien*. That all sounds very promising," he said, ending on a jovial note. "When are you going to see her again?"

Five minutes later, I was having a fight with my best friend.

"You don't have her cell number?" He was beside himself. "Oh boy, how stupid can you get? You waffle on for hours about some dumb films and bridges and you don't even ask her the most important thing. Tell me it isn't true, Alain!"

"But it is true," I replied curtly. "At the time, I didn't think it was the most important thing. It's as simple as that."

I was annoyed with myself. Why on earth hadn't I asked Mélanie for her number? The shameful truth was that I'd just forgotten to. On that first evening, which we'd wandered through like sleepwalkers, with every confidence in the fact that there was more linking us than modern technology, something as profane as a cell phone had had no place at all. But how could I explain that to my friend?

Robert could no longer remain calm. "You meet the woman of your dreams and don't even get her number?" He laughed in disbelief. "That really takes the cake. What planet are you living on? Hello! This is the third millennium. Do you really understand anything at all? Are you going to communicate by carrier pigeon?"

"Good grief, I'll ask her next time. I'm seeing her on Wednesday, after all."

"And if you don't?" Robert asked. "What if she doesn't turn up? I find it funny that she didn't ask for your number. Or at least give you hers. My students always want my cell number." He laughed with quiet self-satisfaction. "That doesn't sound much like a very successful evening, if you ask me!"

"But I'm not asking you," I said. "Why should I care about your students? We have a firm date, and even if it's beyond your understanding, there are still people who can wait a week, looking forward to seeing each other again, and simply stick to a fixed date without having to call each other ten times and throw the whole thing over just because something better has turned up." I realized that I was beginning to feel like wringing Robert's neck. "It's not always a matter of a quick conquest, even if that's all you're after with your little students."

"It's all a question of how attractive you are," said Robert, unmoved. "But everyone has the right to his own views. Either way, I wish you a lot of fun with your 'looking forward.' I hope you're not looking forward in vain."

It was impossible to miss the sarcasm in his voice, and I began to get mad. "Why are you getting all bent out of shape?" I asked. "I mean, what are you trying to prove to me? That I'm a complete dumbass? Granted. Yes, of course I should have asked for her number. But I didn't. So what? Mélanie knows where my cinema is, after all. And I know where she lives."

"Her name's Mélanie?"

It was the first time I'd mentioned her name to Robert. "Yes, funny coincidence. isn't it?"

"And the rest?"

He had me there, and I was unable to speak. What could I have said? I *was* a complete dumbass. It was only now that I realized I didn't know Mélanie's surname. That was unforgivable. I tried to shake off the panic that was welling up in me. And what if Robert was right?

"Well . . ." I said, embarrassed.

"Boy oh boy, you really are beyond help!" Robert sighed.

And then my friend gave me a short lecture about why life is not a film where people find and lose each other, only to meet again by chance the following week at the Trevi Fountain because they'd both—at the very same time—hit on the idea of throwing in a coin and making a wish.

"But I know where she lives," I repeated stubbornly, seeing in my mind's eye all the nameplates beside the gate on the rue de Bourgogne. "If for any reason she doesn't turn up next week, I can always go and ask around. But she will come; I'm sure of it. My feelings tell me that. You don't understand these things, Robert."

"Oh yeah?" he said. "Well, it may be so. Perhaps everything will run according to plan." He gave a skeptical little laugh. "And if things turn out differently, you could always stand on the bridges of Paris, waiting for Mélanie to pass by one evening—she does love bridges, after all."

Mélanie had left a message for me at the Cinéma Paradis that very same day. That was a triumph, because it proved my friend a liar. And a pity, because I wasn't there to receive the message myself, because then I could have seen Mélanie once more before she left. And this time, I would definitely have asked for her number.

So it was François who gave me the white envelope as I arrived at the cinema at half past four. I stared at it in his hand. It had my name on it.

"What's this?"

"From the woman in the red coat," explained François calmly, giving me a quizzical look from behind his steel-rimmed glasses. "She asked for 'Alain' and then gave me this letter."

"Thanks." I literally tore the letter from his grasp, fleeing with it into the auditorium, which was empty at the time. I hastily opened the envelope in the rash hope that it might contain something nice. It was just a short letter. After hastily scanning the lines written in dark blue ink, I gave a sigh of relief and settled down to read the letter once more, sentence by sentence.

Dear Alain,

Did you get home all right last night? I would really have loved to walk back to the rue de l'Université with you, but in that way, we'd just have wandered back and forth all night, and I had to get up early this morning. But I still couldn't sleep. I'd hardly gotten up to the apartment when I began to miss you. And when I looked out of the window after I got up, this morning and saw the old chestnut tree, I suddenly felt very happy.

I don't know if you'll be in the cinema later (that would be the nicest thing) or if I'll just have to leave my letter behind the grille, so that you'll find a little sign from me before I go away. I'm not adventurous, Alain, but I'm looking forward to next Wednesday, to you, and to everything that is about to happen.

Kisses, M.

"I'm not adventurous," she had written, and it moved me, even though it was a quotation. Or perhaps precisely because it was. The words came from the film *The Green Ray,* which had been showing in the Cinéma Paradis the previous evening. The somewhat diffident Delphine says them to her friends: "I'm not adventurous."

"Oh, sweet Mélanie!" I murmured in the semidarkness of the auditorium. "No, you're not adventurous, but that doesn't matter. That's precisely what I love about you. Your vulnerability, your shyness. This world is not just for the rash and the fearless, for the loud go-getters—no, the shy and the quiet, the dreamy and the eccentric have their place there, too. Without them, there would be no nuances, no light blue watercolors, no unsaid words that give the imagination space to work. And isn't it precisely the dreamers who know that the truest and greatest adventures take place in the heart?"

I would probably have continued my apologia for humanity from the second row for some time had there not been a rustling noise that made me look up. There in the doorway of the auditorium, Madame Clément in her flowery apron was leaning on a broom and watching me with fascination.

"Madame Clément!" I called, and cleared my throat to try to regain my composure. "Are you eavesdropping on me?" I stood up hastily. "How long have you been standing there?"

"Oh, Monsieur Bonnard." She sighed, not answering my question. "Those things you were saying were so lovely, with the still waters and the blue pictures and the dreams. I could have gone on listening to you for hours. I had a box of watercolor paints when I was a child—I've no idea where it's gotten to. At some stage in life, you give up painting, and dreaming.

It's a shame, isn't it?" A dreamy smile played on her lips. "But when you fall in love, you start dreaming again."

I nodded in some confusion, folded the precious letter, and put it in my jacket pocket. I hadn't known that there was a philosopher slumbering in Madame Clément.

"Has she written to you? What does she say?" She looked at me with a conspiratorial grin.

"What!" I exclaimed. "Well, really, Madame Clément, I must say!" I felt like I'd been caught out, and I was not prepared to reveal the state of my heart to her. How on earth did she know that?

"François told me about the letter, of course." She gave me a benevolent glance.

I raised my eyebrows. "Of course," I repeated, glad to hear how well communications in my little cinema were functioning.

"We were all wondering how your evening with the pretty woman in the red coat panned out," Madame Clément continued. She actually said "all," as if she were part of a great royal court that spent all its time following the activities of its beloved ruler. "But if she asked for you today and even left you a love letter, it must have been a pleasant evening."

"And so it was." I had to laugh. "And why are you so sure it's a love letter?"

She tipped her head to one side and put her free hand on her hip. "Now listen, Monsieur Bonnard, I wasn't born yesterday, and you only have to look at your face to see what's going on. She wrote you a love letter. *C'est ça!*" Her large hands grasped the handle of the broom and swept it along the floor to emphasize her words. "And now please get out of the way so that I can sweep this place before the performance begins."

I sketched a bow and left the room. When I saw my face in the big Art Deco mirror in the foyer, I had to admit that Madame Clément was right. The tall, slim man with the thick dark hair, the telltale gleaming eyes, and that very peculiar smile was in love. Anyone with eyes in their head could see that.

I turned away and reached for the letter in my jacket pocket. Was it a love letter? I took it out once more and smiled as I scanned the tender words. I smiled, but little did I know that I would be reading this letter over and over again in the next few weeks, and clutching it as a drowning man clutches a straw, because it was the only evidence to show that that happy evening that ended under an old chestnut tree in the rue de Bourgogne had actually happened.

I stared at the poster for *The Things of Life,* which I'd hung in the foyer the previous afternoon with a notice saying "Next Wednesday in the series *Les Amours au Paradis,*" and wished it was already next Wednesday. I would gladly have done away with the laws of time and given up a whole week of my life to see Mélanie right then, but she was presumably already on the way to Brittany.

For the next few days, Mélanie's letter sat in my jacket pocket like a talisman. I kept it with me all the time—as a kind of insurance policy for love. I read it in the evening as—under Orphée's watchful gaze—I sat on the sofa with a glass of red wine, not wanting to go to bed; I read it the next morning as I drank my espresso at one of the round tables in the Vieux Colombier, staring absently at the rain pattering on the sidewalk.

Of course it was a love letter. And it was also the loveliest surprise that exciting week had brought me. At least that's what I thought until the moment on Friday evening when I lowered the shutters on the cinema after the last performance and a little man in a trench coat stepped out of the shadows and spoke to me.

I knew the man, and I knew the woman beside him. But I only realized that a few seconds later.

No one could blame me for opening my eyes wide and letting the bunch of keys slip from my hand. The whole scene was—in the words of the shy bookseller from *Notting Hill*— "surreal but nice."

As if he had fallen from the skies, the famous New York film director Allan Wood was standing in front of me, and at his side was a breathtakingly beautiful woman whom I had often admired on the screen.

Solène Avril, one of the best-known actresses of our times, shook my hand as naturally as if we were old friends. "*Bonsoir, Alain,*" she said, giving me a radiant smile. "I'm Solène, and I love this cinema."

Eleven

....

"*Mon Dieu,* it really is exactly as I remember it, wonderful—
c'est ravissant!"

With childlike enthusiasm, Solène Avril was going through
the rows of seats, stroking the old red plush upholstery. "Isn't it
just incredible, *chéri?* Was I exaggerating? You must admit we
would never have found anything like this in America."

Allan Wood pushed his horn-rimmed glasses up on his nose
and was just about to answer, when Solène fell into one of the
seats and gracefully crossed her silk-stockinged legs. "It's perfect, simply perfect," she went on, leaning her mop of blond hair
against the back of the seat. For one moment, all I could see of
her was her hair, flowing like liquid gold over the red velvet,
and the tip of her well-formed knee, excitedly jiggling up and
down. "And so *madly* atmospheric. Just the smell in this old
auditorium inspires me. . . . Aaaah, lovely, isn't it? Come and sit
here beside me, *chéri!*"

Allan Wood, who had been standing near me the whole

time to allow the "great atmosphere" of my cinema to work on him in a rather more restrained way, gave me an apologetic smile before moving toward the front and threading his way along the row where Solène was sitting. I watched him with some astonishment, and this unreal scene made my own cinema suddenly seem almost alien to me.

The heavy red velvet curtain that reached the floor and was now drawn across the screen; the thirty-two rows of seats rising in a slight rake toward the back wall of the auditorium with its little rectangular window that allowed the projectionist to see the screen and the audience; the black-and-white portraits of Charlie Chaplin, Jean-Paul Belmondo, Michel Piccoli, Romy Schneider, Marilyn Monroe, Humphrey Bogart, Audrey Hepburn, Jean Seberg, Cathérine Deneuve, Fanny Ardant, and Jeanne Moreau, smiling from their root-wood frames on the dark walls as if the glow of the spherical lamps were awakening them to new life. But the finest thing of all was the dome, which I rarely looked up at, though it was now attracting the admiration of my late-night guests. Its dark green foliage, where birds of paradise and golden oranges played hide-and-seek, arched over the auditorium.

"Do you understand now why I could only play those scenes here?" Solène Avril stretched her arms out and spread her fingers in a dramatic gesture. "I don't want to get oversentimental, but this place here . . . this place here is something completely different from a mock-up in a studio, *n'est-ce pas, chéri*? I can be authentic here. I can act from the heart here. I can just feel it." She sighed happily.

Allan Wood sat down beside her, leaned his head back, and stretched his arms out over the seat backs to the left and right of him. For a moment, he said nothing. Then he said, "Yeah, it seems like the perfect place. I really like it! And it has a really . . . nostalgic aroma." He waved his little white hand in the air, and in his comic accent with the strongly rolled *r*, it sounded like "arrrroma." "It smells"—he clicked his finger as if he'd just had a brainstorm, "of historrry."

I stood dumbly by the rear wall of my cinema, no longer capable of judging whether Allan Wood was right or not. To be honest, I was no longer capable of judging if I was actually hallucinating.

It was just before midnight, and I was expecting the two heads in the cinema seats to dissolve into thin air, leaving me to wake up in my own bed, shaking my head and muttering that I'd dreamed that a famous American director and one of the most beautiful women in the world had come to my little cinema, wanting to use it as the location for a film. I mean, that's how it works in dreams, isn't it?

I shut my eyes for a moment and breathed in deeply. A heavy scent hung in the air of the auditorium. It had entered with Solène Avril and wafted over toward me every time she moved. If that's what history smelled like, it was a pretty intoxicating smell.

"Is it original—or do you use some kind of spray, Alain?"

"Er . . . I beg your pardon?" I opened my eyes again. Allan Wood had turned toward me, and his dark eyebrows shot upward. "Oh, you know. A kind of air-freshener spray. I have one at home. It smells like an old library, makes everything feel very homey," he explained, standing up nimbly from his seat.

I shook my head. "No, no," I replied. "Everything here is genuine. . . ." I glanced at my watch. It was midnight, and nothing happened. I spread my hands in a gesture of resignation. It

was obvious that I wasn't dreaming and that this strange nocturnal incident, which was to turn my life upside down in the weeks
to come, was actually happening. It was unbelievable!

Allan Wood and Solène Avril were really here, in the
brightly lit auditorium of my cinema. And they were totally
determined—if I agreed, of course—to shoot a film in the Cinéma Paradis in the next few weeks.

I shook my head again and burst out laughing. "Everything
is real, even if I have to admit that you two still seem a bit unreal to me." I shrugged my shoulders. "I mean, things like this
don't happen to a normal guy like me every day."

Allan Wood took a couple of steps toward me and stopped
right in front of me. He was shorter than I, and his friendly
brown eyes twinkled with amusement as he looked up at me,
stretched his arm out, and plucked at the sleeve of his trench coat.

"But we *are* real," he said. "Come on, touch me. Totally real!"

I plucked at his sleeve and grinned. He really was "totally
real."

In spite of the fact that I had initially thought him to be an
apparition, I took an immediate liking to the little man in the
trench coat. He politely overlooked my obvious confusion. I,
however, still found it difficult to get used to the reality of Solène
Avril, even though she was standing less than a yard away from
me, looking at the famous photo of Audrey Hepburn with her
cigarette holder.

"Very elegant. Perhaps I should get myself one of those things.
What do you think, *chéri*?" She pouted thoughtfully, then sighed.
She turned to me. "But today you can't even smoke in a bar.
Our world has become so vulgar, don't you agree, Alain?" She
smiled at me. "Everything's changing, mostly for the worse."

She wrinkled her brow, and I admired the play of expressions on her face. "It's a good thing that Tiffany's is still there. I find that very reassuring."

We went back out into the foyer, and I looked out at the street, thinking of the strange encounter of an hour ago. I'd been as little prepared for it as I might have been for an alien landing. Someday, I'd probably be telling my grandchildren how I'd found Allan Wood and Solène Avril standing outside my cinema one night.

"Allan Wood?" I had stammered, after the little man in the trench coat had introduced himself to me, thus confirming my vague feeling that I knew him from somewhere. "That's really something. The Allan Wood from New York? Of course I've heard of you."

Allan Wood was modesty itself. "I'm so glad that you know me, Monsieur Bonnard. I see that we have the same name. That's quite amusing, isn't it? Can I call you Allan?"

"Alain," I said in a daze, correcting him.

Allan Wood seemed not to hear the difference. "That's great, Allan," he said with a friendly nod.

"Alain, *chéri,* his name is *Alain,* not Allan!" cried Solène Avril, giving me a sly smile. This Hollywood star had grown up in Paris and was well aware of the nasal pitfalls of the French language.

Allan tried once more, this time emphasizing the second syllable of my name. "Oh, I see . . . Al-lang. So . . . Al-lang, please excuse our little intrusion. Solène—what's the French word?— dragged me here. She insisted on showing me the Cinéma Paradis, and it's such a stroke of luck that we found you here."

Solène nodded and winked at me with a smile. I nodded back, grinning like a village idiot. And I was actually finding it difficult to follow the conversation.

"I'd like to talk to you about my new film, Al-lang," said the little man in the trench coat. Apart from his accent and a few minor errors, Allan Wood spoke French surprisingly well. He gazed up at the old facade and clicked his tongue in admiration. Then he handed me his card, which I stuck in my breast pocket. "I may well need your fine old cinema," he said.

"Aha!" I replied. To be honest, nothing better came to mind. What did Allan Wood need my cinema for? Gossip in the business had indeed suggested that the American director with the big horn-rimmed glasses had a number of quirks, but I had not been aware that buying up old French art-house cinemas was one of them. And at that particular moment, I didn't actually give a damn. I was completely under Solène Avril's spell. I stared like a sleepwalker at the beautiful blonde as she straightened her woolen stole. It lay on her shoulders like a fluffy cloud and made her look quite angelic. She actually seemed to be floating above the cobbled street.

"Oh, this is all so *exciting*," she whispered. "I feel just like a little girl. . . . Could we come in and look around a bit, Alain? *Please!*" She looked at me and put her hand on my arm. I could feel myself going weak in the knees.

"Of course," I said. "Of course." And I fell backward against the closed shutters. I have to say that I was finding all this quite exciting, too. I would never in my wildest dreams have imagined that a screen icon like Solène Avril would one day ask me for something. That was already like something from a movie.

So I'd picked the keys up from the sidewalk and a short while later we'd gone into the foyer, where we were now standing, and where Solène Avril had immediately found some familiar things. Her excited outbursts ("No! I recognize this mirror!" or

"Look, *chéri*—*La rêve est réalité*—that used to hang above the box office. I told you about it, didn't I?") continually interrupted Allan Wood as he explained what he wanted in great detail and with a great deal of gesturing, while Solène lost herself in her little trip down memory lane.

Initially, it wasn't very easy for me to work out the reason for this nocturnal visit, as both of them seemed to be very skilled at permanently cutting each other short. That made listening difficult, but after a while I understood this much: Allan Wood intended to make a new film starring Solène Avril. The film was to be called *Tender Thoughts of Paris* and, of course, would be set in Paris. It was a love story, about a woman searching for the lost love of her youth, revolving around an old art-house cinema.

This was why they'd traveled to Paris. And it had to be the Cinéma Paradis, because the capricious Solène remembered it from her childhood, and had developed the fixed idea that she could act this part well in only that very cinema. At the same time, after ten years in America, she was going through a phase of sentimentality about the French capital. Ultimately, it was probably his favorite actress's reminiscences of Paris that had inspired the aging director's latest project.

"Oh, you should be so happy that you're living in Paris, Alain. I'm *vraiment* fed up to the back teeth with America," said Solène, taking my arm as if it were a matter of course when, after an hour in which every nook and cranny of the cinema had been minutely inspected, we went back out onto the street. "How I've missed the crooked alleyways, the wonderful old houses, the reflection of the lights in the Seine, the smell of the streets after rain, the scent of the chestnut trees in the Tuileries and all the little cafés, bistros, and colorful stores in Saint-Germain. The tiny *tartes au citron*, the *méringues.*" She continued to chatter to me as we walked down the street to the quay and Allan Wood kept an eye out for a taxi.

"In California everything's gigantic, you know. The pizzas, the ice creams, the stores, the people, the friendly smiles of the waitresses—it's all XXL. It gets on my nerves. And the weather is always the same. Sunshine every damn day. Do you realize how boring it gets when you have no seasons anymore?"

I thought of the atrocious February weather that had plunged the majority of Parisians into deep depression and shook my head.

"There! A taxi!" Allan stopped and waved. Seconds later, a car pulled up beside him with its indicators flashing.

Solène planted a good-bye kiss on my cheek, while Allan held the rear door of the cab open for her. Then he turned to me again.

"Well, Al-lang . . . It was really nice meeting you." He fumbled in his jacket pocket and then handed me—for the second time that evening—his card. "If you have any problems, just call me. Otherwise, I'll see you in the Ritz on Sunday evening. Then we can discuss the whole *chose,* okay?" He took my hand and shook it. For a man of his size, he had a surprisingly firm handshake. "Think my proposal over, my friend. If you make your cinema available to us, it will bring in loads of money. . . ." He winked at me as if he were Al Pacino in person. "I mean *real* money." With these words, he got into the taxi. The door slammed shut and the car zoomed off and joined the stream of lights moving along the left bank of the Seine. On the other side of the river, the massive black silhouette of the Louvre stood out against the dark blue night sky. It was half past twelve. I was standing on the bank of the Seine, totally overwhelmed by the events of the last three days. I had kissed the woman in the red coat, I had received a love letter, and I had a date at the Ritz with Solène Avril and Allan Wood, who called me, respectively, Alain and Al-lang.

If my new, exciting life continued like this, I'd never find the time to see any films at all. By now, I felt as if I were Jean-Paul Belmondo, and that *Breathless* was a boring story compared with what I had experienced. I stuck Allan Wood's second card in my pocket, where Mélanie's letter still nestled, and all at once had the feeling that I was right in the middle of things—right in the middle of life. It was an intoxicating feeling.

"Who says that life no longer throws up any surprises?" Robert stubbed out his seventh Gauloise, trying to keep cool in spite of everything, but his demeanor spoke volumes. I had rarely seen my friend as impressed as he was that Saturday afternoon. We'd been sitting for two hours under the red-white-and-blue-striped awning of the Bonaparte, to which I had summoned him with the cryptic statement that I had sensational news.

"Oh man, Alain, you're waking me just for that? I'm still half-asleep. What could possibly be so sensational in your life?" he had asked reluctantly. "*I* had a sensational night with Melissa, believe you me."

"I do believe you," I replied, wondering which of his students Melissa was. "But that's still nothing compared with my news."

"Let me guess—you've gotten her cell number. Sensational. Congratulations." He yawned loudly. "Can I hang up now?"

"No, no, Robert, you're not getting away with it that easily. When I say sensational, I mean sensational. You'll never guess who I'm having dinner with at the Ritz tomorrow evening."

"Don't keep me in suspense."

I maintained an iron silence.

"Angelina Jolie? Har-har-har." He laughed at his own joke.

"Hey, not a bad try," I said, and the laughter died.

"What? Is that supposed to be a joke?"

"No joke," I said. "Just come."

I'm reluctant to admit it, because it perhaps shows me in a bad light, but after all those years as "periphery man," it did me a lot of good to see Robert dumbfounded for once. After I had told him everything, he sat in silence for a long while, speechless for the first time in his life. This was, of course, not, as you may well realize, due to the fact that the lovely Mélanie had sent me a very encouraging letter and—in spite of Robert's withering prognosis—definitely did want to see me again. For my friend, this was no more than a minor, peripheral bit of news, on which his only comment was, "Fine, fine—is that all?" But the business with Solène Avril—that was something else.

"*Solène Avril?* Wow, that's cool!" he said, lighting yet another cigarette. "Totally awesome! Tell me, is she as much of a knockout in person as she is on the screen?"

I nodded, tore open the little paper packet beside my cup, and trickled some sugar into my coffee. "You can say that again. It really knocks your socks off to see that woman suddenly standing right next to you in the flesh."

Robert sighed and took a deep drag on his cigarette. "Oh man. When I imagine that, I get a warm feeling all around my heart. And that sweetie was in your cinema for a whole hour, you say?"

"With Allan Wood."

"Allan Wood? What does the old fogey want from that sex goddess?"

"Nothing at all, as far as I can see. He just wants to make a film with her—in my cinema."

"Pull the other one!" mocked Robert. "I mean—*Solène Avril*! Really, anyone who kicks her out of bed for eating crackers must be nuts." He gave me an unmistakable look. "And you're meeting again tomorrow evening? At the Ritz? I bet that woman has a suite there with a gigantic king-size bed. Boy oh boy, are you lucky!"

"Good God, Robert!" I burst out. "We're meeting to discuss the film shoot. Don't you ever think about anything else?"

Robert shook his head. "No," he said decisively. "Not with that woman!"

"Well, at least I don't feel the need. I'm already in love, re-- member?"

For a moment, I thought about Mélanie, who would only be returning to Paris on Wednesday, and wondered what she was doing at that moment. Perhaps she was walking on the seashore, thinking of me, as well.

"What's love got to do with it?" Robert gave me an uncomprehending glance, and behind his wrinkled brow I could see the word *idiot* beginning to form. Then a new thought clearly shot through his mind and his expression brightened. "Say, Alain . . . do you think I could come along on Sunday evening? As your friend?"

I gave a satisfied laugh. "No way, José! The dinner at the Ritz is strictly a business meeting."

"Aha! Purely business—only you could believe that!" Robert pouted. "Then at least invite me along when they begin shooting."

"I'll see if it can be arranged." I grinned.

"Hey, what do you mean, man? Do you want to ruin my life? I only want to meet her." He looked at me with disarming innocence in his light blue eyes, and I began to understand why most women were unable to resist him. It would be hard to escape this leopard in rabbit's clothing.

"And what about your sensational Melissa?" I asked, although I already knew the answer.

"What about her?" Robert looked at me in amazement and drained the last drop of coffee from his cup. "Melissa is a very nice girl who's got to learn all about Newton's laws because she has her exams coming up. And anyway, everything is relative, as the highly esteemed monsieur Einstein tells us."

"I'm sure he didn't mean it like that."

"Of course he meant it like that." A sly grin crept over Robert's face. "Now, are you my friend or not?"

I pushed my cup away with a resigned sigh. "No worries—I'm your friend."

"And I'm yours. Do you have anything suitable to wear to dinner at the Ritz? I bet you'd even manage to show up there in a pullover. At the Ritz!"

You can say what you like about me, but my best friend, Robert Roussel, professor of astrophysics and babe magnet to all his female students, would have lost that bet outright. Because as I drove up to the Ritz in a taxi that Sunday evening, I was wearing a dazzling white shirt with a tie and an elegant dark blue suit. My getup left nothing to be desired; even Robert would have had to admit that.

But my friend turned out to be right about one thing. That dinner with Solène Avril was to end very differently from what I'd imagined. And in a way that was not strictly business at all.

Twelve

....

The dramatic structure of a good film is based on a director's choosing a moment in the life of his hero when an unexpected occurrence or a sudden realization changes everything. This turning point, which divides the lives of the people on the screen into a before and an after and changes them for the better or the worse, is the core of the action. And very often chance or fate—in the last analysis, it doesn't really matter which—has a hand in it.

A man sees someone being murdered on a passing train. A clerk finds a ticket for Rome in a phone booth one morning and decides not to go to work, but to risk the journey. A woman discovers a suspicious hotel bill in her husband's suit pocket. A child dies in a car accident, and its death throws a whole family out of its equilibrium. A man discovers during a picnic in the Bois de Boulogne that he actually loves his fiancée's best friend. Three quarrelsome siblings are forced by the terms of their mother's will to travel the pilgrim road to Santiago together before they can touch their inheritance. The daughter of a millionairess hides the good-looking thief who hammers on her hotel door. Five years after the war, a married man unexpectedly meets his first love again in a café.

Oh, yes, there's one more: The owner of a small cinema takes an evening stroll on one of the loveliest squares in Paris with a famous actress.

It's always a single moment that sets everything in motion and creates new connections. Cause and effect. Action and reaction. The butterfly that flutters its wings and causes a hurricane many thousands of miles away. In real life, however, unlike in the movies, you can't choose the moments that bring about groundbreaking changes. In fact, you often don't have the faintest idea that you are heading for such a moment.

The place Vendôme lay silent and majestic in the twilight, an untouched island that seemed to have been forgotten by the bustle of the city. On an impressive column towering in the middle of the square, the cast-iron statue of Napoléon kept lofty watch over time and all things human. In the arcades around the edges of the square were a whole lot of banks and also the most elegant stores and most expensive jewelers in Paris. You don't just chance to pass through the place Vendôme, and as my taxi stopped outside the entrance to the Ritz, I tried to remember when I'd last been in this square. Without success.

The porter opened the taxi door for me; I got out and, for the first time in my life, entered the oldest grand hotel in the world.

I looked around uncertainly in the lobby—the reception desk was on the right-hand side—and less than a second later a gray-haired hotel clerk came up to me and asked discreetly if he could help me.

"*Bonsoir.* I have an appointment with Monsieur Allan Wood and . . . er . . . Madame Avril," I said, and for a moment was a bit worried that he wouldn't believe me.

"Of course, Monsieur Bonnard. They are expecting you. Please follow me." The elderly man in his livery seemed totally unimpressed and walked in front of me with a measured pace. I, on the other hand, was deeply impressed, if only by the fact that he knew my name. We crossed the lobby and passed an inner courtyard with stone and marble statues, where a few guests were sitting at the tables, smoking.

At teatime, they serve little *tartes aux framboises* and delicate sandwiches on silver cake stands—I knew that from Robert, who valued the discreet privacy of the place when he came here with one of his chosen ones and didn't want to be seen. "Even a poor professor can afford the occasional afternoon tea at the Ritz," he joked. A thick carpet with an orange pattern swallowed the sound of our steps as we headed for an old-fashioned sofa and chairs. Behind them, on a marble fireplace, a gigantic flower arrangement of deep blue gladioli, purple tulips, white orchids, and pink roses reached almost to the ceiling. Fascinated, I looked around. Wherever my gaze fell, there were flowers, pictures, mirrors, antiques, and even the occasional person sitting with a drink or an iPhone in his hand.

"This way, please, Monsieur Bonnard!" The man in the red livery opened a gigantic door, behind which I could hear the low hum of voices. It looked as if we'd reached the restaurant.

It felt like entering a temple of spring. A light blue sky dotted with white clouds arched over the tables with their white cloths—a *trompe l'oeil* painting whose appearance of reality was enhanced by a real blooming tree in the center of the room. I looked up, expecting to see birds flying and chirruping through the restaurant, but their re-creation of nature didn't go quite that far.

A young waiter with gelled-down hair came up and took over convoy duties after a whispered conversation with the elderly man.

"This way, please, Monsieur Bonnard." He wove his way lithely between the tables, and I was no longer surprised that he knew my name. I was gradually beginning to get a real VIP feeling.

"Please, Monsieur Bonnard. Of course, Monsieur Bonnard. With pleasure, Monsieur Bonnard." The frequency with which my name was being used had grown exponentially since I had entered the old grand hotel. I honestly wouldn't have been surprised if someone had suddenly asked me for an autograph.

But that was reserved for the blond woman in the sleeveless little black dress who waved casually to me from one of the tables at the back of the room as a corpulent man took his leave of her with an autograph on his menu.

I raised a hand, put on a winning smile, squared my shoulders, and walked calmly over to the table where I was expected.

"She's like a sun—everyone wants to be close to her." Allan Wood watched his favorite actress admiringly as she tripped through the restaurant on her high heels "to freshen up."

I nodded. Solène was without doubt the shining polestar of this evening. She was charming, entertaining, extremely amusing. She automatically knew how to draw attention to herself without anyone being able to say exactly how she did it. Perhaps it was the way she told a story, how she threw her head back and broke out in infectious laughter, how she said *"Oh là là, chéri"* to Allan Wood, or simply the way she spread butter on her baguette. Everything she did, she did with enthusiasm and yet also with the greatest of ease.

The nervousness I'd been feeling all day vanished in the very moment that I sat down with the two of them at the table and Solène said, "Come on, Alain, drink a glass of champagne— we're having such fun!"

And we proceeded to have even more. It may sound strange, but after just a quarter of an hour I had completely forgotten that I was sitting at a table with two famous people. I got caught up in the relaxed atmosphere that emanated from this odd couple—who, as I had surmised, were not actually a couple.

In the weeks to come, it became clear to me that Solène Avril called every male being around her *chéri*. She actually did this because it was so much easier than remembering everyone's name. "I have to learn such an awful lot of lines, I can't be expected to burden my brain with names as well," she would say with a laugh. Cameramen, lighting technicians, journalists she'd chatted to for more than ten minutes—she called them all *chéri*. Even the waiters at the Ritz, who served food and drink expressionlessly with all the respect and propriety you would expect, were no exception. They were the only ones who occasionally reminded me that evening that this was not a casual dinner with friends at La Palette.

Men that Solène didn't like were, of course, not called *chéri*. They were "idiots" or "bores"—and the latter was clearly the worse insult of the two. "He was a bore, wasn't he, *chéri*?" she repeated emphatically in a broad American accent to Allan

Wood when talking about her latest lover, the Italian racing driver Alberto Tremonte. "Can you imagine it—a racing driver and yet so boring? I tell you, I almost died of boredom."

Strangely enough, this headstrong actress never called men whom she was in a relationship with *chéri*. These chosen few were given names like *mon lion* or *mon petit tigre*. Her latest tiger was a big Texas landowner who was actually named Fred Parker. Funnily enough, she managed to remember my name.

"Alain," she said, "tell us a funny story about your life." She was highly amused by the way that Allan Wood kept on mispronouncing my name, and loved pointing it out to him. "It's Alain, not Al-lang," she would say, correcting him. "But that's what I've just said: Al-lang," he replied every time, raising his eyebrows in good-humored surprise. "Al-lang—bang bang!" Solène poked me in the ribs and we laughed till tears ran down our cheeks.

Allan Wood joined in the laughter. He had a great sense of humor, and was one of those enviable people who are capable of laughing at themselves. I'd seen that when the starter was served. Allan had chosen *œuf cocotte* from the gigantic menu. "*Oeuf cocotte*—that sounds kind of sexy," he had said, only to find himself half an hour later leaning over a little dish in which half-cooked eggs and chopped-up mushrooms were floating in a slimy brown sauce. "Good God, what on earth is that?" he blurted, staring distrustfully at the warm goo—which, incidentally, is said to have an aphrodisiac effect. "Has this already been in someone else's mouth? That wasn't necessary. I may be old, but my teeth are still up to scratch!"

"That's what you eat when you have something else in mind, *chéri*," Solène explained, the corner of her mouth twitching suspiciously.

"Would you believe it?" said Allan, shaking his head as he fearlessly dunked a big chunk of baguette in the egg mixture and chewed on it gingerly. "Interesting," he said, and nodded a couple of times. "Tastes interesting. But I somehow prefer fried eggs, sunny-side up." He quickly washed the gloop down with a big gulp of red wine, threw his napkin down on the plate, and looked at me. "Now I'm looking forward to my steak. But first you and I have something to discuss."

With these words Allan Wood very quickly came to the actual reason for our meal, and Solène, who found everything to do with business "frightfully boring," stood up and reached for her little black patent-leather purse to go and freshen up, as she said.

Even before she came back, the essentials had been worked out. Even if I'd previously had reservations about making my cinema available for the shooting of *Tender Thoughts of Paris,* these had quickly been allayed—Allan Wood's engaging manner and the prospect of the not inconsiderable sum that the director was offering me for my inconvenience and the fact that I'd have to shut the Cinéma Paradis for a week were just too convincing. "A week should be enough to get those few scenes in the can," he said, and it sounded so innocuous and simple.

As we happily raised our glasses to our "mutual project" and Allan Wood explained to me that he intended to start shooting in three weeks' time, I had no idea what that would mean for my little cinema, and above all for me. I had not the slightest clue about the excitements of the coming weeks, nor about my despair, my hopes, nor about the whole complicated tangle, which had begun with a sad little story that had taken place in Paris many years before.

While our main course was being served and I listened to Allan Wood talking about his new film, I wondered what Uncle Bernard would have said about it all. Even if *Tender Thoughts of Paris* wasn't, strictly speaking, going to be a truly *impressionist* film, the whole thing still sounded like a story he would have liked. I would have loved to have been able to tell him that his old cinema was being so highly honored. And that I had found the love of my life in the Cinéma Paradis.

Allan Wood had come to the end of his story. "So, what do you think of the plot?" he asked.

"Sounds as if it'll make a really good film," I replied, suddenly proud and happy. I thought of Mélanie and would have liked her to be with me. I was eager to see her reaction and was sure that she'd be just as impressed as I was.

In my mind's eye I could already see another framed photo in the cinema. It was of Solène Avril and Allan Wood, and written above it in black pen was the caption: *We loved it here in the Cinéma Paradis—Allan and Solène.*

"I'm really glad that we can shoot the film in Alain's cinema rather than with those boring people in La Pagode," said Solène after we had, by mutual consent, given up on dessert and gone straight to cups of espresso, which were served on a little silver tray with cookies. "It'll be a really fun week. I'm already looking forward to it."

La Pagode, in the rue Babylone, was the oldest cinema in Paris. Uncle Bernard had watched Laurel and Hardy films there as a child, and he'd told me that La Pagode had originally been a Japanese-style dance hall built by the architect of the department store Bon Marché for his wife at the end of the nineteenth century. It was in the seventh arrondissement and was surrounded by an enchanting garden in which Solène had had her first kiss at the age of thirteen.

"The garden was lovely, but the kiss was gross," she said with a laugh. "But I never went to the cinema itself. My parents lived in Saint-Germain, after all, and when we went to the cinema as children, which, to be honest, wasn't very often, we always went to the Cinéma Paradis. We must have just missed each other there, don't you think, Alain?"

I smiled at the thought that we could have met back then. There were, I imagined, about five years between me and Solène. Five years that are so important in childhood and so totally meaningless later. I thought of the many afternoons in the Cinéma Paradis, of Uncle Bernard, whom I had told them about the evening of my first kiss and the little girl with the braids, and somehow had a feeling that things were coming full circle.

"I have an idea! How do you feel about holding the premiere of the film in the Cinéma Paradis?" Solène was already back in the here and now and was completely carried away by her brainstorm. She picked a little white flower off Allan Wood's jacket. "That would be very *charmant, chéri,* don't you think?"

Shortly after midnight, we were sitting in the bar. Because after he'd charged the check to his room, Allan Wood had had yet another idea. "And now we'll have one more little drink in the Hemingway Bar," he'd said. "I think I could do with a nightcap."

"Oh, yes, a last nightcap. Come along, Alain!" Solène had already taken my arm and guided me along an endlessly long corridor. Lining its sides, there were massive showcases displaying expensive jewelry and fine purses, cigars, and porcelain, dresses, swimsuits, and shoes for the rich and beautiful people of this world—certainly they would be out of most people's reach. But Solène pulled me along with her, not even deigning to look at all the displays.

And so we found ourselves a little later sitting on a leather sofa in the wood-paneled hotel bar, surrounded by photos and sculptures of Hemingway, hunting rifles, fishing rods, and old black typewriters with little round keys. Mojitos in hand, we celebrated Paris, because Paris was a festival of life.

I must admit that my two new friends would have had no trouble fitting in with the wild party mood that had swept Paris in the twenties, when people were celebrating life to banish the horrors of war.

"'If you are lucky enough to have lived in Paris as a young man,'" Allan started for the second time, and his voice sounded a little slurred as he quoted the great Hemingway, "'then wherever you go for the rest of your life, it stays with you . . .'" He waved his glass and the mojito almost spilled over the edge.

"To Paris!"

"To Paris!" we replied.

"And to the greatest writer of all time!"

"To Hemingway!" we shouted boisterously, and some of the guests looked over at us and laughed,

I was more than a little surprised when I realized that the weedy New York director, whom I could hardly imagine—if only for reasons of his own safety—with a shotgun, had, of all people, chosen as his idol the man who was a synonym for big-game hunting, war, and danger and who, so they say, never missed the opportunity for a fistfight.

"Do you know, Al-lang, I'm a big Hemingway fan," Allan had confided in me as we walked into the bar. "I mean, what a man!" He'd run his hand over the bust of Hemingway standing in a corner near the bar. "I admire him. He could fight. And he could write! I'd like to see anyone else do the same." Then he'd stopped at the black typewriter that stood on a pedestal to the rear of the bar and tapped tentatively at a couple of the keys. "Someday I'm going to make a film where Hemingway plays a role," he'd said with a decisive nod.

It wasn't the first time Allan Wood had been here. The bartender, a loquacious man who loved signing copies of his own cocktail book, which was on sale in the bar, had greeted him with a handshake, taken the RESERVED sign off the table, and invited us to sit down on the sofa.

While we drank our mojitos, Allan became talkative. He talked about his daughter, whom he had last seen a few years before in the Hemingway Bar. "I'm afraid it wasn't a very pleasant meeting," he said pensively. "I believe my daughter has never forgiven me for leaving her mother and marrying another woman. I've heard nothing of her since that disastrous evening." He raised his hands in a gesture of regret.

I knew that he had three marriages and several relationships behind him, and that they had produced some children. But the fact that he had a daughter in Paris was new to me.

A young woman in a white blouse with her dark hair wound in a perfect chignon put a new dish of nuts and salted almonds on our table. She had a little name badge on her chest. Allan Wood straightened his glasses. "Thanks . . . Melinda," he said affably.

The tall, slim girl went away smiling, and Allan Wood looked sadly after her. You could see that he was thinking of his daughter. "She always walked very upright," he said. "Like a ballet dancer." Solène stood up, and several guests looked over with interest.

"Oh, come on, *chéri,* it's been such a lovely evening, let's not get miserable. I certainly don't want that. You'll see your daughter again someday. In the end, you always see people again." She reached for her purse. "I'd like a cigarette now, and I'd like a little stroll in the fresh air before I go to bed. Who's coming with me?"

Allan shook his head. He wanted to stay, and joined the barman at the counter. As we left the Hemingway Bar, the two men were already deep in conversation.

Two guys in leather jackets were lounging in the seats near the door. They were sitting under a photograph of Hemingway with a fish. They looked after us and whispered to each other.

It was only as I was giving Solène a light outside the hotel and she leaned toward me for a moment and puffed the smoke out with a satisfied sigh that I realized that we were alone. At this hour of the night, there wasn't even a doorman standing at the entrance.

I lit a cigarette for myself, too, and looked up at the victory column towering like a golden obelisk against the night sky in the beam of the spotlights. Not that there was any reason for it, not that I had any intentions, but I felt strangely self-conscious, and, in the silence of that great square, I became suddenly aware of how extraordinary this situation was.

"What are you thinking about, Alain?" asked Solène.

"Nothing. No, that's not true. I was just thinking . . . well . . . how quiet it is here," I said. "Like on a lonely island."

"Happiness is always a little island," said Solène, smiling. "I guess we were both thinking the same thing. Come on, let's take a little walk."

She took my arm. Our steps rang out as we passed the stores, whose displays were still lit up even at this hour of the night, and the smell of our cigarettes mingled with the heady scent of her perfume.

"You have a very unusual perfume. What is it?" I asked.

She gave me a sidelong glance and with her free hand tucked back a stray lock of hair. "Do you like it? It's Guerlain. L'Heure Bleue. A very old perfume. Just imagine, it's been around since 1920."

"Incredible. I like it a lot."

"And I like you, Alain."

"Me? Oh my goodness." I grinned in embarrassment. "As a man, I'm a disaster. I don't hunt, I don't box, and I can't even play the piano."

"That really is a disaster." She laughed. "I bet you can't even dance, but that's not important. What's up here"—she tapped my forehead—"that's important, that's attractive, and that's what I like so much about you. You know a lot, you're intelligent, and you have imagination. I can see that right away." She gave me a roguish look. "It's true. You have a good mind. A real intellectual, a bit shy perhaps, but I find that very sweet."

A shy intellectual! I shook my head. It's astonishing what people project onto you just because you don't chatter away the whole time.

"Come on, I'm not that intellectual!"

"You don't know Texan farmers." Solène sighed, then came to a sudden halt and looked at me. "And me? Do you find me attractive? Purely theoretically, I mean." A few fine light blond hairs drifted across her face and she drew her lips into a smile. She stood there, a shining light in the darkness, and waited for an answer.

I felt very strange. Was I being propositioned by Solène Avril? Everything seemed unreal. The ground seemed to quiver beneath me and I could feel the earth moving. I swallowed and cleared my throat. "Goodness, Solène, what sort of a question is that? Of course I find you attractive. And not just in theory. Just look at yourself! You're as far removed from theory as a summer day from a . . . from a filing cabinet. I mean, is there any man at all who could resist you? You're so beautiful and radiant . . . and really very . . . very seductive . . ." my voice trailed off and I ran my hands through my hair.

"Do I hear a 'but' there?"

"Solène . . . I . . ."

"Well?" A strange glint came into her deep blue eyes.

It really wasn't easy, and I was probably the greatest idiot the world has ever seen, because this was without doubt one of those moments in life that will never be repeated. But then another image crossed my view like the face of the moon. I saw an old chestnut tree and a girlish young woman in a red coat whispering, "Might this be the moment?"

"I'm sorry," I said. "It's not the right moment."

"So there's someone?"

I nodded. "Yes. And it's not just anyone, Solène. I've really fallen in love—with a woman who's been on my mind for several months. I kissed her for the first time on Wednesday. And it feels as if I've always loved her, even if I haven't always known her. Can you understand that?" I put my hand to my heart. "I hope you're not angry with me."

Solène was silent for a moment. Then she smiled. "Oh dear, it obviously seems to be our fate just to miss each other." She took my arm again. "Of course I'm not angry with you, but couldn't you have waited a couple of days with that kiss? Then at least I might have had a slim chance."

I laughed, relieved that she had taken it so calmly. Solène Avril definitely had all kinds of chances, as she very well knew. As we continued on around the square, she gave me a coquettish look and sighed. "Okay, fair enough, since you're head over heels in love. Then I wish you luck—and I'll drop by in ten years' time."

"In ten years' time, you'll have long forgotten me."

"Or you me."

"That'll be hard, with you smiling down from every screen."

"Serves you right."

By this time we'd made a complete circuit of the place Vendôme, and Solène pulled me over to the display in a jewelry store a few yards from the entrance to the Ritz. She looked at the watches, the sparkling rings and necklaces that were on sale at astronomical prices. "Perhaps you should buy something nice for your girl?"

"I'm afraid they're not exactly in my price range."

"But they are in mine," she said. "At least they are nowadays. Cartier, Chanel, Dior—all no problem. Have you got another cigarette for me?"

I held out the pack to her and gave her a light.

"Thanks." She exhaled the smoke and watched it thoughtfully. "My parents didn't have much money. They found it difficult to make ends meet. Our whole apartment was about as big as my bathroom today in Santa Monica. I was beautiful, ambitious, and obnoxious. As soon as I got the chance, I left Paris with an exchange student from San Francisco—Victor." Her expression darkened a moment and she flipped her ash away. "Then I lived in Carmel for a couple of years." Memory made her voice go soft. "Do you know Carmel?" I shook my head, but she seemed not to notice. "Carmel. Even the name sounds precious, don't you think? A little place right on the Pacific shore. There's an old monastery there, and an endless golden beach. You can hardly imagine the distance. When you're sitting there, you forget everything."

She smoked on in silence and I just stood there and waited. Night was a good time for confessions.

"Then I was approached on the beach at Carmel," she said. "I had a job in a coffee shop to keep my head above water. Then I was suddenly the face they were looking for. Screen tests, auditions, my first film. And then everything moved very fast. It was uncanny." She laughed. "All at once, I had money. A lot of money. I could hardly take it all in. Everything was so easy." She shook her head. "With my first wages I gave my parents a trip to Saint-Tropez. To the Hôtel Belrose." She leaned against the wall of the jewelry store and pulled her dark stole around her shoulders. "My mother always dreamed of a once-in-a-lifetime holiday in Saint-Tropez with my father. They couldn't afford expensive journeys. She thought Saint-Tropez was the greatest. There was an old poster of the Côte d'Azur hanging in her sewing room, and she always used to gaze at it. Before they set off, Maman called me one last time. Her voice was full of excitement—she sounded like a young woman again. She was so happy. 'I think this is the happiest day of my life, child,' she said." Solène swallowed. All of a sudden, she seemed sad, and I wondered why.

"What a wonderful idea," I said hesitantly. Solène looked at me, her dark eyes shining.

"No, not such a wonderful idea," she said bitterly, and threw her glowing cigarette butt on the ground. She pressed her lips together, and I was afraid that she'd burst into tears.

"My parents had a fatal accident on the way. Some overtired truck driver who didn't look in his mirror before changing lanes. They never reached Saint-Tropez."

"Oh my God, Solène, that's terrible!" Without thinking, I put my arm around her. "I am so sorry!"

"It's all right," she said, wiping her eyes. "It was all so long ago. I don't know what suddenly made me think about it again. It's so strange to be back here in Paris after all those years—perhaps that's why."

She attempted a smile, and then with a quick movement she brushed a lock of hair from my forehead. "Thanks for the walk anyway, Alain. You're really very sweet. Your girlfriend is lucky."

And then it happened. Out of the blue. At first, I thought a lightning storm had crept up on us. I hunched my shoulders and waited instinctively for the growl of the thunder. A blinding flash pierced the darkness, then another. I raised my hand in self-defense and closed my eyes, blinded. When I opened them, I was looking straight down the lens of a camera.

Thirteen

....

Three things in life are inevitable, Solène had said: love, death, and paparazzi.

These words came to mind as I walked unsuspectingly along the boulevard Saint-Germain that Tuesday morning. I'd used the morning to sort out a few things, and they were now all dealt with. I'd delivered my quarterly tax return to my accountant, I'd picked up my shirts from the cleaners and bought fresh cat food. I hadn't been to the cinema on Monday, and apart from the fact that Orphée had profited from a moment when I wasn't watching her to pull the chicken intended for me off the kitchen shelf and wolf most of it down, the previous evening had been almost totally uneventful. I'd almost forgotten what it felt like to wake up refreshed after a good night's sleep.

The day was still young, and the sun was casting its springtime spell on the streets of Paris. A perfect morning to sit outside somewhere and read the paper while drinking a large *café crème*. I put on my sunglasses and, full of the joys of spring, walked past two girls in light coats with scarves wound several times round their necks who were standing at one of the newspaper kiosks, leafing through the magazines.

I was just thinking that I would have to talk to Madame Clément and François that afternoon about the fact that in three weeks' time we were going to have important visitors and that the cinema would have to be closed for the film shoot, when I was almost trampled down by a group of Japanese tourists. Laughing and chattering, armed with cameras and brightly colored shopping bags, they were following a tourist guide as she thrust her red umbrella into the air in time with her footsteps. I stood aside to get out of the way and found myself standing in front of a newspaper kiosk.

RINGS FROM CARTIER—IS THIS HER NEW MAN? The headline in *Le Parisien* hit me right in the eye. I was dumbfounded as I looked at the photo. A young man with dark brown curly hair was looking back at me. He was staring into the camera in a state of shock and seemed to be quite surprised himself. Beside him stood a smiling blonde in a black evening dress. It took a couple of seconds for me to realize who the man was. "I don't believe it!" I said.

The newspaper seller was very friendly. He even offered me a carrier bag. I bought not only *Le Parisien* but also *Le Monde, Le Figaro, Libération, Les Echos, L'Equipe,* and, just to be on the safe side, the current edition of *Paris Match.* Then I rushed excitedly, carrying cat food, shirts, and papers, the few yards to the Café de Flore and went up to the first floor.

At this time of day, not much was going on on the first floor of the Flore, and you could sit there undisturbed. We Parisians normally avoided establishments like the Deux Magots or the

Café de Flore, where tourists would sit every day, trying to soak up the atmosphere of the old days, but if it couldn't be avoided, we preferred the Café de Flore, which was a bit farther from the church of Saint-Germain, and then we went for the first floor, where tourists rarely penetrated, unless they were looking for the bathroom.

I crossed the sunlit room, where there were only two ladies deep in lively conversation, looking suspiciously like denizens of the publishing world. They looked up quickly as I came in, then turned back to a list that was lying on the table in front of them. One of them was talking, underlining her words with lively gestures. The other was nodding with interest and making notes in a little black Moleskine.

I found refuge at one of the rear tables by the window. Just to be on the safe side, I kept my sunglasses on. A waiter in a black vest came over to take my order. After ordering my *café crème* and scrambled eggs, I almost expected to hear "Of course, Monsieur Bonnard." But the waiter didn't even say "Of course, monsieur." He just growled an indifferent "*Oui*" and took back the menu. The waiters in the Flore are not easy to impress and are usually in a bad mood. Still, over the years very important guests have sat at the tables in their café and held important conversations about art, philosophy, and literature. Compared with them, what was the owner of a small cinema who had just made his way onto the front page of *Le Parisien,* where he didn't look particularly intelligent?

"Paparazzi, damn it!" Solène had hissed as we were surprised by the flash of the two photographers on the deceptively quiet place Vêndome on Sunday evening. "Come on, Alain. Just keep cool."

She'd taken me by the hand and quickly led me the few paces to the entrance of the Ritz, paying no attention to the two men in their leather jackets, who followed us to the hotel, trying to tempt the actress out of her reserve with their questions. I admired the self-control with which Solène ignored the paparazzi. She said nothing, looking obstinately forward as she hurried to the hotel entrance. Then she turned round briefly and smiled thinly.

"Messieurs, if you have any questions to do with my new film, all you have to do is come to the press conference at two o'clock tomorrow afternoon. Good evening."

It was clear that those two gentlemen were not necessarily desperate for information about a new Allan Wood film. The question of who was sleeping with whom was far more interesting.

"The shadow side of fame," Solène had explained with a laugh after we had run past the porter like two kids who'd just broken a window. We were now sitting in the lobby. "For a moment, I'd almost forgotten that." She raised her hands in mock desperation. "At first, I always got terribly upset when one of those stupid snappers jumped out from behind a hedge and then published the craziest stories in the tabloid papers. But it's best to stay cool. Publicity is part of the job; that's the way it is. If there's nothing about you in the papers, you're on the way down. Then you can take early retirement, or become an animal rights activist." She grinned. "But if those press dummies get too cheeky, they get it in the neck from my lawyers."

She'd crossed her legs and was contemplating her pointed black patent-leather shoe. "You wouldn't believe the people they've foisted on me—three months ago, it was the gardener. Headline: 'She calls him *chéri*. Is he Lady Chatterley's lover?'" She smiled broadly. "Kind of sweet, isn't it? Those gossip sheets really will clutch at any straw to one-up the opposition." She gave me a sly glance. "I hope you weren't too shocked, Alain."

"Aw, it wasn't that bad," I replied with a grin.

The incident on the place Vendôme had catapulted Solène back to the present. Her melancholy seemed to have vanished. And so had the paparazzi when I made my way home a little later.

I sank back in the leather upholstery of the Café de Flore and studied the front page of *Le Parisien*. It was quite amazing to see what fairy tales the paper had invented about the snapshot of Solène and me.

Is the lovely Solène Avril cheating on her Texan landowner? On Sunday evening she was seen standing outside a jeweler's on the place Vendôme with an attractive man.

I smiled at the flattering thought. The attractive man was me!

The waiter came and slammed a tray with a silver coffeepot, a glass of water, and a jug of hot milk down on the table. I poured myself a coffee, and nearly burned my tongue when, without thinking, I took a great gulp as I read on.

Were the couple looking for an engagement ring? The Hollywood film star, who lives in a luxury villa in Santa Monica and has come to Paris with director Allan Wood to make a new film in the next few weeks, seemed relaxed and happy as she disappeared into the Ritz with the unknown man.

I shook my head in amazement, then put the paper down for a moment because my scrambled eggs had arrived. While I ate it with a chunk of baguette, I looked through the other papers, as well. These papers also reported on Allan Wood's film and its star. Although she'd been living abroad for many years, Solène Avril was very popular in France—probably mainly because she came from Paris and spoke fluent French. None of these papers had anything about the attractive stranger who'd been seen buying engagement rings at Cartier, though they did mention that some of the scenes would be shot in the Cinéma Paradis. Solène Avril had obviously mentioned this at the previous day's press conference, and the journalists had zealously taken down all she'd said.

"It's the cinema I used to go to when I was a little girl. Shooting the film there means a lot to me. And Paris is still Paris. I've only just realized how much I've missed this city," quoted *Le Figaro,* and *Le Monde* had an article under the headline *PARIS, JE T'AIME!* SOLÈNE AVRIL AND ALLAN WOOD IN PARADISE! which dealt with the content of the new film a little more extensively.

> Tender Thoughts of Paris *is the story of Juliette, who accompanies her fiancé, Sam (played by Ron Barker), on a business trip to Paris and, in the cinema she went to when she was young, meets the great love of her youth, Alexander (Howard Galloway), quite by chance. They have three days to visit all their old favorite haunts together and to conjure up a time when everything seemed possible and feelings had an intensity that never comes back in later life.*

"Of course, many things in life are irretrievable. In Tender Thoughts of Paris *I'm trying to show that the dreams of the past are never totally lost. They may get overlaid with other things, abandoned, or suppressed. But they're always there. All you have to do is find them," says Allan Wood. The shy director appeared at the press conference for only a short while.*

Solène Avril, the leading lady in Wood's new film, is particularly pleased that the Cinéma Paradis, with its rich history, will be one of the original locations.

"In America, these little art-house cinemas have almost died out," said the French star. "I find it so reassuring that there are people like Alain Bonnard, who maintain quality and traditional values even if that is out of step with the spirit of the age."

Beneath the article was a photo of Solène Avril and Allan Wood standing in front of an old fireplace. And even in *Paris Match,* there was a photo collage of Solène Avril, Howard Galloway, and the Eiffel Tower, with a short paragraph about the forthcoming visit of these stars to Paris, which ending with the question of whether the lovely Solène and the handsome Howard might become a couple in real life, as well.

I folded the papers and put them in my plastic bag, then looked around for the waiter, who had not shown himself upstairs for quite a while. In the end, I folded the check and a twenty-euro note, stuck them under my cup, picked up my jacket and all my bags, and headed for the stairs, where a display case had ashtrays and mugs from the Café de Flore for sale. When I passed the cash register downstairs, three waiters were standing there together, chatting. They gave me an indifferent glance and then went on chatting. The ignoramuses did not know whom they were dealing with: Alain Bonnard, a man who stood for quality and traditional values.

After reading those papers in the Café de Flore, which had amused me while at the same time giving me an idea of what it was like to be the focus of public interest, I began to think for the first time that the coming weeks could be quite exciting for me. And I turned out to be right.

I'd hardly taken a couple of paces along the rue Bonaparte with my bags and shirts when my phone rang.

"*Wow!*" said Robert. "I take my hat off to you, Monsieur Bonnard! I always knew that there was a real dandy hidden somewhere in you. You're faster than sound!"

"You, too, it seems," I replied. "Since when have you been reading *Le Parisien*?"

"Since my friend took over the front page." Robert gave a sly laugh. "It did take a bit of time till I recognized you. I have seen better photos of you!"

"It was a snapshot." I grinned as I thought how dumb I looked in the photo. "The paparazzi never sleep."

"And?"

"And nothing," I said. "It was a very pleasant evening. And afterward we smoked a cigarette outside."

"A cigarette *afterward*?" I realized that he was teasing me, but I still blushed.

"Yes, afterward," I said. "*After* the meal. All the rest is just fairy stories."

He sighed. "You're destroying all my illusions."

"I'm inconsolable. Have you ever thought of a career with

Le Parisien? You seem to have the kind of imagination needed for a job like that."

"I know." He took it as a compliment. "But I prefer astrophysics. Will I see you for lunch?"

"No, no time. I'll call you."

"Aha. 'Don't call us; we'll call you'—you're already starting to sound like a bloody celeb."

I laughed. "Absolutely, my friend. I'm famous now, you know."

I swear it was meant as a joke, but when I got to the cinema that day, I learned better.

"Oh, Monsieur Bonnard! Just imagine what's happened," said Madame Clément, beside herself with excitement and waving a copy of *Le Monde* in my face. "A man from the paper was here asking for you. He wants to write about the Cinéma Paradis. Here . . . his card. You should call him *right away,* he said. And he thinks our old cinema is fabulous. I took him around and he looked at everything very carefully. Isn't it all just too exciting? We're famous!" She stroked her short gray hair and gave a self-satisfied glance in the foyer mirror. "*Mon Dieu*, just wait till I tell Gabrielle . . . Solène Avril and Howard Galloway in our cinema!"

Good God was what I thought, too. I had obviously totally underestimated the speed with which that sort of news gets around. In the Cinéma Paradis, at least, everyone was very clearly in the picture.

"Why didn't you tell us about the film shoot, Monsieur Bonnard?" asked François. His voice was as calm as usual, and only the fact that he raised one eyebrow slightly betrayed his irritation.

My projectionist is a laid-back kind of guy who takes things as they come. He's absolutely imperturbable. Even now, he only gave me a questioning look, while Madame Clément went on muttering, listing the people from her circle of acquaintances she could tell the great news to.

"I've only known for a couple of days," I said a little guiltily. "In fact, the whole thing was only definitely decided on Sunday evening, and I was going to tell you both today anyway. And now it seems the gentlemen of the press have gotten in before me."

I looked at the card the journalist from *Le Monde,* a certain Henri Patisse, had left. At the bottom he'd scribbled a note, asking me to call him. I frowned. I was already more than fed up with journalists. "What exactly did the man want? I can't tell him anything about engagement rings from Cartier."

"Engagement rings from Cartier!" blurted Madame Clément. "What do you mean, Monsieur Bonnard? Are you getting engaged?" She opened her eyes wide. Unlike my friend, she seemed to have heard nothing about the nocturnal incident on the place Vendôme.

"Don't you read *Le Parisien,* then?" I said, sounding more cynical than I intended.

"*Le Parisien*—what do you think I am, Monsieur Bonnard?" Madame Clément was visibly piqued. "You probably think that because I sit in the box office and sell tickets, I only read the tabloids. I'm from a respectable family, monsieur. In our house, we read *Le Figaro* at breakfast. I haven't always worked in a box office, you know. In the past, I even worked in a library, and it was only when my husband died and I had to bring the children up all on my own that I took the job in Bon Marché because it paid much better, and I'm sure that's nothing to be ashamed of."

"Madame Clément, please!" I raised a reassuring hand. I'd obviously hit a sore point. "It was a joke, that's all. Just forget it, okay? And as far as today's concerned, I'm really glad you don't read *Le Parisien*, because it's full of total garbage."

Madame Clément nodded, mollified.

"Now, what exactly did this Monsieur Patisse want?"

"Oh, he was a very serious gentleman." An expression of great satisfaction crossed Madame Clément's face. "And very friendly and attentive. He's already taken some notes about the things I was able to tell him—that the cinema once belonged to your uncle, and that you took it over even though you were trained for a totally different profession." She looked at me with almost maternal pride, and I couldn't help thinking that my own mother had found my decision to give up the lucrative trade in bathroom fittings for the United Emirates to go back to the cinema to be a total "head in the clouds" move. "Have you thought it over carefully, son? Giving up such a great job for a stuffy old cinema . . . well, I just don't know," she had said in desperation, and my father had weighed in on her side with a grave expression. "Good jobs don't grow on trees these days, Alain. Everyone has to grow up sometime." Those were his words, and that was the first time I asked myself if growing up necessarily meant betraying your dreams to earn as much money as possible. Obviously, it did.

I gave an involuntary sigh.

"It was all right to tell the gentleman from *Le Monde* those things, wasn't it, Monsieur Bonnard?" Madame Clément looked at me anxiously, and I nodded.

"Yes, yes, of course. It wasn't a secret."

"And he was very enthusiastic about our *Les Amours au Paradis* series, too. 'My goodness—*Jules and Jim*,' he said when he looked at the program leaflet. 'I haven't seen it in ages. I must come and see that.'" Madame Clément pointed at the old black-and-white poster in the foyer, which showed Jeanne Moreau in a baker boy's cap and sporting a painted mustache as she laughed and ran across a bridge with her two friends. "He stood in front of it for a long time, then shook his head and—well, anyway, he wants to write an article about the Cinéma Paradis and about you, Monsieur Bonnard. About what it's like to run an art-house cinema these days. It's not always easy, is it? We all know that!"

She looked over at François, who growled an agreement, and then they both looked at me as if I were d'Artagnan. It wouldn't have taken much to get me to shout out "All for one! and one for all!" Madame Clément and François had been there from the very beginning, but I still found the way they were standing behind me and the little cinema quite moving.

"*Bon.* I'll call the gentleman of the press later." I nodded to them both and smiled. In actual fact, it was not very easy to be the proprietor of a small cinema, but it had a charm of its own and could sometimes be quite exciting, as the last few days had shown.

But I wasn't naïve enough to believe that the sudden appearance of a journalist had anything to do with me or the rediscovery of the Cinéma Paradis. For a paper like *Le Monde,* a story about a cinema like the Paradis was of very limited interest. Unless it was August and they were racking their brains for something to fill the summer gap until the *rentrée* brought people back to the city. Or it was April and an actress by the name of

Solène Avril had, for sentimental reasons, declared a particular cinema to be her favorite.

Before vanishing into my office behind the box office, I turned around once more. "Oh, yes. And about the film shoot—we'll be closing the cinema for a week at the beginning of May to make it available for the actors and crew. The performances for that week are canceled. Apart from that, nothing will change."

At that moment, I'm sure I believed what I was saying. But a lot did change. Everything, in fact.

Fourteen
....

There was a bright blue sky over Paris when I opened the window the next morning. I saw a little white cloud that seemed to be hovering just over my head, and my first thought was of Mélanie, whom I was going to see at last that evening. I remembered her cutely disheveled hair and her lovely mouth and sighed longingly. A week had passed since we had parted with a thousand kisses that night under the old chestnut tree, but it might as well have been four weeks—so much had happened in recent days. Most of the time, I hadn't even had the breathing space to indulge in my new favorite activity, dreaming about the woman in the red coat, but all those extraordinary events had helped to shorten the time for me. And so this one week had seemed at the same time both longer and shorter than a normal one.

At the moment, nothing was normal anyway. On the previous day alone, three more journalists had called wanting to write something about the Cinéma Paradis and inquiring about the beginning of the filming. Monsieur Patisse of *Le Monde* had insisted on returning that same afternoon to ask his questions and then photograph me beside my old projector, which brought a gleam to his eyes of the kind you normally only see in six-year-olds when they get their first model train.

"Great, Monsieur Bonnard! Wonderful," he'd said, looking at the display on his camera. I didn't know if he meant me or the projector. "And now once more, please . . . smile!"

My reputation grew by the hour. Robert, with whom I absolutely had to go out for something to eat that evening—he'd even dropped the sensational Melissa to do so—was deeply impressed by my new, exciting life. And even my parents, who had probably seen the article in *Le Figaro,* had left a message on my voice mail congratulating me on my "great success." "This is really great, son. Make something of it," Papa had said, and I wasn't quite sure what he'd meant by that. Should I make my cinema permanently available for filming? Did I have any say in the matter? Still, I can't deny that I was pleased to hear his words of recognition.

The last few days had swept through my otherwise-tranquil life like a whirlwind, and yet the whole time I felt that I was carrying Mélanie with me in a corner of my heart. From time to time, I touched the letter, which I always carried with me, and asked myself what she would say about all these goings-on. There was so much I wanted to tell her about, to share with her. But there would be time for that. Because the most important things I wanted to say to her were only to do with us, and us alone. Waiting had increased my longing, and a thousand words came into my thoughts that I wanted to whisper in her pretty ear as the evening turned to night and night to morning.

I made myself an espresso, and imagined how Mélanie would come along the street in her red coat with her light upright walk and an expectant smile. I would wait outside for her and take her in my arms. No, I would run toward her, full of impatience. "You're here at last," I would say. And I'd never let her go.

It was a long time since I'd sung in the shower. That morning, I did. I sang the chorus of an old Georges Moustaki song over and over. I'd rarely felt myself to be so real as I did that morning. I was just waiting for Mélanie, who would be there that day. Everything was possible, there were no limits, and life was an endless spring day full of promise.

I hummed as I tidied the apartment. I put food and fresh water out for Orphée, who could sense my nervousness and kept rubbing herself against my legs, put two bottles of Chablis in the fridge, and ran downstairs to buy an armful of roses from the little florist's shop in the rue Jacob, which I then spread around the whole apartment.

I decided to reserve a table at the Petit Zinc, a good restaurant diagonally opposite the church of Saint-Germain, just a stone's throw from my apartment. I'd get a table right next to the window, in one of the niches with their pretty light green Art Nouveau pillars, which made you feel as if you were sitting in an arbor outside in a garden.

I put the rest of the roses in a glass vase and set it on my polished round cherrywood table. The opulent pink, red, and light yellow blossoms bent their heavy heads over the edge of the vase. A sunbeam, caught in the water of the vase, painted quivering flecks of light on the wood. For a moment, I saw this as a reflection of the state of my heart—so bright and warm and full of joyful agitation.

I stopped for a moment, ran my hand through my damp hair, and looked around the apartment, contemplating with satisfaction the results of my labors. Everything was perfect. I was well prepared for an extraordinary evening and for love, which would enter my home that day with the light-footed steps of a girl.

When I left the apartment that afternoon, I smiled at myself in the mirror. Never in my life had I been so prepared for happiness.

The Cinéma Paradis was sold out that evening. Half an hour before the first performance, there were already no tickets left. I think it was the first time I'd ever had to turn the tubby little man with the briefcase away when he, as usual, rushed into a foyer thronged with customers only a few minutes before the show began. Nor was there any room for the woman with the black curls, who that day had wound an emerald green scarf in her hair and come without her little daughter. I raised my hands apologetically and watched as my two regular customers left the cinema in disappointment, exchanged a few words of astonishment, and then crossed the street together. They were just as surprised as I was. Or, in the words of Madame Clément, "just as surprised as *all* of us."

Of course, Julie Delpy's *2 Days in New York* was in every respect a remarkable film. And even more so was Claude Sautet's *The Things of Life,* which was the late show that Wednesday evening: You could always find something new about what really matters in life in that film. But that didn't explain this sudden invasion, which the Cinéma Paradis was barely able to cope with.

Like a tsunami, a wave of interest had swept over our cinema, engulfing everything in its path, and it would not ebb for the following weeks and months. The friendly reports in the press, which just for a change had capriciously chosen an art-house cinema where there was no popcorn—which was obviously felt to be both unusual and *très sophistiqué*—the forthcoming filming of *Tender Thoughts of Paris,* and the surprising suggestion of the film academy that the Cinéma Paradis and its proprietor should be given an award for "exceptional service to French film" drew in whole crowds of customers.

People I'd never seen before thronged to the performances and discovered their love for the *cinéma d'art* and the magic of an old, rather comfy, and almost forgotten cinema, where time seemed to have stood still and the monotony of everyday life was held at bay for a couple of hours.

Even if most of them came out of voyeurism, curiosity, or a desire not to miss anything at any cost, many of them left the Paradis different people from when they had entered. You could see it in their faces. The magic moment at the core of every good film seemed to be reflected in their eyes. The audience came out of the cinema borne on images that were bigger than they were, moved by gestures whose gentle fingers had imperceptibly left their mark on their hearts, and enriched by words of wisdom that they could take home like a handful of diamonds. And that was at least as good as the pleasing side effect that I was suddenly the owner of a relatively successful cinema—carried on a wave of sympathy and admiration, wooed by journalists and ultimately even by a major cinema chain that offered a friendly takeover with astonishingly good conditions and the assurance that even under their auspices "everything would remain the same" for me.

Even the owner of an upmarket Parisian discotheque approached me with the suggestion of turning the Cinéma Paradis into a kind of luxury cinema where the sybarites of the city could chill out with cocktails and exquisite finger food while watching the films.

I turned them all down gratefully, knowing all too well that the price of security was my freedom. In those turbulent weeks, the Cinéma Paradis seemed to be offering me both financial security and entrepreneurial freedom. And what could have been more attractive for a man who had followed his idea calmly and with determination and was now making the pleasant discovery that this idea was actually bearing fruit?

"Alain Bonnard has succeeded in doing something absolutely magical, something that has become very rare in our time. One could almost envy him," Monsieur Patisse had written in his article.

It was clear to me that the catalyst that had produced all this sudden attention had been Solène Avril's support. I was not so deluded as to think that Paris was going through some sort of nostalgic revolution, of which I had been the harbinger—but every success has its share of luck. And luck had just arrived on my doorstep. Without doubt—and in my father's words—this was "the high point" of my professional career in the cinema business.

And so that second Wednesday in April should have been the shining prelude to the loveliest weeks of my life. It would have if something hadn't happened, or, rather, had definitely *not* happened—something I would not have believed possible as I happily decorated my apartment with flowers that morning.

The woman in the red coat didn't come.

The moon shone high over the city's old houses. Its round disk snuggled up against a cloud that floated lonely in the deep blue sky. And as I finally made my way hesitantly to the rue de Bourgogne, I thought that the night seemed made for two people in love. But I was walking through the narrow streets alone, the echo of my steps ringing heavily from the walls— and my heart was heavy, too.

Mélanie hadn't come and I didn't know why.

Just before eight, as the audience for the second performance were sitting back in their seats to enjoy Julie Delpy and her unconventional French father, I went out of the cinema to meet Mélanie. When she still hadn't appeared at twenty past eight, I was firmly convinced that she'd been held up. Perhaps she was one of those people who just couldn't be punctual. I hadn't learned anything about that aspect of her character yet. I smiled understandingly. Which of us has not been late at least once in our lives? These things happen. Perhaps a call had prevented her from leaving her apartment on time. Perhaps the train from Brittany had been late. Perhaps she'd been trying to make herself look particularly beautiful. There were a thousand explanations. I shook a cigarette out of the pack and smoked as I walked a few steps up and down outside the cinema. But as the minutes became quarters of an hour, my smile took on a degree of anxiety.

If something had cropped up, why hadn't Mélanie telephoned the cinema? Even if she didn't have my private number, she could easily have gotten the number of the Cinéma Paradis and left a message.

While the second performance of that evening headed to its conclusion and the culture-shock complications of the extended French-American family in New York reached their dénouement, I prowled back and forth in the foyer.

Could it be that Mélanie hadn't returned from Brittany at all? Perhaps the old aunt had had a serious attack of pneumonia and Mélanie was sitting at her bedside, having forgotten our date in all the commotion.

Against my better judgment, I took my cell phone out of my pocket and looked at it. There were actually three missed calls on the display. I didn't recognize any of the numbers, but I anxiously returned the calls.

Two journalists answered—no idea how they'd gotten my number—and a charming old lady who'd keyed the wrong number into her new cell phone, a gift from her daughter for her eighty-third birthday. She apologized to me a thousand times. "The keys are so small, I'm always pressing the wrong ones," she said, giggling. I said, "No problem, really," and put my cell phone back in my pocket. Then I went outside once more to keep a lookout. All of a sudden, I was no longer sure that Mélanie and I really had a date for that Wednesday.

Had she said she was going to her aunt's in Le Pouldu for one week, or two? But I had the letter, her little billet-doux, which I'd been carrying around with me for a week, and whose lines I knew by heart. And there it was, unmistakably: ". . . but I'm looking forward to next Wednesday, to you, and to everything that is about to happen." And the 'next Wednesday'—that was today. I had no doubt about that. With a sigh, I put the letter back, stuck my hands in my pockets, and went over to stare out through the glass door.

Madame Clément, who was sitting in the box office reading the paper—I didn't even notice that it was *Le Parisien,* which she shamefacedly put down whenever I came past—looked at me with concern. "Is everything all right, Monsieur Bonnard?" she asked. "You seem so nervous. Or is it just that there are so many people this evening?"

I shook my head. No, it wasn't the number of people. It was just one woman who was making me nervous that evening. A woman who otherwise turned up automatically here every Wednesday, but who had not done so tonight.

The film was over, I opened the auditorium doors and the audience streamed out past me into the street. Some of them took the program leaflets that were lying near the box office, and their laughter and chatter mingled with that of the new audience coming in for the late show.

The foyer was almost too small for all the people who were looking around curiously and lining up at the box office to get tickets for a film from the seventies whose motto was that it told a story without telling a lie.

I saw the old professor among those in the audience for the late show. He arrived last, clutching his ticket in his hand, and as he entered the auditorium, he whispered to me in surprise that he'd never thought it possible that *The Things of Life* could attract so many people. "I think it's great!" he said, smiling at me.

I gave a curt nod and closed the door behind him. In our *Les Amours au Paradis* series, an audience of just one woman would have been enough for me.

I looked in on François in the projection booth and stared through the little rectangle that gave a view of the screen. When Michel Piccoli crashed into the tree in his Alfa Romeo Guilietta and lay there silently on the grass recalling the events of his life, I was overcome with panic. What if Mélanie had had an accident? What if she'd run across the boulevard Saint-Germain, forgetting in her excitement to look right and left, and been knocked down by a car? I grimaced, chewing my lower lip, then waved to François, who was sitting over his books, as usual.

Then I took a couple more turns of the foyer under the watchful eye of Madame Clément. Finally, I decided to go and have a *café au lait* in a nearby bistro.

"If a young woman asks for me, please tell her to wait for me no matter what," I instructed my cashier.

"You mean the pretty girl you went out with last week?" she asked, raising an eyebrow. I nodded, giving no further explanation, then went out into the street.

In a few minutes, I was in the bistro, where I sat down on one of the worn wooden stools and quickly drank my coffee. The warmth that permeated my body did me good but didn't banish my disquiet.

When the late show was over as well, I waited in the Cinéma Paradis for another hour. Contrary to all probability, Mélanie might just suddenly turn up, out of breath, with her light step, a smile that asked for forgiveness, and words that explained everything.

"Don't you worry about it, Monsieur Bonnard," said Madame Clément as she put on her coat to leave. "I'm sure there's a perfectly simple explanation."

There may well have been; in fact, there definitely must have been. Yet I had a bad feeling about it and decided to go to the building where Mélanie lived. Just as I had done the previous week, I crossed the boulevard Saint-Germain, passed the Brasserie Lipp with its orange-and-white-striped awning, and then hurried impatiently along the rue de Grenelle, which took some time, until I finally reached the drugstore on the corner of the rue de Bourgogne and turned left. Then I was standing in front of the big green entrance gate, which was, of course, locked. I looked indecisively at all the names beside the bell pushes. I couldn't possibly get someone out of bed at that time of night, and I didn't even know which bell to ring.

I hung about near the entrance to the building for a while, then went over to the stationer's where, the week before, the old man in the slippers had lurched past, shouting "Look at the lovers." I was almost sorry not to see the old guy. I lit a cigarette. I waited—I didn't really know what for, but I didn't want to move away from the building, which had behind its walls a courtyard and an old chestnut tree, and possibly also a girl named Mélanie.

And then I got lucky. The gate in the old building opened with a low hum. A taxi drove up slowly, concealing for a moment the man in the long, dark woolen coat who now came out of the entrance and got quickly into the taxi. Before the taxi even stopped, I'd crossed the street and slipped through the gate, which closed behind me.

The moonlight fell gently on the courtyard and I heard a rustling in the branches of the old chestnut tree. I automatically looked up, but I couldn't distinguish anything. Only three windows in the upper floors of the rear building were lit, and I thought I recognized one of them as the one behind which Mélanie had disappeared the previous week. But I wasn't sure.

I stared helplessly up at the high window, which was wide open, spilling out warm golden light. I wondered if I should call out Mélanie's name, or if that might be stupid or inappropriate. Then a white feminine hand appeared in the frame and pulled the window to with a decisive tug. The light went out, and I was left there distraught.

Had it been Mélanie's hand I'd seen for a moment on the window catch? Was she therefore in Paris and had failed to keep our date? Or was it another woman's hand and I'd been totally wrong about which apartment was which? And who was the man in the dark coat who'd driven away in the taxi a few minutes before?

There was another rustle in the branches above me, which startled me. Then something jumped, and all of a sudden a big black cat was standing in front of me, looking at me indifferently with its green eyes.

At the time, of course, I didn't realize how everything fitted together, and I had no clue that the black creature with the iridescent eyes could have given me the answer to at least one of my questions.

At that moment, absurdly, the only thing that came into my mind was an image from an old Preston Sturgis film, where a black cat runs through the scene and the woman asks the man what that means, and he says, "Depends what happens next!"

The rue de Bourgogne was absolutely dead and I didn't see a soul on the rue de Varenne, either, as I made my way home, pensive and somewhat confused. There wasn't even one of those inevitable guards who are usually standing outside the old government buildings with their sandstone facades. The newspaper and antiques stores, the little groceries, the *boulangeries*, which every morning gave off the tempting aroma of fresh baguettes, the *pâtisseries* with their fancy *tartes* and little cakes and the pastel-colored meringues, which remind you of clouds and dissolve into sweet particles at the first bite, the restaurants and cafés, the *traiteurs,* which served *coq au vin* with chicory and a glass of red wine for next to nothing all day long—their shutters were all down.

At this time of night, Paris was a deserted star. And I was its loneliest inhabitant.

Fifteen

....

"Yeah," said Robert, obviously unimpressed, and spread his croissant with butter and jelly. "I told you it was a mistake not to ask for her telephone number. Now you're up that proverbial creek. It doesn't look good, if you ask me."

Stupidly, I had asked him. I was the one who'd called him early in the morning and asked him to come. I needed to speak with a good friend. But the trouble with really good friends is that they don't always say what you want to hear.

Since nine o'clock, we'd been sitting outside the little café by the Hôtel Danube on the rue Jacob and arguing. I waved to the waitress, a giantess of a woman whose head stuck forward in a very strange way and whose heavy, dark hair was worn in a chignon, and ordered my second *café au lait,* in the hope that it might bring my thoughts into some kind of order.

I'd slept badly, and of course it had been good of Robert to agree to come over on this morning when he had no lectures to listen to the events of the last night and the convoluted windings of my thoughts. I know I was ungrateful, but I'd been hoping for slightly stronger moral support. I stared indignantly at my friend as he chewed away without a care in the world.

"What are you saying, Robert? We don't know enough to tell if it looks good or bad," I replied, trying to gloss over my own doubts. "Good, at first sight it may seem strange that she didn't turn up or call, but that doesn't necessarily mean that she, that she . . ."

I swallowed and thought of the man I'd seen in the rue de Bourgogne. Had he been coming from Mélanie's apartment? Or from any apartment at all? Was he the reason Mélanie hadn't appeared at our rendezvous? Or did he just happen to live in the same building? The uncertainty stabbed me to the heart. I heaved a deep sigh.

Robert drank his coffee and swept a few crumbs from the table. "Why are you making things so difficult for yourself? Alain? I tell you, forget the chick. Believe you me, things are bound to be more complicated than you think." He leaned forward and looked at me with his bright, incorruptible eyes. "That's quite obvious."

I shook my head. "I can't be that wrong, Robert. You didn't see the look she gave me as we parted. She intended to come. I know that for a fact," I insisted. "Something very serious must have happened. Something that prevented her from coming or calling me."

"Yeah, yeah, you've already said that." Robert squirmed uncomfortably on his chair. "But the likelihood that your chick has been run over by a truck or fallen downstairs and broken a leg is extremely small." He rolled his eyes and calculated. "A hundred thousand to one, I'd say. Of course you're free to call every hospital and police station in Paris, but I don't think much would come from that."

"It doesn't have to be an accident," I said. "Perhaps it's something else . . . something we just haven't thought of yet."

"Well, I've got some pretty clear ideas. Do you want to hear them?"

"No," I said.

"Good," he went on, taking no notice. "So, let's leave your sixth sense and all your wishful thinking to one side and concentrate on the facts." Robert raised a finger. "I'm a scientist. I see things as they really are."

The giantess with the chignon came over, bringing fresh coffee. I held fast to my cup as Robert got into his stride. He did that very well, and I could see why his seminars were so popular. There was something very manipulative about him. It was barely possible to resist the magnetism of his words, the logic of what he was saying.

"So, to sum up: You talk to a woman you've had your eye on for some time. She's obviously single, at least that's what she says—didn't she tell you she always ends up with the wrong guy, or something like that? *Bon.* You spend a great evening together, walk, kiss, cast searching glances, the whole caboodle, right?"

The way Robert described it made it seem a bit reductive, but in principle he was right. I nodded.

"You part. You make a date for the next"—he paused for effect—"Wednesday."

"Because she's going to see her aunt," I interjected.

"Right. She's going to see her old . . . *aunt*," he repeated, and it suddenly sounded like a lie. "So, lots of schmoozing in the courtyard. It's the middle of the night. Everything is hunky-dory. She *doesn't* ask you up to her place. She *doesn't* give you her telephone number."

I said nothing.

"She's off to spend a week with her aunt and doesn't hit on the idea of giving you her number? When you've just fallen in love? I mean, at times like that, you spend every possible minute on the telephone. She's a *woman,* my friend. Women love the telephone. And now, my friend, we come to the crux of the matter." He pointed his knife at me. "She doesn't want to be called. Perhaps it's too dangerous. Someone might hear the call. Someone might check her cell phone. . . ."

"Baloney!" I said, beginning to feel a bit uneasy. "*Honi soit qui mal y pense.* Now you're basing deductions about other people on your own character, *mon ami.* And stop waving that knife under my nose." I leaned back in my chair. "Those are supposed to be facts? You're just throwing out one assumption after another."

"I know women," he said baldly.

It wasn't even boasting, he did really know a lot of women, and I often got the feeling that he studied them as assiduously as the stars in the Milky Way.

"This one is different," I said.

He gave me a pitying look. "Fair enough. Let's drop that subject. Let's look a bit more deeply into our little story. Mé-lanie—"

"Mélanie writes me a letter," I said triumphantly, interrupting him. "Why would she have done that? Why would she have written me a letter if she doesn't care about seeing me again?"

Robert raised his hand. "One moment, please. That's just another argument in favor of my theory. Just think about it! She writes you a letter, but she doesn't want to telephone. Otherwise, she'd have asked for your number."

"Okay, leave the letter aside," I said, slightly miffed. "People like you probably don't even know what a pen is anymore."

"No insults, please." Robert smiled winningly. "To each his own." He banged on the table with his knife. "The fact is, she doesn't call you all week, not even when she stands you up. And that's even though she knows the address of your cinema. But perhaps she's so old-fashioned that she can't even find a telephone number on the Internet. She works in an antiques store, doesn't she?"

"I'm astonished at how carefully you've been listening."

"I always listen carefully, Alain. After all, you are my friend, and your joys and sorrows are very close to my heart."

"If you have one, that is."

Robert nodded earnestly and placed his hand on his chest. "Oh, yes, I certainly do. Healthy, red, and extremely lively. Do you want to feel it?"

I shook my head.

"Fact two: She doesn't appear at your rendezvous even though she is—as you yourself later established—at home—"

"I'm not sure if it even was her apartment!" I said, interrupting again. "Good grief, I was only there once, and God knows I didn't really notice if it was the first, second, or third floor."

"Fact three: In the middle of the night, a strange man comes out of the building—probably even from her apartment. That would, of course, also explain why she had no time for you. That was probably one of those 'wrong guys.'" Robert leaned back smugly. "I think your Mélanie was having you on with all her maidenly airs. Perhaps it's a kind of number she does. She wanted to do a bit of two-timing and you turned up at just the right moment. The way I see it, she'd just had a bust-up with her boyfriend; then she went on holiday with him and everything was okay again. Or she was really in Brittany with her aunt and the guy just turned up. Big reconciliation in the *grand lit*, QED."

He speared a chunk of baguette with his knife and held it up like a trophy. "Don't make such a face, Alain, things like that have happened even to me. You get mixed up in a story and have no idea what's happening to you. It's not your fault. You had no chance from the very start."

"No, no, no, Robert, I know it's not like that," I said, trying to free myself from the spell of his chain of argument. "Why do you always assume the worst?" I saw the giantess leaning against the café door, looking over at us with interest.

"My friend is a pessimist, you see," I said in her direction. She smiled her broad Carmen smile, but she was too far away to catch what I was saying, and she made a sign in the air, asking if we wanted more coffee. I shook my head.

"Your friend is a realist," said Robert.

"But we have no idea if it was her apartment," I reminded him. "If the light wasn't on in her apartment after all, then your theory falls apart."

"Well then, there's only one thing left to do," Robert waved his trophy, looking indulgently at me. "Go back to the rue de Bourgogne and find out."

"Just imagine: I'd already hit on that idea. I'll do it this evening. And then we'll see."

Robert grinned. "So we will. At any rate, I hope you have a lot of fun with your bell ringing."

"I'll ask my way around, don't you worry. It can't be that hard."

"Oh, no. I imagine it'll be extremely entertaining. You're sure to make a lot of new acquaintances." Robert obviously got great pleasure from the thought of my standing by the row of bells, trying one apartment after the other.

"How great that you've only got her first name; otherwise, it would be far too easy." He laughed.

"How great that you're so witty!"

"Ah, here comes Melissa!" Robert jumped up and waved as a slim girl with long, straight red hair ran toward us. She was wearing jeans and bright sneakers and a brown suede jacket over her brightly patterned T-shirt. She was smiling.

"Melissa, this is my friend Alain. Sit down for a moment; we'll be finished right away." He put his arm around the redhead and kissed her on the lips.

Melissa nodded to me and let Robert pull her down onto the chair next to him. The most astonishing thing about her were her eyes—very clear and very green.

"*Salut,* Alain. *Ça va?* I've already heard a lot about you. Robert's best friend. *Oh là là!*" She stressed the last three words, and I liked her jolly, friendly manner from the start.

I smiled, wondering what Robert might have told his new girlfriend about me. "I've heard a lot about you, too," I replied, and her green eyes sparkled.

"Oh! Really?" With a cheeky gesture, she ruffled Robert's hair. "What do you tell people about me, then, *mon petit professeur*? Nothing but good, I hope!"

"Of course, *ma petite*," said Robert. "What else could I do?" He ignored the "*petit professeur*" with his usual aplomb and winked at me. His expression spoke volumes: Did I promise too much? Sensational, or what?

I grinned.

Robert reached playfully for Melissa's hand and twined his fingers in hers. "My sweet, I hope you'll forgive me for rushing off like that this morning, but this young man here has problems."

"Oh. I'm so sorry. I hope it's nothing serious."

"It is, actually," I said.

"It's peanuts," said Robert.

Melissa looked from one of us to the other in amazement.

"Alain was dumped last night by a woman he's kissed only once, and he thinks this is the bitterest blow fate has ever dealt him," explained Robert, spreading his hands in a theatrical gesture. "And unfortunately . . . unfortunately he knows only her first name—Mélanie. Do you know a Mélanie?"

"*Mais oui!*" Melissa laughed. "My cello teacher's named Mélanie. Mélanie Bertrand, but I'm certain it's not her. She has iron gray hair and saws away madly at her big cello. A skinny little witch. And when I play a wrong note, she always gives me a very stern look—like this!" She wrinkled her pretty forehead and narrowed her eyes. "'Mademoiselle Melissa, you must practice, practice, practice. This will never do,'" she croaked in a disguised voice.

We laughed and I said, "No, that's not the Mélanie I'm looking for, for goodness sake!"

"My good friend has taken it into his head to find this girl again. I advised him against it," said Robert. "There are better ways of spending your time." He put his hand on Melissa's knee and smiled like a man who had a very good idea of better ways to spend his time.

"I'm going to look for her anyway," I said, smiling like someone who knows even better. "Still, thanks for coming." I got up and reached for my wallet.

"He'll just never learn," said Robert. "That's what I value about him so much. No, no, this is on me, please." He shoved my hand with the wallet aside. "But to be serious just for once, Alain. Hang loose! You could just relax and wait instead of getting so stressed out. She knows where your cinema is, and if she's serious, she'll get in touch, won't she?" He looked at Melissa, expecting confirmation.

"Not necessarily," replied Melissa, and I found I really liked her. She cradled her slender face in her hand and looked coquettishly up at me. With her gleaming eyes and her long center-parted hair almost completely covering her forehead, she looked a bit like a water nymph.

"Well, I find it all very romantic," she said with a blissful little sigh. "Don't give up, Alain. Keep searching!"

Sixteen

....

There were twenty names—all of them surnames. I stood at the green entrance gate in the rue de Bourgogne and studied the metal nameplates with their black engraving very carefully.

"This is more complicated than you think," Robert had said, but he didn't know what he was talking about. Nobody knew that. With hindsight, there is a certain degree of irony in the fact that my friend, in complete ignorance of the facts, had hit the nail right on the head. It was in actuality far more complicated—not to say complex—than any of us had thought. But that Thursday as I stared—uncertain but still determined and with a certain basic optimism—at the nameplates, there was a remnant of the day's warmth in the narrow street, and I thought, Okay, this is a bit tedious, but still totally in the realm of possibility.

I had decided to proceed systematically. Since Mélanie's apartment was probably on one of the upper floors at the rear of the building, I planned to concentrate first on the top row of nameplates. I glanced along the row—often enough, first name and surname can form a certain unity—and murmured them under my breath. "Bonnet, Rousseau, Martin, Chevalier, Leblanc, Pennec, Duvalier, Dupont, Ledoux, Beauchamps, Mirabelle . . ."

Mirabelle? Mélanie Mirabelle—they seemed to go well together.

But first I'd just ring any old bell to get myself into the building under some pretext or other. That way, I could cross the courtyard and reach the rear of the building. I pressed firmly on the bell beside one of the nameplates on the lower floor, which appeared to belong to the front of the building, and waited. Nothing happened. I was just about to ring somewhere else when the intercom crackled.

"Hello?" It was a quavering voice, obviously an old lady's. *"Hello?"*

I took a deep breath and tried to appear hurried and yet indifferent, like one of those UPS deliverymen who double-park their truck in the street with the hazards flashing. "I have a delivery for Mirabelle. Could you let me in please?"

"Hello?" The intercom crackled again. "I can't hear anything."

"Yes, hello!" I tried to speak louder. "Excuse me, madame, I have a delivery here for—"

"Hello? Dimitri? Dimitri, is that you? Have you forgotten the key again, darling?"

I stepped as close to the intercom as possible and shouted, "No, this is not Dimitri. It's the delivery service! Could you please open the gate for me, madame?"

"Aaah . . ." The old lady gave a short cry and there was a suspicious crackle in the intercom. "For heaven's sake, don't shout like that. You scared me. I'm not deaf."

There was silence, then slyly she asked, "Do you want to see Dimitri?"

"No," I shouted back. "I have a—"

"Dimitri's not here," she shrieked, and I wondered who this Dimitri actually was. I felt like I was in a bad espionage thriller. And Dimitri was beginning to get on my nerves.

"That's good," I replied, trying to keep calm. "Because I'm not here to see Dimitri."

"Hello?" she shouted again. "You'll have to speak more clearly, young man. I can't understand what you're saying. Dimitri won't be back till later. Do you hear? Come back later!"

The old woman was either deaf or crazy, or both. I decided to change tactics and reduce things to essentials. "I have a delivery for Mirabelle!" I said loudly. "Please open the gate for me, madame. I only want to deliver something."

She seemed to be listening carefully to what I said, and I could almost hear the cogs turning in her mind. Then she shouted, "Isabelle? Isabelle is not here, either!"

I laughed out loud. Was I in a madhouse? Then, overcome by the black humor of the situation, I asked, "And Mélanie? Is Mélanie there? Does a Mélanie live here? Do you know?"

"Mélanie?" she shouted back. "There's no Mélanie here." She muttered something incomprehensible. It sounded indignant. "Strange people keep ringing at my door and want me to tell them names. But I've just moved here—from the rue de Varenne. There's no Mélanie here. I don't know anything." Her voice became shrill and took on a hysterical note. "Who are you anyway?"

"Alain Bonnard," I said loudly. "Open the gate for me!"

"Never! Go away!"

There was another crackle in the intercom, and then deathly silence. I hoped I hadn't scared the old lady to death. Or she'd be lying in the hall until Dimitri came back and found her.

With a sigh, I pressed the bell beside the next nameplate. The name was Roznet. This time, the reply was quicker. Within a couple of seconds, I heard a sonorous masculine voice. It sounded a bit halting, but otherwise it was totally normal. I breathed a sigh of relief.

"*Oui?*"

"I have a delivery for Mirabelle at the back of the building," I said slowly and clearly. "Would you kindly open the gate for me?"

"Sure. No problem."

A moment later, the buzzer went off and the gate slid open. The staircase at the rear of the building was cool and dark and there was a strong smell of peaches. The cleaner had obviously just finished. There was an elevator, but it seemed not to work. I ran up the worn steps, determined to begin my inquiries on the top floor. It was 6:25 in the evening. My heart thudded. I rang Mirabelle's bell.

I could hear light footsteps behind the apartment door. Then a woman's voice. "Someone's rung the bell. Could you get the door?"

Pattering feet sounded in the hall. The heavy wooden door flew open. A little blond girl with a ponytail stood in the doorway and looked at me curiously. She must have been about five. "Are you the drinks deliveryman?" she asked me.

Could it be that Mélanie had failed to tell me she had a daughter?

"Marie? Who's there?"

"A man," replied Marie truthfully.

There was a clatter in one of the rooms at the back of the apartment and then a woman in a flowered dress came into the hall. She'd quickly wound a towel around her wet hair and was fixing the dark blue turban on her head as she approached. She looked at me and smiled expectantly. "Yes?"

It would have been just too good if I'd hit the jackpot at the first try.

"*Bonsoir,* madame," I said. "Please excuse the intrusion. I had hoped to find a woman called Mélanie here. She works in an antiques store," I added clumsily.

Madame Mirabelle gave me a friendly look and then shook her head. She obviously found me likable. "I'm afraid not. My husband and I and our daughter are the only people living here. What's the lady's surname? Perhaps you've made a mistake about the floor."

I shrugged. "That's precisely my problem: I don't know her surname."

"Oh," said Madame Mirabelle.

"She's in her mid- to late twenties, dark blond hair, brown eyes, wears a red coat," I said.

Madame Mirabelle shook her head regretfully. Marie wound her arms around her mother's legs. "Is that a riddle, Maman?"

Madame Mirabelle stroked her daughter's hair. "Shh—I'll explain it to you later." Then she turned to me again. "I'm afraid I can't be much help. We haven't lived here very long. I've never seen a young woman in a red coat in the building. But that doesn't necessarily mean anything. Perhaps you could try Madame Bonnet on the ground floor—I'm sure she sees more than we do up here. And she used to be the concierge."

"Yes, thanks," I said miserably.

"I'm really sorry," said Madame Mirabelle sympathetically. "We have visitors coming; otherwise, I'd have asked you in for a coffee."

I thanked her and turned to go. There was another door on the opposite side of the landing.

"That's just Monsieur Pennec and his wife," she said. "A grouchy adman. He already complained when Marie was having her birthday party. But it's certainly not his wife you're looking for." She pulled comic grimace as she shut the door. "They're both really awful!"

On the second floor, nobody answered at the Leblanc apartment. I heard a strange scratching behind the door, then meowing. I pressed the bell once more, longer this time. I was suddenly convinced that the window with the lights on must have been on the second floor. I waited a moment, then rang one last time.

A door flew open behind me. I turned in surprise and found myself looking directly into the hate-filled eyes of a little Japanese man who was scrutinizing me suspiciously through the thick lenses of his glasses.

"How many more times are you going to ring, monsieur? You can see there's no one in," he shouted.

I seized the moment. "I'm looking for a young woman with dark blond hair. Her name is Mélanie. Do you know if she lives here? Mélanie . . . Leblanc?" I pointed to the door, and for some reason it enraged the little man.

"Mademoiselle Leblanc is not there," he spat. "You can keep ringing as long as you like. She's never there in the evening, and when she gets back in the middle of the night, she always slams the door and wakes me up."

There was excited meowing from behind the apartment door, the little Japanese man was swearing like a trooper, and I could hardly suppress a smile. Was it Miss Holly Golightly who lived there?

"I'm sorry about that. Could you possibly tell me if Mademoiselle Leblanc's first name is Mélanie?"

"No idea," growled the Japanese man. "Why do you want to know that—is she wanted?"

"Only by me," I assured him.

"Are you her boyfriend?"

"You might say that."

He sniffed. "Don't get your hopes up. No one lasts very long with her. She's the type that drives men to ruin."

"Aha," I said. This was beginning to get to me. "Who says that?"

"Monsieur Beauchamps, my landlord, told me."

I took a step closer and glanced at the nameplate. "Aren't you Monsieur Beauchamps?"

He looked at me as if I were crazy. "Do I look like a Beauchamps? I'm Tashi Nakamura." He pulled himself up to his full height, but he still only reached my chest. "Pierre Beauchamps was a colleague of mine at Global Electronics."

"Was?" I was understanding less and less.

He nodded. "Until that little black-haired witch drove him out of his mind. Her nose is too long for my taste, but so what? Anyway, he got himself posted to Michigan for two years and sublet the apartment to me." He shook his head. "After she broke up with him, he couldn't bear to stay here—with their doors facing each other."

"I see," I said. I was sorry for that Beauchamps guy, but I was even sorrier for myself. Mélanie had a totally normal nose, and although I know that Asian people think that all whites have big noses—they call us "long noses" behind our backs—and everything is relative anyway, even the size of a nose—the woman I was looking for definitely didn't have black hair.

In spite of that, I asked, "Does she sometimes wear a red coat?"

"I've only ever seen Mademoiselle Leblanc in black."

I sighed in disappointment. "And I suppose her name isn't Mélanie, either?"

He thought for a moment. "No idea. Or—no, wait a moment—I had to take in a package for her once. It was . . . it was . . ."

"Yes?"

"Lucille or Laurence or Linda—something beginning with L at any rate." Tashi Nakamura waved his index finger decisively.

"Hmm. I was afraid of that." I could have sworn that the light that had gone on and off the week before had been on the second floor. I was wrong.

Monsieur Nakamura nodded to me and started to disappear back into his apartment.

"Oh, Monsieur Nakamura?" He sighed. "You don't happen to know another Mélanie in this part of the building?"

He looked at me, narrowing his eyes until the dark irises were hardly visible. "Tell me, monsieur—what exactly is the matter with you? Does it *have* to be a Mélanie? You seem a bit obsessive to me."

I kept smiling.

"No," he said finally. "And if I did, I wouldn't care anyway. I'm not that interested in women." With these words, he slammed the door, leaving me standing outside.

No one was in at the Dupont apartment on the first floor, so I rang at the second door: Montabon. It took a little while until the door was opened very carefully. In front of me stood a distinguished-looking elderly gentleman in a light gray suit. The curly white fringe of hair around his brown pate, which was speckled with age spots, suggested that he once must have had very thick hair. In spite of the fact that it was evening and that the landing was quite dimly lit, he was wearing dark sunglasses. He straightened them with a wiry, freckled hand and said nothing. He was obviously waiting for me to speak first.

"Monsieur Montabon?" I asked.

"I am he," he said. "What can I do for you?"

I knew at once that I'd rung the wrong bell. Nevertheless, I asked my question.

Monsieur Montabon was an extremely courteous man, and he invited me to come in, because it was not his nature to hold conversations on the doorstep. He lived alone, liked listening to the music of Ravel, Poulenc, and Débussy, and played chess. He had been ambassador in Argentina and Chile for a long time but had retired from the Diplomatic Service fifteen years ago. He had a housekeeper who came in every day, kept the apartment in order, did his washing and shopping, and cooked for him. Her name was not Mélanie, but Margot.

I'm sure that if it had been in any way possible, this friendly gentleman would have helped me. But Monsieur Montabon had not seen a woman in a red coat. Jacob Montabon was practically blind.

By this time, it was eight o'clock, and my mood had noticeably worsened. All those conversations had been effortful and not very productive. This was to change as I trudged dejectedly down the stairs to the ground floor and fell into the arms of a rather plump woman of about sixty, who was standing in the hall in a black skirt and purple cardigan, as if she had been waiting for me. In view of the weight she must have been carrying, her feet were surprisingly dainty. They were clad in well-worn little purple ballet flats. The lady in purple greeted me in a friendly way, and so, without ringing any bells, I made the acquaintance of Madame Bonnet.

Francine Bonnet's favorite color was indubitably purple. When, with lively gestures, she began chatting to me, I noticed that even her earrings, which dangled like raindrops beneath her short silver-gray curls, were made of purple glass beads.

In an earlier life, Madame Bonnet had been the concierge in one of the old town houses on the place des Vosges. Then her husband had gotten pancreatic cancer, died within a few months, and left her with a handsome pension.

"Poor Hugo—it all happened so quickly." She sighed sadly.

She hadn't needed to work since then. But she knit brightly colored scarves for a little fashion store in the rue Bonaparte (silk and wool mix, mainly in shades of purple, of course), and these scarves, each one a unique creation with an oval label saying *Les Foulards de Francine* in script, were obviously very popular. In this way, Madame Bonnet had something useful to occupy her and could still stay at home all day. And she also knew things about the inhabitants of the rue de Bourgogne. As soon as I mentioned the name Mélanie, she remembered that was Madame Dupont's (*Madame,* not Mademoiselle, but dark blond, pretty, and single) first name, too.

"A delightful person, Mélanie Dupont," she told me. "Although she hasn't had much luck in her life."

I felt an inward surge of elation.

"But she's not at home. I've rung her bell," I said.

"I know," replied Madame Bonnet, the soft jangling of her earrings underlining her words. "Madame Dupont won't be back until tomorrow, or very late tonight. She had to go away for a couple of days, and she asked me to collect her newspapers from her mailbox."

I could hardly contain my joy. This was Mélanie, no doubt of it! I clenched my fists in my pockets to conceal my excitement. After what had admittedly been a somewhat laborious start, I had now finally found Mélanie. And the reason why she hadn't come to the cinema was also clear. She just hadn't returned from Brittany. Who knows what had held her up there. At least it wasn't a strange man in a dark coat! It looked as if he'd actually been coming from Mademoiselle Leblanc's apartment. I suppressed a chuckle. I was also becoming very familiar with the old house on rue de Bourgogne and its inhabitants.

I decided to leave a message for Mélanie, a letter. And after I'd rushed excitedly across to the stationer's, almost getting run down by a car that was definitely traveling too fast along the narrow street, and then discovering that they were closed, Madame Bonnet was friendly enough to help me out with a sheet of paper and an envelope.

I hastily scribbled a few lines on the paper and put it in the envelope. Then I went past the old chestnut tree for the fourth time that evening. I hesitated for a moment, toying with the idea of pinning the letter, which was simply addressed "For Mélanie from Alain," to the old tree—I found the idea that Mélanie would come into the courtyard late that night or early the next morning and find my letter on the tree deeply romantic. By now, I was feeling the same way the young Goethe had felt in the film of the same name—a lover who gallops, or practically flies, across a vast green landscape, prepared to do anything at all to get to his girl. The film *Goethe!*—a German production with young, almost unknown actors—had run in the Cinéma Paradis only a couple of months before.

I'm sure Goethe would have pinned the letter to the old chestnut tree. But I didn't feel that was safe enough. The letter might fall off or even be taken by someone else, even though it seemed highly unlikely to me that in this building, where the majority of the tenants seemed not really to know one another, or, if they did, not to be on speaking terms, there could be another Mélanie.

I crossed the courtyard, went into the front of the building, and stood by the black mailbox for a moment with my letter in my hand. This is what I'd written:

Dear Mélanie,

You didn't turn up on Wednesday, and I was beginning to worry. I would have called you, but I don't have your number. Now I've been told that you're only coming back this evening or tomorrow morning.

I hope everything's all right. I was so delighted by your little

letter and have read it at least a hundred times. I've just been
standing under the old chestnut tree where we kissed. I miss you!
Please get in touch when you get back, my little nonadventuress.
I await your call with tender impatience.
　　Alain

I'd written my telephone number at the bottom of the message.
I pushed the letter through the little metal flap of the mailbox
with the name Dupont on it and heard the rustle as it fell down
inside. Now all I had to do was wait.

Looking back, I've often thought that it might probably have
been better to do what Goethe would have done and follow my
initial instinct.

About an hour after I had left the building in the rue de
Bourgogne, feeling so lighthearted, someone walked past the
old chestnut tree—a person who would have known what to
do about the addressee and the sender of the letter. If I had
pinned my billet-doux to the old tree, it might possibly have
reached the hand of the woman it was intended for a very short
time later. I might have saved myself a lot of hassle.

Possibly.

Seventeen

....

The moment the telephone rang, I knew it was Mélanie. That afternoon I'd actually intended to make a new selection of films for the next few late-night *Les Amours au Paradis* shows. I was just watching *Benjamin or the Diary of a Virgin* with Catherine Deneuve when the theme tune from *The Third Man,* which I'd chosen as my ringtone, began to play. I grabbed for the telephone on the table in the projection room, almost knocking my soda over in the process.

There was a crackle on the line, then "This is Mélanie."

My heart was thumping madly.

"Mélanie! At last," I said hoarsely. "Oh, it's you!" Goodness, was I glad to hear her voice.

"Am I talking with . . . Alain?" The voice at the other end sounded hesitant. It was a musical female voice; it sounded a bit strange to me, but that was probably because of the line.

"Yes!" I said. "Yes, of course. This is Alain. Did you get my letter? Goodness, am I glad you've called. What happened?"

A long silence followed, and I was alarmed. Something awful must have happened. Perhaps her old aunt had died.

"Mélanie?" I asked. "You sound so funny. What's up? Are
you at home? Should I come over?"

"Oh . . ." The woman sighed. "I knew it must be a misunderstanding."

I listened in confusion. A misunderstanding? What did that
mean? "What's that?" I asked.

"I'm not Mélanie," said the voice.

What was she saying? She was Mélanie and she wasn't Mélanie? I pressed the handset to my ear and had a definite feeling
that our conversation was going in totally the wrong direction.

"I mean, yes, I am Mélanie—Mélanie Dupont. But we don't
know each other."

"Don't know each other?" I echoed, completely lost.

"I found your letter this morning," she said. "I don't know
who you are, Alain, but I fear you're confusing me with another Mélanie."

My heart sank with every word. It was gradually dawning on
me that the strangeness in her voice wasn't due to the connection. It was a different voice, but I simply didn't want to accept it.

"But, but . . ." I stuttered. "You . . . do live in the back of
the building on the rue de Bourgogne, don't you?"

"Yes," said the other Mélanie. "That's right. But we've never
had a date. And we've never kissed under the old chestnut tree.
I don't know you, Alain, and I knew right away that the letter
wasn't intended for me. I just wanted to let you know."

"Oh," I murmured. "That's . . . that's . . . very unfortunate."

"Yes," she said. "I think so, too. It's been a long time since
I've had such a lovely letter. Even if it wasn't meant for me."

I took a few seconds to pull myself together. Thoughts were crowding into my head and I tried to bring some degree of logic into all this confusion.

"But . . ." I said, "but there *must* be a Mélanie. I walked her home myself—into the courtyard. We said good night. She went into the rear of the building, I saw it with my own eyes. I saw the light going on and going off again. I mean, I'm not crazy," I said a bit lamely.

The other Mélanie was silent. She probably thought I was getting hysterical. I even thought I was a bit hysterical myself.

"That is really curious," she said finally.

"Do you know if there's another Mélanie in the building?"

"No," she said. "I'm really sorry."

I nodded a couple of times, pursing my lips in disappointment. "Well . . ." I said, "well, then please excuse the mix-up, Madame Dupont. And thanks anyway for calling so soon."

"No problem, Alain," said the other Mélanie. "Just call me Mélanie."

All I remember of the days that followed is that I felt as if I were being wrapped in cotton wool. The sounds of the world retreated, and I felt my way, strangely insecure, through my own little film, whose ending was getting lost in uncertainty. I didn't know what I had done to make fate play such a trick on me. I went to the rue de Bourgogne three more times to try to find signs of Mélanie. I went at all times of day to increase my chances, but it was all in vain. I met Madame Bonnet again, I saw grumpy Monsieur Pennec with his irascible wife, a superannuated, extremely well-groomed blonde with combed-back hair, hung from tip to toe with gold jewelry and looking like the Christmas decorations in

Printemps. On one of these fruitless afternoons, I even encountered Madame Dupont, the other Mélanie—a charming woman in her late thirties with ash-blond hair and a melancholy look—at the mailboxes and introduced myself to her. She greeted me like an old acquaintance and took her leave with a promise to come to the Cinéma Paradis very soon.

Mademoiselle Leblanc, the night owl who broke men's hearts, was, as usual, away. Her neighbor, Monsieur Nakamura, had set off laden with gifts for a family occasion in Tokyo—I heard this from Madame Bonnet, of course. The genteel Monsieur Montabon obviously left his apartment very seldom—at least I never saw him. By this time, I had rung at the doors of all the other neighbors, even those in the front of the building, but no one had been able to help me. And then I had crossed off all the names on my list.

I stepped out onto the street and felt like I was going crazy, just as the old man who slouched up to me in his slippers on this last visit to the rue de Bourgogne obviously already was. He was hunching along, then stopped as he saw me and gave a wicked little smile. "Dilettantes. All dilettantes," he said, and spat. There was no way of knowing whom his anger was directed at. As far as I was concerned, he was right. I'd never felt so useless. My thoughts were bitter as I returned home.

It was about noon as I walked back along the rue de Grenelle, my head bowed low. Most of the stores close for lunch around then, and the street was quiet. I querulously kicked a Coke can out of my way, and it rolled across the sidewalk and came to rest in front of a shop with closed shutters. The white enamel sign said A LA RECHERCHE DU TEMPS PERDU, and it seemed to me like a mocking sign from the heavens. With a curt, bitter laugh, I left the can lying there. I was indeed in search of a few happy hours that now seemed to be irrevocably lost.

The following week, I even ran after any red coat or mane of dark blond hair that appeared on the street. On one occasion, I saw a woman with a red coat and caramel blond hair getting on the bus outside Bon Marché, and I was sure it was Mélanie. I ran panting beside the bus as it left, shouting and making signs until I got a stitch and grabbed my chest like Yuri Zhivago in that deeply tragic scene where he sees his Lara behind the window of a bus and collapses in the open street when she doesn't notice him. Unlike the unfortunate Zhivago, I even succeeded in attracting Mélanie's attention. With a final surge of strength, I jumped up and hammered on the window, but when the woman in the red coat turned toward me, all I saw was an expression of surprise.

After every setback, I would defiantly take out Mélanie's little letter and read it. But that was all a sham. The woman in the red coat had disappeared without a trace.

Finally, I called Robert. "She doesn't live in the building," I said sheepishly, and told him about my investigations. "Nobody there knows a woman named Mélanie."

My friend whistled through his teeth. "The case is beginning to get interesting," he said, to my surprise. "Perhaps your Mélanie is a secret agent. Perhaps she was involved in some dubious affair and had to go undercover. Or she's in a witness protection program, hee hee hee." He cackled at his own joke, and I said nothing, upset because he wasn't taking my troubles seriously.

"Jo-hoke!" he said when he calmed down. "But let's be serious, Alain. Perhaps she just gave you a false name. Women do that sometimes. Perhaps you're looking for the wrong name and it is actually the little witch from the second floor that the Japanese guy hates so much. She seems interesting to me."

"Oh my God, Robert, can it, will you? Why would anyone do a thing like that? After all, no one forced her to spend an evening with me. And she came to the cinema every week before that wearing a *wig,* or what? Mademoiselle Leblanc has black hair, you dope! That's what Monsieur Nakamura said, and he should know. He lives in the apartment opposite and he hates the woman. And apart from that, she obviously *doesn't* work in an antiques store!"

"Yes, well . . . That could have been something she made up, as well," said Robert, and I heard him lighting a cigarette. "This Mélanie has somehow pulled the wool over your eyes, that's definite. I only believe what I see; no one gets the better of me." My friend obviously liked seeing himself as Daniel Craig. Hard as nails and impossible to influence.

"That's absurd, Robert. *You're* absurd. Can't you see that none of this makes sense?" I sighed. "It's enough to drive you mad. For once, I meet the right woman, and then she disappears—just like that. What should I do now? What *can* I do?"

Robert sighed, too. "Oh, Alain," he said. "Just drop it. Accept it once and for all. The whole thing is doomed. I said so from the very start. And your mood is getting worse and worse. Let's go to the jazz club this evening with Melissa and her friend and drink a few whiskey sours. Let's have some fun."

"I don't like whiskey sour. Don't you have any better suggestions? I've got to find that woman again. I've just got to find out what has happened. Do you have any other ideas or not?"

" 'I've got to find that woman again. I've got to find that

woman again.' Jeez, you really get on my nerves sometimes," said Robert. But then he did have an idea.

When I set off that evening to see my friend in the rue Huyghens in the fourteenth arrondissement, I'd done my homework.

We were sitting in the roomy kitchen of Robert's bachelor pad on the fourth floor, bent over what my friend called the "schedule of all the facts." In front of us were two water tumblers full of red wine, a big crystal ashtray with a number of stubbed-out butts, and a dish of wasabi nuts, which stung my nose every time I inadvertently allowed one of the green-coated spheres to explode in my mouth.

The door to the bedroom was ajar. Behind it, on a bed with an incredible number of pillows, Melissa was lolling in a pale green kimono, listlessly studying a pamphlet with the impenetrable title: *Interstellar Regularities in Connection with Black Holes and the Gravitation of Celestial Bodies.*

"Don't mind me," she'd called as I hung up my jacket in the hall. "I'm studying." Nevertheless, she listened in on our conversation, shouting her comments through from the bedroom.

"Well then, let's see," murmured Robert, scrutinizing the list. "We need to look for clues."

I nodded thankfully. Robert was a good guy at heart—I'd always known that.

"Make a list. Write down everything that comes into your head," he'd said at the end of our phone call. "What she was wearing, what she said, what she talked about. Try to remember. Take your time. Concentrate. Any little detail might turn out to be vital."

He was Sherlock Holmes and I was Dr. Watson, a hanger-on

who was allowed to share in the great genius of the master detective.

That Sunday, I had not gone to the cinema. Madame Clément and François were understanding about it. "We can cope on our own, Monsieur Bonnard, don't worry," Madame Clément had said. And so I'd sat in my apartment the whole afternoon, talking occasionally to Orphée, who jumped up on my desk and butted me with her head every time I stopped writing and began chewing pensively on my pen. I was hungry but decided to ignore my rumbling stomach. I could eat later.

After an hour and a half, I had written down everything that I could recall about that Wednesday evening, especially about Mélanie. I made an effort to be exact, which was not very difficult. I could remember some of the things she'd said almost word for word. Not to mention her delightful face. My chair creaked as I leaned back and read through the list with its heading "What I Know about Mélanie" once again.

What I Know about Mélanie

1. Appearance: medium height, slim, upright walk, big brown eyes, dark blond hair—a particular blond, reminiscent of shiny caramel candy, or brittle.
2. Often (always?) wears a scarlet knee-length coat. Old-fashioned cut.
3. Wears a gold ring with carved roses on her ring finger.
4. Always comes to the late show on Wednesdays.
5. Always sits in row seventeen.
6. Favorite film: *Cyrano de Bergerac.*

7. Has an aunt Lucille (Lucie? Luce?), who lives in Le Pouldu.

8. Was there for a week on vacation before she disappeared.

9. Obviously does not live on rue de Bourgogne (or does she?). Lives in Paris, in any case. (Also comes from Paris? Brittany?)

10. No family in Paris, has never been married (at least, that's what she says), lives alone (completely alone!).

11. No pets, but likes cats.

12. Her last boyfriend cheated on her (jade earring). Always meets the wrong men. ("I have a talent for falling in love with the wrong men.")

13. Mother dead (the rose ring was hers); sad memories. Family? Men?

14. Her friend works in a hotel bar.

15. She works in an antiques store. Her boss is in the hospital with pneumonia (heavy smoker); there is one other colleague.

16. She works until 7:00 P.M., even later on Thursdays.

17. Shy at first sight, but also smart.

18. Likes old things.

19. Favorite bridge: the pont Alexandre. ("Do you know how lovely it is to walk over the pont Alexandre when the reflection of the city lights starts sparkling in the water and the sky turns lavender? I sometimes stop under those old lamps for a moment . . .") Suggests: Lives/works near the bridge? If she doesn't live in the rue de Bourgogne.

20. Goes to the cinema when she's looking for love.

I smiled with satisfaction. "That's not at all bad for a beginning," I murmured. Orphée looked at me with her inscrutable little cat's face and I stroked her tiger-striped fur. I took her purring for agreement, but a certain professor of astrophysics, whom I then went to see, was not so easily convinced.

"Hmm," said Robert, glancing over my list with narrowed eyes. "Is that all?"

"Well, there *are* twenty points," I said.

Robert clicked his tongue, unpersuaded. " 'Goes to the cinema when she's looking for love,' " he read out. "How's that sort of thing going to help us along? He shook his head with a sigh. "I'm afraid that the fact that the color of her hair is reminiscent of brittle is not a real clue." He read on. " 'Always comes to the late show on Wednesdays.' " He looked at me. "*Came* is what you mean. Tut, tut, tut. 'Always sits in row seventeen.' Should we go and search under the seats there, do you think?"

"You said I should write down everything that came into my head," I said, defending myself. "Everything. And that's just what I've done. If you want to make fun of it, go ahead, but that's the last thing that will help us get anywhere."

"Okay, okay," said Robert. "No need to go off the deep end. I'm doing what I can." He wrinkled his forehead and stared at the paper, concentrating deeply. "Le Pouldu? Where is that?"

"In Brittany. She has an aunt there. Do you think we should try there? The way it looks at the moment, it's not even certain that Mélanie's even come back from Brittany." I pulled the kitchen chair nearer to the table.

"No, no," said Robert with a dismissive gesture. "Needle in a haystack. Do you really seriously want to travel to Le Pouldu and ask people there if a girl called Mélanie has been staying with an aunt Lucille or Lucie or Luce, whose surname we unfortunately don't know, either?"

Disappointed, I said nothing. Somehow I'd hoped that my list would reveal new connections or that my friend would hit on a decisive clue.

"Her friend works in the bar of a grand hotel," I told him.

"Yeah, if the friend had a name, that might be a hot tip," said Robert.

"Sorry. I don't even know if Mélanie mentioned her name at all. I only know that she said that her friend's cat always drinks out of a flower vase."

"Aha." Robert raised an eyebrow. "Do you at least know the cat's name?" He grinned. "That would be a new starting point."

"Yeah, yeah, Mr. Holmes, mock on." I wondered for a moment if I should mention the black cat I'd seen in the courtyard of Mélanie's building in the rue de Bourgogne. But I had no desire for further witticisms at my expense. So I let it go. The rue de Bourgogne had turned out to be a dead end anyway.

"Hmm," said Robert again. "The only useful clue I can see here is the business with the antiques store. We might be able to find something out about that." He looked at me. "Did she mention the name of the store? Or where she works? Or at least what arrondissement it's in?"

I shook my head gloomily.

"Perhaps she said something like 'I work quite near here.' Think, man!"

"I would have written it down if she's said it."

"And the boss? Did she mention his name? Most antiques stores are called after their owners."

I nodded in desperation. "Yes, she did. I can even remember

that she was talking about her boss as we crossed the boulevard Raspail. But with the best will in the world, I can't remember his name anymore."

"Come on, Alain, think about it." Robert tried to coax me. "I'm sure you'll remember it. You only have to want to. It's possible to call up any memory."

I closed my eyes for a moment and tried to beam myself back to the boulevard Raspail. I wanted this; I wanted it so much.

"I have a nice boss," Mélanie had said. "But he smokes far too much. Now he's in the hospital with pneumonia. When we visited him, the first thing he did was to joke that the thing he missed most was his cigars. "Monsieur"—this is where she'd said his name—"is so unreasonable."

Monsieur . . . Monsieur . . . I made so much of an effort that I felt I was going to make the kitchen table float in the air at any moment.

I opened my eyes again. "Lapin," I said. "His name is Lapin."

It was just a single letter that was keeping me from my happiness, but it was an important one.

Robert really had the bit between his teeth. "Leave it to me, I'll deal with this. Make sure you get some sleep; you look terrible," he said.

And then he set three of his research students to work looking for Monsieur Lapin and his little antiques store. The students were charming and, indubitably, highly motivated to do their favorite professor a special favor. But after several days of diligent Googling and telephoning, the ladies threw in the towel. There were hundreds of little antiques stores in Paris, but obviously none of them was called Lapin or registered under an owner of that name.

"Either this cigar-smoking Lapin has since gone to the happy hunting grounds and his shop has been closed or we're on the wrong track," said my friend. "There must be something wrong there." And Robert was absolutely right about that. The simple fact that I'd confused a *P* with an *L* doomed us to failure.

I was restless, nervous. I just couldn't understand it. My courage was failing, my mood was bad. During the following two weeks, I always woke up with a feeling that something was not right with my life. I smoked too much—far too much. I'd soon be following the unhappy Monsieur Lapin to the happy hunting grounds. I imagined Mélanie finding me too late and collapsing on my grave. First the boss, then the lover. Tragic.

"Alain, you're exaggerating wildly. Man, it's just a woman; you'll get over it," said Robert in his friendly, direct way. I was aware that my pain was making me exaggerate, but what use was that to me? It was no consolation at all.

Every afternoon, I went to the Cinéma Paradis, and when evening came, I stared out at the street. Madame Clément and François exchanged concerned looks. I ran into my office to get away from their questions.

The more time passed, the more unlikely it became that I would ever see Mélanie again. Every Wednesday, my turmoil increased out of all proportion. Wednesday had been her day. Our day! And it was only five days till the filming, which I'd totally lost sight of in the interim.

Deciding to send a signal, I changed the film for the late show at short notice. Instead of *The Passerby*, *Cyrano de Bergerac* would be shown in the *Les Amours au Paradis* series. For one short, senseless moment I imagined that I could cast a spell on the universe that would tempt Mélanie into the cinema. Oh, how you grab at straws when you want something so much!

The show was sold out that Wednesday evening, too. No woman in a red coat. She's probably no longer wearing it, I thought bitterly. May had just arrived, and the weather was far too warm for winter coats.

When I stepped out of the cinema that evening to smoke a cigarette, the air was mild and those arriving at the Paradis were strolling over the cobbles in spring clothing. Skirts blew up, delicate scarves in pastel colors waved in the breeze, and pullovers were thrown loosely over people's shoulders. Their steps were lighter than before, and their eyes were smiling.

I looked longingly down the street as a couple walked up to me arm in arm. I almost failed to recognize them. It was the woman with the dark curls, who had always looked so unhappy before—this time without her daughter—and beside her, floating on air and without his briefcase, walked the tubby little man who'd always arrived late in the foyer, looking harassed. It looked as if they were really looking forward to *Cyrano de Bergerac*. Possibly—or even probably—they were just happy. They walked past me without a care in the world, and didn't even notice me.

I don't know what it was, but the woman with her red lipstick suddenly seemed much less miserable and the man, who had exchanged his suit jacket for a light blue pullover seemed a great deal less fat.

I took a last puff and threw the cigarette butt into the gutter. That first Wednesday in May, I was probably the only unhappy person around.

Eighteen

....

As is so often the case in life, help came from an unexpected direction. It was to be Allan Wood who provided the decisive pointer, because he recognized the obvious link, the connection that Robert and I had missed and which took the whole thing in a new direction.

"My idea may seem a little offbeat at first glance, but you must admit there could be something in it." Allan Wood sank into the cognac-colored leather sofa and contemplated the strawberry that had been elegantly stuck to the rim of his strawberry daiquiri.

I nodded. It was Sunday evening, and I'd been sitting with the New York director in his favorite bar for quite some time.

That morning, I had been surprised by a call from Solène Avril, whom I hadn't seen since that walk around the place Vendôme. "We're going to take a trip to Montmartre with the whole gang. Would you like to come along, Alain?" she said. "That way, you'll get to meet everyone at once."

Everyone—that meant the most important members of the film crew, who would be invading the Cinéma Paradis the following morning. The cameramen, the lighting crew, the makeup artists, the director and his assistants, Solène Avril's personal assistant, and, of course, the actors. You can read the credits at the end of any film, but you seldom think how many people are necessary to make a film—or even just a couple of scenes.

At the very beginning, and in the comfortable atmosphere of a dinner with Allan Wood and Solène Avril, the filming had seemed a great idea, but now it was upon us I was somewhat apprehensive about all the hassle—just as I was always apprehensive about anything that disturbed my normal daily routine. Unlike Robert, Madame Clément, and François, who were anticipating the event with excitement and the most varied of expectations, I had decided to stay away from my cinema as much as possible for the next few days.

FROM MAY 3 THROUGH MAY 7 THE CINEMA WILL REMAIN CLOSED FOR FILMING. Even as I hung the sign on the entrance with very mixed feelings, a few passersby had stopped to look, but even without the sign you would have noticed straightaway that things were different from usual. A part of the narrow street had already been cordoned off, there was a trailer parked on one side, looking very alien among the old buildings, and behind that sat the catering truck and the production trailer.

I was definitely going to look in on Monday to get to know everyone—Solène had insisted on that—but the idea of spending several hours with the whole crew on Sunday—and in Montmartre, of all places—made my stomach churn.

From a distance, the sugary white church on its hill high

above the city—which can also be reached by the *funiculaire,* a little cable car—is just about bearable. But when you're there, especially during the daytime, Montmartre is very dreary. At the foot of the hill, there are rows of cheap stores, and dubious characters can be seen rummaging in the mountains of underwear that are on sale on the tables in front of them. Farther up, tourist buses that are far too big squeeze their way through the narrow streets and past the restaurants. In each one of them, at least one great painter has eaten, painted, or drunk, as you can read on the notices outside. On the steps beneath the church sit necking student couples and camera-toting tourists from all over the world—a little disappointed that you can't see the Eiffel Tower from there.

Hordes of Gypsy girls descend, like the pigeons in the Piazza San Marco, on everything that moves, trying to read your palm, or steal your wallet, or get you to sign a petition, perhaps all three at once. Most of the people who wander around here as if they were looking for something they don't quite understand are tourists, and that is nowhere more noticeable in Paris than here. Here, within the magic circle surrounding the church of Sacré-Cœur, you might easily get the impression that the waiters in the bars and restaurants are the only natives—and you wouldn't be far wrong.

On the picturesque place du Tertre, painters try, with more or less successful pictures, to maintain the old traditions. Around the square crowd both visitors and little restaurants.

At night, in the flattering light of the old street lanterns, Montmartre indubitably has, even today, something of its old picturesque magic, which seems indestructible. But in the bright light of day, it reminds you of a woman with her best years behind her, wearing too much makeup.

Montmartre by day depresses me, and I was already in a melancholy mood. So I said no to Solène and wished her a lot of fun.

Half an hour later, Allan Wood called to ask if I *really* didn't want to join them. It was such a perfect day for Montmartre. They'd hired three cars and drivers to explore the artists' quarter, and were all really excited at the prospect.

I couldn't imagine that there was any such thing as a perfect day for Montmartre, but after all, *I* wasn't an American tourist. So I politely said nothing.

"Solène has been waxing lyrical about how beautiful it is there," said Allan Wood. He seemed to have been totally overcome with excitement, and I could only assume that ten years in the United States had made the lovely actress's memories not only tender but also highly sentimental.

"We're going to look at the Musée Montmartre and then we're going to take a little snack in Le Consulat—Picasso painted there once."

I grinned, not sure if that was right, but I knew Le Consulat well. It was quite high up in the acute angle of two cobbled alleyways and had a little terrace, where I had sat and eaten onion soup. I must admit the soup was really good.

"Good choice," I said. "Have the onion soup."

"And you're really not coming with us?"

"No, I really am not."

Allan Wood was not the kind of person who insisted; he was too clever for that. "Okay, Al-lang. Then you'll join me at the

Hemingway Bar this evening and we'll drink a strawberry daiquiri together. Okay?"

"Okay," I said.

And so it came about that I was sitting in the Hemingway
Bar with Allan Wood on Sunday evening, with jazz music
playing softly in the background. Among the fishing rods and
hunting rifles, a confidential conversation "between men" developed.

At first, we'd just discussed a few organizational things about
the filming, but then Allan suddenly leaned over toward me and
gave me a penetrating look. "You are so blue, Al-lang," he said.
"What's the matter? You seem kind of delected." He waved his
hands in the air, looking for the word. "Is *delected* the word?"

"Dejected," I said, and took a large gulp of my daiquiri with
an embarrassed smile. But it didn't change anything. I was indeed dejected. "Oh, well," I said, shrugging my shoulders. "I'm
a bit tired, that's all."

"No, no, you're defected, Al-lang. I can see these things."
The director shook his head. "When I was with you last time at
our amusing dinner at the Ritz, you were so cheerful and happy.
And now you've totally changed. I feel very familiar with you,
Al-lang. Really, I like you." He looked at me with concern.
"Won't you tell me what's wrong? Perhaps I can help you."

"I don't think so. It's rather complicated."

"Let me guess. It's about a woman."

I nodded dumbly.

"A very beautiful woman?"

I sighed my agreement.

"You're in love?"

"I'm totally smitten."

"But your love is not returned?"

"No idea." I flipped the strawberry from the edge of my glass and watched it sink in the third daiquiri of the evening.

"At first, I thought that she returned my feelings. Everything seemed perfect. Once in a lifetime. I've never felt like that before." I laughed bitterly. "And it was once in a lifetime. After that, she didn't turn up for our date, and she hasn't been in touch since. Sometimes I think I imagined the whole thing. It's as if it never happened. You understand?"

He looked at me sympathetically. "Yes," he said simply. "I understand exactly what you mean." He sighed. "Oh boy, I was afraid of that. It's so typical. She can be so enchanting. *So* thrilling. And then she suddenly changes her mind and just drops you." He snapped his fingers. "She did the same with Carl." He took a mournful sip of his drink.

"Carl?" I asked. "Who's Carl?"

Carl Sussman was the cameraman. He had a full black beard, his family had come from Brazil, and he'd had a short but passionate affair with Solène Avril before she dropped him in favor of a major Texan landowner called Ted Parker. According to Allan Wood, Carl was a real man. But where the lovely actress was concerned, he was like wax in her hands. He was still suffering. And now he had his hopes up again, since Ted Parker had remained on his ranch in Texas.

Fascinated and slightly tipsy from the alcohol, I listened to Allan Wood's profuse explanations, which were meant to console me. "For God's sake, don't take it personally, Al-lang," he told me. "Solène is a very seductive woman. And doesn't she know it! She is what she is. But she likes you, Al-lang; I know that. At least she was very disappointed that you didn't come with us today." He looked around the bar. "Well," he said. "How odd! This is where everything began a couple of weeks ago. Oh boy!" He shook his head. "I'm really sorry, old man."

I stared at him in shock. What on earth was he talking about?

"Listen, Allan," I said. "I think you've got the wrong end of the stick. . . . Solène and I . . ."

"Don't worry," he said. "I'll be as silent as the grave. Solène has no idea that I know about it."

"But Solène has nothing at all to do with it," I said. "I'm in love with Mélanie."

Allan Wood opened his eyes wide. "Mélanie?" he said. "Who is Mélanie?"

I told him everything—from the very beginning. The director kept picking at his corduroys and interrupting me with little interjections. "But that . . . that's really funny. And I thought you'd fallen in love with Solène," he said. "What a story!" When I finally told him about my list and the unsuccessful search for a little antiques store, he gave me a sympathetic look. "Oh boy," he said. "That really is complicated." He waved to the waitress and ordered two more daiquiris. "What are you going to do now?"

"I haven't the faintest idea." I sank back into the soft leather sofa and stared vacantly into space. Allan Wood was silent, too. And so we sat on the sofa together for a while. Two men in a bar, drinking in silence, lost in thought, yet understanding each other without saying a word. I'm sure Hemingway would have liked it.

"Have you ever thought that there might be a connection between the filming in your theater and the disappearance of this woman?" Allan Wood asked, suddenly interrupting the dying strains of Ella Fitzgerald's "I Got the Spring Fever Blues."

"What?" I was startled out of the comfortable serenity that had enfolded me.

"Well, I mean, isn't this all very strange? We appear . . . and a short time afterward this woman disappears without trace. Perhaps there's some connection there."

"Hmm," I said. "What kind of connection might that be? Fortune smiles on a little cinema proprietor and as a result he loses the love of his life? Is that it? Lucky at cards, unlucky in love?" I shrugged my shoulders. "Am I being punished by the Fates because I'm starting to make money at last?"

"No, no, that's not what I mean. No Fates. I'm not talking about retributive justice or nemesis." Allan Wood tried to think how he could explain it to me. "What I'm trying to say is, could there possibly be a connection between the two things? Some kind of link? Or do you think it's just a coincidence?"

"Hmm," I said again. "I've never looked at it like that. I mean, things happen simultaneously all the time—good things and awful things—and as a rule they have nothing at all to do with each other. That's the way the world works." I was starting to talk like my friend Robert. "Someone has a birthday . . . and his father dies the same day. A car is stolen . . . and its owner wins the lottery the same day. An American director comes to Paris to make a film in a little cinema . . . and a girl named Mélanie, whom the cinema owner has just fallen head over heels in love with, disappears without trace." I leaned forward and ran both hands through my hair. "There may be a connection, but I can't see it." Then I smiled wearily and made a stupid joke. "Unless the director turns out to be the young woman's great love, thought to be lost forever, and they have now found each other again and don't know how to tell me." I laughed. "Although I would find the age difference a bit questionable."

Allan Wood looked at me for a long time without saying anything, and I began to worry that I'd offended him with my off-the-cuff remarks.

"And if the director was her father? What then?" Allan said.

At first, I thought it was a joke. I thought Allan Wood was in an inventive mood. It's not unusual for creative people to let their imaginations run away with them. But as Sir Arthur Conan Doyle once so elegantly put it, "When you have eliminated the impossible, whatever remains, however improbable, must be the truth."

"What do you mean?" I asked.

"Exactly what I said." Allan Wood took off his glasses and began to clean them laboriously. "Your Mélanie could be my daughter."

"Purely theoretically, you mean?" I had no idea where his remarks were heading. He'd obviously fallen into a state of elderly sentimentality of the "Oh my God, she could be my daughter" kind. But Allan Wood shook his head.

"No, seriously. I mean it!"

I looked at him in disbelief. "Is that meant to be a joke?"

He put his glasses back on. "No joke." Lost in thought, he leaned back in the sofa, dangling his arm over the side. "My daughter must now be twenty-five. As far as I know, she lives in Paris. When I said recently that she'd never forgiven me for leaving her mother, I was understating matters. She hates me. I tried to visit her once—at the stud farm that her horse-obsessed mother ran on the Loire—but she just ran away. She vanished for four weeks. Unbelievable, right? She was sixteen at the time. After that, we only met once more—here in this bar. But the evening ended in disaster." He sighed. "She takes right after Hélène—just as stubborn and self-righteous. And just as pretty! Those big brown eyes!"

Allan Wood became lost in his memories and I began to wonder if all those daiquiris had been a little too much for this rather slight man.

"Yes . . . and?" I asked a little impatiently. "What has all this to do with me? And Mélanie?"

"Oh," he said, looking at me in surprise. "Didn't I tell you? I'm sorry, I'm getting a bit confused myself. Her name is Mélanie. But we always just called her Méla—that's why I didn't hit on it right away. But my daughter's proper name is Mélanie. Mélanie Bécassart."

It ended up being a long evening, because Allan Wood told me a story from his past that—it turned out—was definitely connected to my story.

When he was in his prime—I guessed he meant that he was about forty at the time—and after his first marriage broke up, he had met Hélène Bécassart during a vacation in Normandy. Hélène, a wild girl with flowing chestnut curls, had literally fallen at his feet when a white horse threw her as she rode along one of the broad sandy beaches of the Côte de Nacre.

This passionate but difficult relationship produced a little girl. Mélanie, whom everyone lovingly called Méla, was a shy little creature with an overdeveloped imagination. Her headstrong mother—who, at thirty-nine, was not exactly young when she had her first child—belonged to an aristocratic family that had a little castle on the Loire. She was a great nature lover, passionate about riding, and, at the beginning, Allan Wood, the city dweller, had found her extraordinarily fascinating. But her increasing mulishness, her deeply felt prejudices against Americans, her refusal to set foot in a city, and her rides—which grew ever longer—finally drove this sensitive man to flee.

"I mean, it really wasn't easy for me, Al-lang. There were no horses at all where I grew up, and I really have no clue about those gigantic beasts with their big yellow teeth. They scare me." Allan Wood shuddered as he said this. "But at the end, it was always just horses, horses, horses. It began at breakfast—I mean, I couldn't even read the paper without her yakking about some Arab she wanted to cover her mare. It was called Fleur, and it was a brute. It disliked me from the very beginning—I could see that from its shifty looks. It was very jealous of me. Once when I was standing behind it, it kicked me with its hoof— right here." Allan Wood put his hands in his lap and grimaced painfully.

The omens for Hélène and Allan weren't good, and so what had to happen happened. The couple grew ever further apart in the most literal sense of the word. And in the end, they were divided not only by the Atlantic Ocean but also an inability to communicate.

When Méla was eight, her father sat down by pure chance on a bench in Battery Park in Manhattan, looking out across the Hudson River. And there, on that bench, with the spring wind blowing around them, he became involved in conversation with a young woman who loved arguing. She was, as quickly became obvious, a lecturer in literature at Columbia University, and she had, which was even better, a deep aversion to horses. Too much nature made her just as nervous as it did Allan Wood. And so the two of them walked the streets of Manhattan, talking and laughing, and Allan, who had become almost dumb during his relationship with the horsewoman, made the glorious discovery of how fresh and new everything becomes once more when you talk about it with a beautiful young woman whose interests seem inexhaustible. Excitement and guilt alternated in quick sequence, but in the end excitement won—both in the intellectual and physical sense.

Allan Wood left Hélène, whom he'd never married, by the way, and wed Lucinda, thirteen years younger, with whom he soon afterward had a son.

Hélène was beside herself with rage. She shook her chestnut brown curls and, consumed with hate, swore that she'd never see him again. Then she went off to an ashram in India. In the meantime, Méla went to a boarding school, but Hélène had infected her daughter with hatred for her treacherous father.

Allan Wood looked into his glass a little guiltily as he came to the end of his story. "Of course that was all rather unpleasant," he said. "But you know, my friend, when you get older and more thoughtful and eventually realize that life is not that long, then it's like a gift from the heavens to be able to be with a young person like that. To suddenly be able to share once more in that carefree lightness that you've lost over the course of the years, but which you never cease to yearn for."

I nodded. Thoughts like that were foreign to me—so far. But Allan Wood remained true to his yearning. A few years earlier, he had separated from the literature lecturer. Since then, he'd married for the third time.

"And you think Méla—I mean Mélanie—could be the woman in the red coat?" I asked, feeling butterflies in my stomach.

"I don't think it can be ruled out. Méla has always been very impulsive. Perhaps she found out that I'm in Paris, in *your* cinema, and then took flight."

"But . . . but where . . . I mean how . . ."

Allan Wood raised his eyebrows. "The papers were full of it—that the film was to be made on location in Paris, and in the Cinéma Paradis."

I squirmed in excitement on the leather sofa and remembered with terror that in the interview with Monsieur Patisse, I had even babbled something about how much I admired Allan Wood, how likable I found him, and that during our very first conversation, I'd already felt that I was talking to a friend. AL-LAN AND ALAIN—BEST FRIENDS was the headline the journalist had given his article, quite proud of the way he'd brought in the film reference.

And if you looked at it carefully, it was a fact that Mélanie had vanished from my life at the very moment that Allan Wood appeared in it. All of a sudden, thousands of thoughts shot through my mind. There was the similarity in name and age. My Mélanie also had beautiful brown eyes. And hadn't Allan Wood said something about walking upright like a ballerina? I began feverishly looking for similarities.

"Does she have dark blond hair? Sort of caramel blond?" I asked.

Allan Wood thought for a moment. "Well," he said. "You know how it is with women. They like changing the color of their hair. As a child, Méla had chestnut brown hair, like her mother. Then all at once she had black hair. The last time I saw her, her hair was blond—even if it wasn't exactly caramel blond." He smiled. "You have a real eye for detail, Al-lang; I thought that when you first told me about your list. One item on the list struck me—you mentioned that Mélanie had said that her mother didn't like jewelry. Hélène was the same. 'I have other charms; I don't like the feel of metal on my skin,' she said when I wanted to buy her a bracelet." He grinned. "Though I suppose she might have accepted a wedding ring." He stirred his glass thoughtfully with his straw. "She did actually get married later, but as far as I know, the marriage broke up very quickly and without any children."

This made me think of Mélanie's ring with the roses. All of a sudden, I was assailed by doubts. Mélanie had said the ring was a memento of her mother. Her dead mother.

"Do you know if Hélène is still alive?" I asked, afraid of hearing the answer.

Allan Wood sighed and shook his head regretfully. "She was so obstinate; even when she was over sixty, she had to get on some stupid nag and go for a ride." He wrinkled his forehead in disapproval, and I felt sick with relief.

So it was true. Mélanie's mother had died and Mélanie wore Hélène's ring—the only thing she had left. She had no siblings. And the fact that she hadn't said a word about her father no longer surprised me, under the circumstances.

"I've always said that those brutes are dangerous, but she always did as she pleased. She broke her neck. An accident—two years ago. I even got a card . . . but not until weeks later. After the funeral, which was a private one for close family. Which I'm no longer part of. I'm persona non grata with the

Bécassarts." He took a sip from his glass. "But I'd still like to see Méla again. Perhaps we'll find a way to make peace with each other. She is my daughter, after all." His voice sounded wistful.

"I'd also very much like to see your daughter again," I said, my heart pounding. All of a sudden, I was wide awake. It was unbelievable and delightful at the same time, and I could hardly believe that after all the effort wasted on trying to find Mélanie, a new line of investigation was opening. I could have hugged the man with the horn-rimmed glasses, who had that evening become a kind of relative. "I'd like nothing better than to finally see Mélanie again," I said once more. "Will you help me with that, Allan?"

Allan Wood smiled and held out his hand to me. "I'll find Méla. That's a promise."

Nineteen

....

Filming had begun. It transformed my little cinema into a bustling, crazy, humming microcosm, a barely controllable, highly
explosive conglomerate of snaking cables, harsh spotlights, rolling cameras and snapping clapboards, bellowed instructions, and
tense silences. It was a world all of its own, which combined
human vanity, heated rivalry, and great professionalism in the
strangest way.

That Monday, when I climbed over the two rows of seats
that had been removed and were now standing across the foyer,
blocking the entrance, I realized that the whole place had been
practically demolished. Massive changes had taken place in the
Cinéma Paradis. Not even Attila the Hun had produced such
devastation when he invaded the plains of Pannonia.

Incredulous, I came to a halt in the foyer, staring at the chaos
that had broken out around me. A panting, sweating man carrying a cable jostled against me; I took a step back and almost
tripped over the foot of a lamp, which began to sway dangerously.

"*Attention, Monsieur!* Out of the way." Two men hurried past me, groaning. They were hauling a massive chandelier into the auditorium, and I tottered to the side once more, this time bumping into a human being—one wearing a floral dress. It was Madame Clément.

"Oh God, oh God, Monsieur Bonnard, there you are at last," she said, gesticulating wildly in the air. "*Mon Dieu,* what a shambles!" Madame Clément's cheeks were bright red and she seemed extremely worked up. "Have you seen what they've done to my box office? I couldn't stop them, Monsieur Bonnard. Those catering people just don't care—even though they've got their great big truck parked outside the cinema." She pointed reproachfully at the box office, which was filled to bursting with cases of drinks, cans, and paper plates. On the wooden counter where the cash register normally stood, a coffee machine was hissing away. "I can only hope they'll put everything back in order when they've finished here, Monsieur Bonnard. My goodness, what a shambles," she repeated.

I nodded with a sigh of resignation. I, too, hoped that my little cinema would emerge from this hurricane undamaged.

"Have you seen Madame Avril yet?" Madame Clément asked. "A delightful person—she's in your office at this very moment with the makeup people," she said with a self-important expression. "And Howard Galloway's in the projection booth, freshening up. He wasn't happy about his part; he wants more lines." She shrugged her shoulders. "I've just taken him a *café crème*; he takes it with three lumps of sugar."

Madame Clément's eyes gleamed, and I wondered how on earth you could freshen up in the projection booth. But I didn't really want to know, and I stared at the caterer as he walked past us in his white apron, carrying trays of sandwiches and finger food in both hands to a folding table that had been set up in the corner of the foyer. A tall, almost bald man who was writing things down in a notebook made his way with all the confidence of a sleepwalker through reels of cable and amplifiers to reach the room that until very recently had been my office. Now it was the wardrobe area. I took a tentative look inside.

Dresses, jackets, and scarves on metal hangers were crammed onto a clothes stand. Peering behind it, I could see a wash basket heaped higgledy-piggledy with files and documents. My desk was bare—or rather, it had been swept bare. Now it was piled with hundreds of jars and pots, brushes and powder puffs, hair clips and sprays. And enthroned in the middle was a Styrofoam head crowned with a hairpiece. They'd hung a gigantic mirror over the desk, and I wondered for a moment what had become of the two pretty watercolors of Cap d'Antibes.

Solène was sitting at the mirror, her back to the door, attended by two women who were busily combing her hair. She didn't notice me. No one seemed to notice me, except perhaps for Madame Clément, who had obviously become one of the crew herself.

I tottered into the auditorium, where the temperature was tropical, and had to shut my eyes, blinded by the lights. When I opened them again, I saw a big bearded man standing behind a camera, taking test shots with the lighting double.

"A bit more to the right, Jasmin! . . . Yes, that's just fine!" The bearded man waved and checked the viewfinder once more.

A screwdriver landed at my feet. I leaped to one side and looked up. Vertiginously high up on a ladder were the two men who had just carried the gigantic chandelier across the foyer.

They were taking down the old ceiling lights. The intention was obviously to increase the nostalgia factor of the Cinéma Paradis by several degrees of magnitude.

I looked over at the two front rows, where the seats had been replaced by cameras and gigantic lights. A little man in dark glasses was standing there talking very emphatically to a handsome man with dark blond hair, an aristocratic air, and a sulky expression, who later turned out to be Howard Galloway. The little man gave a friendly wave when he saw me. It was Allan Wood, my new friend, the man who was holding all this chaos together.

"Ah, Al-lang! Come here. Come here!" he called, beaming widely. "So, haven't we done a great job on your little film palace?" He pointed up at the ceiling, where the oversize chandelier was now swinging dangerously. "Now it looks really old, don't you think?"

Three hours later, the man who was holding everything together was nervously wiping his forehead with his handkerchief. His face was no longer beaming. His patience seemed exhausted. I'd been told that when you're shooting a film, there are good days and bad days. And then there are the very bad days. This was obviously a very bad day.

"So let's do it all over again. Concentrate! Three, two, one aaand . . . *action!*" shouted Allan Wood. He was standing behind Carl, the cameraman, watching the scene with his thumb under his chin and his index finger to his lips: It was the ninth take. It was supposed to be the first meeting of the main characters, Juliette and Alexandre, in the cinema.

A few seconds later, he waved his hand impatiently to cut

the scene. "No, no, no, that won't do at all! Solène, you should turn in a bit. And a bit more surprise, please. You haven't seen Alexandre for years. You thought he was long dead. The way you're talking to him looks like he's just coming back from the toilet. So, once more . . . with feeling!" He wiped his forehead wildly with his handkerchief. "And the line is 'I've never forgotten you, Alexandre,' not 'I've thought of you every second, Alexandre.' Then look into the camera. Close-up. Cut."

"Do you know what? I have an idea," said Solène. She said it as if she'd just invented the formula for eternal youth, and everyone on the set raised their eyes to the heavens. Solène Avril was well known for having "ideas" that wreaked total havoc with everything.

Allan Wood's right eye began to twitch. "No, please! No more ideas for today, Solène. I'm the director. I make the decisions."

"Oh please, don't be so stuffy, *chéri*." Solène smiled winningly. "We'll just change the whole passage. 'I've thought of you every second, Alexandre'—that sounds better, don't you think? It sounds so beautifully . . . intense. Let's change it."

Allan Wood shook his head. "No, no, that's totally . . . I mean, that's totally illogical. Don't you get that?" He sighed. "You haven't seen Alexandre for thirteen years, so you can't have been thinking of him *every second*."

"No, it's Ted she's thinking of every second," said Carl, the cameraman.

Solène looked angrily at the big bearded man in the blue polo shirt. "Interesting! I never knew that you could read thoughts, too. I thought you only read SMS that were not addressed to you." She pursed her pretty lips, and Carl looked grimly at the ground. "In any case, I don't want any close-ups today—I didn't get a wink of sleep last night."

Carl narrowed his eyes. "That's all that stupid cowboy's fault," he growled. "Why does the guy have to call in the middle of the night. Doesn't he realize that the clocks in Paris aren't set to Texas time?"

"Give it up, will you, Carl? What are all these constant gibes supposed to mean? Do you have a problem with Ted?"

Carl shook his head. "Not as long as he stays on his damn ranch," he said grimly.

Solène laughed. "I can't promise that, stupid. You seem to have done your very best to convince him that it would be better if he came to Paris."

"Could you fight your private feuds later? It's getting on my nerves!" A bored Howard Galloway glanced at his perfectly manicured nails. "I'd like to get on with it. I'm hungry."

"*Chéri,* we're *all* hungry," said Solène. "And you're not *always* the center of everything—even if you are, of course, the handsomest man on the set and think that entitles you to the biggest part."

"Quiet! I must have quiet! Absolute quiet!" Allan Wood was rocking backward and forward and slipped something that looked suspiciously like a stomach tablet into his mouth. Then he held up his hand to attract everyone's attention. "Now, pull yourselves together. Just this one scene and then we'll have a coffee break."

He waved Elisabetta over. The makeup artist—everyone just called her Liz—was a good-natured creature with a round, friendly face. You would have thought she belonged in a farm-

yard rather than on a film set. With a couple of skilled movements of her powder puff and brush, she conjured up a rosy
freshness on the cheeks of the querulous actress and refreshed her
lip gloss.

A few minutes later, they were all back in their places. Allan
Wood gave a sigh of relief when, a quarter of an hour later, the
scene was safely in the can without any more mishaps. "Okay,
guys. Let's take a break," he called, sticking a final little pill in
his mouth.

Solène already knew about it. She'd led me into my former office
with a conspiratorial smile, pointed me to a stool, and pulled the
door to behind us. Now she was sitting opposite me on her chair
with a plastic beaker of hot coffee in her hands, and looking at
me with shining eyes.

"*Quelle histoire!*" she said enthusiastically. "I mean, what a
story! The owner of a cinema falls in love with a mysterious
woman who turns out to be the estranged daughter of a director who's filming in his cinema. That's better than any film!
Ha-ha-ha!" She laughed gaily.

I nodded, realizing with surprise how familiar this silvery
laugh had become. Solène, this capricious, pleasure-loving
woman of many ideas, was beginning to grow on me.

"Yes," I said. "It's really an incredible coincidence. Allan
Wood's daughter! I mean, you can't make that stuff up." My
thoughts returned for a moment to the Hemingway Bar and
what Allan had told me about Hélène and his daughter. "I just
hope he really does find Méla." I was quite concerned. "There
isn't a woman called Bécassart living in the rue de Bourgogne
anyhow. I would have noticed."

"Of course he'll find her," said Solène, twirling a lock of hair that had freed itself. Then she put her hand on my arm. "Don't worry, Alain. He'll find her. After all, we all want the tragedy to end up as a comedy, *n'est-ce pas?*"

"All?" I asked. "Who else knows about this?" Solène fiddled with her pearls. "Oh, just Carl—I had to tell him, of course; after all, we were once very close—and Liz. She's really into complicated love stories and finds it all extremely romantic." She smiled. "And so do I." She looked at me for just a little too long, and I decided to change the subject.

"What was going on with Carl just now?" I asked.

Carl Sussman was an excellent cameraman who had won several Academy Awards. And he was also, if you were to believe Solène, the biggest idiot that the French sun had ever shone on. I already knew from Allan Wood that the bearded colossus simply refused to accept that the flighty actress had ended her affair with him and had turned to a big Texas landowner. But since the team had been reunited in Paris to start work on filming *Tender Thoughts of Paris,* the hot-blooded Carl had stuck to Solène like glue. He stole her cell phone, read all the messages Ted Parker had written to her, deleted them, and then wrote to the Texan, "Keep your hands off Solène, cowboy. She's my girl."

Of course the actress had explained everything to her outraged lover on his ranch in Texas and given Carl the tongue-lashing he deserved. She'd even threatened that she would insist on a change of cameraman if he didn't control himself. But Carl refused to be impressed by her anger. He just kept saying, "We're made for each other, *corazón,*" and threw everything into winning Solène back with red roses and passionate declarations of love. Carl was not a man to accept a refusal. He followed her when she went to buy shoes in the rue de Faubourg; he went to the Ritz and hammered on the door of her room in the middle of the night. And when she tried to get rid of him, saying, "*Alors, va-t'en, Carl. Je ne veux pas!*" he'd gasped a determined "*Ta gueule, femme! Tu fais ce que je dis!*" and kissed her. And Solène had shut up and let herself go one more time—one single, final time.

"Yes, well . . . Carl is a very attractive man, and we'd been drinking margaritas," she explained with some embarrassment. "But did the idiot have to pick up my phone that night?"

When, instead of Solène's sweet voice on the line, there was the deep bass of a man with Brazilian roots who had no problem with identifying himself and growled "This is Carl" into the handset, the result had been a transatlantic catastrophe of major proportions. It was the perfect storm. Carl was very pleased with himself, Solène was beside herself with rage, and the jealous rancher, who, far away in Texas, studied the French yellow press exhaustively to get some idea of what was going on during the filming in Paris, was deeply disturbed. Even when Solène assured him that it had only been the room-service waiter, who'd brought a club sandwich to her suite at four in the morning, she was understandably unable to convince her rather stolid but by no means stupid lover.

"I can only hope that Ted will calm down. He's always so impulsive, you know," Solène explained with a dreamy smile. She leaned forward and looked at me. Sitting there with her big blue eyes and her sky blue silk dress with its tulle-lined skirt billowing around her slim legs, she looked like an innocent Ophelia who had been deeply wronged. Finally, she gave a little sigh. "Oh, all these jealous men around me! It's really too stressful, Alain, believe you me."

Solène sank gracefully back in her chair and crossed her legs. Then she fluttered her eyelashes at me and gave me a challenging poke in the knee with her pointy blue fifties shoe. "In my next life, it might be better to try a sweet French intellectual. What do you think?"

Twenty

It was like a fairy tale. Three is a magic number there, too. The miller's lovely daughter has three chances to guess Rumpelstiltskin's name. The enchanted princess appears to the king in the night three times. Cinderella shakes the tree over her mother's grave three times to get a gown for the ball.

Three days after Solène Avril said to me, "Don't worry, Alain. He will find her," my dearest wish seemed to be fulfilled. In a fairy tale, it would probably have been a mounted courier who brought the glad tidings. In my reality, firmly fixed in the twenty-first century, it was simply the ringtone of my cell phone.

Contrary to his usual practice, Allan Wood came straight to the point. "I know where she lives!" he said, and I whooped with joy, thrust my fist in the air like a footballer who's just scored the deciding goal, and gave a delighted leap in the air on the corner of Vieux-Colombier and the rue de Rennes.

A lady who was just leaving a jeweler's shop with an elegant carrier bag and a satisfied smile gave me a curious look, and I felt I had to share my happiness with someone right away. "He's found her!" I called to the astonished lady. She raised her eyebrows in amusement and in a sudden rush of humor said, "Well, that's terrific!"

"He's found her!" I said barely five minutes later to my friend Robert, who was just on his way to give a lecture.

"Great," said my friend. "We'll talk about it later."

It was Thursday, early in the afternoon, and the world was the best of all worlds. Allan Wood, director, master detective, and my new friend and ally, had done it. He'd found his daughter, the woman I had given my heart to.

It had been quite difficult at first, but after a few tense phone calls with members of Hélène's family on the Loire, mainly characterized by the fact that the receiver was slammed down as soon as Allan gave his name, there was a nephew twice removed who took pity on the agitated ex-lover of his deceased aunt Hélène and was ready to reveal the address of their daughter to him.

It turned out that Méla had moved back to Paris from Arles only about a year before, after the dramatic breakdown of her marriage to a southern Frenchman (the nephew was unable to give any more exact details). She was now living under her maiden name in the Bastille quarter, not far from the place des Vosges; the nephew was not exactly sure of the street name, but he was at least able to give Allan Wood her telephone number.

"I've already done a search," Allan said proudly. "She lives in the rue des Tournelles. There is actually someone living there called Bécassart."

"Wow, that's sensational!" I shouted down the line, and the Japanese man with the big camera who was walking past me at that very moment flinched, flashing me an embarrassed smile. I was in seventh heaven, but then I thought back to my experiences in the building on the rue de Bourgogne.

I sighed. "My goodness, Allan, that's really too good to be true. Let's hope it's really her this time."

"It is her—I've already called."

"*What?* And what did she say?"

"Nothing. I mean, just her name." Allan Wood sounded a bit embarrassed. "I didn't dare say anything, so I just hung up straightaway. But it is her—that was definitely Méla's voice."

Excitement shot through me like an electric shock. I would really have liked to take the Métro immediately and go to see her. But Allan Wood advised caution.

"Let's not get too hasty, my friend. This is not just a one-day affair, and we need a good plan," he said with panic in his voice, and asked me to wait till he'd finished filming in the Cinéma Paradis, because that was taking all his emotional energy. With any luck, it would be the next day. Until then, Allan Wood didn't think he'd be up to a confrontation—the result of which was so uncertain—with his daughter.

"I understand your impatience, Al-lang, but I'd like to have a clear head. After all, it's not just about your girlfriend, but about my daughter, too. We need to pull together in this affair, okay?"

Although disappointed, I agreed. As far as I was concerned, we could have set off immediately. But Allan implored me to remain calm and trust him. He made it clear to me that this highly sensitive situation would require a very delicate touch. There were definite reasons why Mélanie Bécassart had refused all contact with her father for years and had also stopped coming to the cinema. Strong emotions were in play, and it was reasonable to assume that the woman we were seeking wouldn't be overcome with joy to see her father and me suddenly standing at her door.

Even though my heart was already rushing to the rue des Tournelles, my head told me that Allan Wood was right. And so we agreed to meet at my place that Friday evening to calmly discuss the best way to proceed.

On Saturday morning at half past seven, the Marais was deserted. The sidewalks were wet, a light drizzle was falling on Paris, and the sky over the city was leaden. It was the perfect morning to sleep in after partying through the night.

Two men in raincoats were sitting behind the misty window of a little café not far from the Bastille Métro station, discussing something over an espresso. Then they fell silent and exchanged conspiratorial glances. Beside them on a black wooden bench lay two gigantic bouquets of flowers. It was not hard to guess that these two men were up to something. They obviously had a plan. Nor is it hard to guess who those two men were—but for the sake of completeness, let us mention at this point that the two men were Allan Wood and I.

I was just saying, "Perhaps it would be better if you went first, Allan." In a very few minutes we'd be ringing the doorbell of Mélanie Bécassart's apartment in the rue des Tournelles, and I was feeling sick with excitement.

"No, no. No way—if she sees me, she'll slam the door in our faces straightaway. You have to go first." Allan Wood rattled his empty espresso cup nervously on its saucer. "Don't lose it now, Al-lang, we'll do it exactly as we discussed yesterday."

Our plan was brilliant, as only the plan of two men who are trying to win back the love of a woman can be. We had done what men always think of doing first. We'd bought flowers. Smiling indulgently, the lady in the flower shop had tied masses of roses, lilac, baby's breath, and hydrangeas into two gigantic bouquets. "Who's the bouquet for?" she had asked, and Allan and I had answered simultaneously, "For my daughter" and "For my girlfriend." The flower seller then asked if it was for a birthday. We had both shaken our heads but had given her to understand that we were totally determined to spend the price of a small car on the two bouquets. "They need to be overwhelming," Allan had said.

And so they were—overwhelming. We could hardly lift the bouquets, but the flowers in their pink-and-blue paper wrapping nevertheless drew benevolent glances from all the female passersby we met. And that was a good sign to begin with.

We'd discussed the matter thoroughly that Friday evening when Allan—somewhat exhausted but happy—returned from the Cinéma Paradis, where the last scene had been shot that afternoon. We'd considered a large number of factors and come to the conclusion that early Saturday morning offered the best-possible chance of finding Mélanie Bécassart in her apartment. When she opened her door, I was to be standing in front to offer her the flowers and say something like "Please forgive me, and give me just a minute. I have to talk to you." Then Allan Wood would appear from behind his bouquet. Allan had said that it was always good to ask a woman for forgiveness.

At nine o'clock, hearts thumping, we were standing at Mélanie's door. We might have found another way of getting in, but fortunately there was a concierge in the grand building on the rue des Tournelles. That extremely friendly lady had readily let us into the building when she saw our flowers and we ingenuously explained that it was Mademoiselle Bécassart's birthday that day and that we wanted to surprise her. Obviously, no one suspects men with flowers of evil intentions.

In the hall, it was peaceful and quiet. The whole building seemed to be still asleep as we climbed the softly creaking wooden stairs. We stopped on the third floor.

I looked at my bouquet, thinking that I'd never bought a woman so many roses before. Then I reached for the bell. Three melodious notes rang out. I listened as they faded away, hardly daring to breathe. Behind me, Allan's flowers were rustling. We waited in a state of high tension. How often in recent weeks had I stood at strange doors and rung the bell. This was going to be the last time.

Nothing moved behind the heavy, dark wooden door.

"Oh, shoot! She's not there!" I hissed.

"Shhh!" said Allan. "I think I hear something."

We listened. And then I heard it, too: footsteps and the creak of floorboards. A key turned in the lock, and then the door opened a crack, revealing a petite shape with disheveled hair, standing there in a blue-and-white-striped nightdress and bare feet, rubbing her eyes.

"Good grief, what's this?" she said as her astonished gaze fell on the sea of flowers at her door and the two men behind them.

The script dictated that I should say my line at this point. But I said nothing. Instead, I just looked at her, and felt the ground giving way beneath my feet. Then, as if from a great distance, I heard Allan Wood's voice. From behind his blue hydrangeas, he could only blurt a single word: "Méla!"

"Papa!" said the woman in the nightdress, too surprised to be angry. "What are *you* doing here?"

Twenty-one

Life is a soap bubble, says Chekhov. And mine had just burst. While Allan Wood emotionally clasped his prodigal daughter in his arms and she—perhaps more grown-up as a result of her mother's death and unexpectedly mild-tempered—invited him into her apartment, I laid my bunch of roses on the threshold as if on a grave and tumbled down the stairs.

Méla was not Mélanie. That was the bitter truth. How I had hoped to look into her heart-shaped face and her big brown eyes as the apartment door opened. How sure I had been that I was only a short moment away from happiness.

Then this strange young woman was looking questioningly at me, and I fell into the abyss. This could not be happening, not after all we thought we had found out. I stood there as if turned to stone and dumbly watched the reunion between Méla and her father.

Allan Wood, himself overcome by emotion, had, after a few words of explanation stammered on the landing, briefly remembered my presence and asked me if I'd like to come in for a coffee anyway. I had shaken my head—that would have been too much.

And while the little man in the horn-rimmed glasses and his pretty daughter clearly had a great deal to tell each other, I ran numbly down the street in the Marais, seeming unreal even to myself. It was still raining, but I couldn't be bothered even to turn up the collar of my raincoat. It was right and proper that it was raining down my collar and that I was getting wet. Or it simply didn't matter. Together with the rain, all the sadness of the city broke over me, and yet rain is only rain, and not something that is passing comment on your life. I wasn't interested in the weather. Who needs a blue sky when he's unhappy? Robert was right. The sky, whether gray or blue, is cold and unemotional, and ultimately even the sun is only a fireball that, unaffected by everything going on here below on earth, simply spews its masses of magma into space.

Heavyhearted, I ran aimlessly through the streets, I can't even say that I was thinking very much, or if I was, I can't remember what. I put my feet forward one after the other like an automaton; I was unaware of anything, not even the damp that was creeping into my bones, not even the hunger that my stomach was trying to make me aware of.

I had been conquered in battle and was beating a retreat just like Napoléon's Grande Armée after the defeat in Russia two hundred years before. To say that I was demoralized would have been a gross understatement. This final attempt had cost me the last of my strength, and my spirit had vanished without trace. I didn't know what else I could have done. I could do no more. It was all over—irrevocably.

I had been fooling myself the whole time. How naïve had I actually been to take seriously the idea that Allan Wood's daughter and the woman in the red coat were one and the same person? How naïve did you have to be to believe that a woman who hadn't been in touch for weeks was in any way interested in you? It was laughable. I was laughable. A fantasist, as Papa had always said.

This all dawned on me as I was marching over the pont Neuf and a passing taxi driver splashed a cascade of water over my clothes. Welcome to reality, Alain! I thought.

With a certain degree of self-destructive cynicism that gave me a strange satisfaction, I remembered Dr. Destouche from *The Lovers of Pont Neuf,* who pasted posters of the heroine—herself going blind—in the tunnels of the Paris Métro in an attempt to find her. A joke! And I hadn't even had a photo. I had nothing. Nothing but a letter and a few fine words. I decided to get the girl in the red coat out of my head once and for all.

Tired, wet, disappointed, and angry with myself, I pushed open the door of La Palette hours later. This was where it had begun, and this was where I would end it. Like a man. I sat down at a table in the rear of the bistro and ordered a Pernod and a bottle of red wine. That would probably be enough to begin with.

It's not actually like me to get drunk in the afternoon. But after the milky anise liquor and four glasses of heavy Bordeaux, which I drank down in steady gulps, I discovered that alcohol in the afternoon can have an extremely stabilizing effect.

Outside, it was still raining, but my wet things were gradually drying out and I'd been taken over by a dull calm that felt quite pleasant. I waved to the waiter and ordered another bottle.

He looked suspiciously at me. "Would you maybe like something to eat as well, monsieur? A sandwich, perhaps?"

I shook my head energetically and uttered an involuntary grunt. What sort of nonsense was this idiot talking? No one had ever gotten drunk by eating. *"Je veux quelque chose à boire!"* I explained with emphasis.

The waiter returned and, without being asked, put a basket with a baguette down in front of me. Then he fussily took the cork out of the new bottle. "Are you expecting someone, monsieur?" he asked.

I found his question downright ridiculous. "Me?" I asked, pointing to myself with an elaborate gesture. "Not at all. For God's sake, do I look like that sort of guy? I'm alone. *Je suis tout seul.* Like all idiots." I laughed at my own brilliant joke and took a great gulp from the big balloon glass. "Would you like to join me? You're invited. But only if you're an idiot, too."

The waiter declined with thanks and went away, looking irritated. He seemed to walk straight into one of the pictures on the wall. I shook my head a couple of times and then I saw him leaning back on the counter with his colleagues. They looked over at me. La Palette gradually began to fill up.

A tall, portly man entered the bistro, his coat flapping in the wind, and shook his umbrella out vigorously before shutting it, exclaiming, "What lousy weather!" My waiter rushed forward and—totally unlike his normal habit—took his coat and umbrella.

I looked over curiously. Every movement the chunky man with the black hair made oozed self-importance. Who did he think he was—the emperor of China? I had a sudden fit of dizziness as he dropped loudly into a chair in the rear of La Palette, not far from my table, and ordered *steak frites*.

He opened a newspaper and looked around with an air of self-satisfaction. I narrowed my eyes and tried to think where I knew this show-off from. And then I remembered. It was Georges Trappatin. He owned one of the biggest multiplex cinemas on the Champs-Elysées. I had once had the dubious pleasure of sitting beside him for a whole evening at an event at the cinémathèque française, listening to his dumb pronouncements. "You small cinema owners are just fooling yourselves," he'd said with a shake of the head. "Films are all fine and dandy for tempting people out of their homes, but the turnover comes from advertising, popcorn, and drinks. Nothing else makes a profit."

I took a sip of wine and noticed, to my horror, that Monsieur Trappatin had seen me, too. He got up and came over to my table with heavy tread. Then his reddish face hovered over me like a Chinese lantern.

"Well, if it isn't Monsieur Bonnard!" he said. "That's what I call a surprise. Long time, no see, har-har-har!"

I watched his fleshy lips carefully as they opened and closed like the movable jaw of a puppet and he uttered an incomprehensible growl.

"Though I have been thinking of you recently, no joke. Little old Cinéma Paradis . . ." He shook his head. "Things are really buzzing at your place, aren't they? Read it in the paper. That's a shot in the arm, isn't it!" His mouth twisted into an appreciative grin.

I stared hard at my bottle of red wine, and he followed my gaze.

"Well, as I see, you're already celebrating hard, har-har-har!"

Georges Trappatin clapped me chummily on the shoulder and I nearly fell off my chair. "A bit of press attention like that is half the battle, eh?" This was followed by another booming laugh, which rang strangely hollow in my head. I twitched painfully. Monsieur Trappatin obviously took this for agreement.

"Well, anyway, I'm happy for you, that your little small-time outfit is getting a slice of the cake for once," he said with condescension. "I personally don't believe there's a future for small cinemas." He leaned heavily on my table and I collapsed back in my chair. "They've had their day, that's clear. You have to move with the times. Nowadays, people want action. Event cinema with all the bells and whistles." He straightened up again. "I was recently at a fair in Tokyo. The Asians aren't really my thing, but I must admit they're miles ahead of us in terms of technology. And they're far from having reached the end of the road; you don't need to be a prophet to see that." He snorted with enthusiasm. "I'm using four-D now. That's the killer, I tell you! Sensory seats and smells—yeah, you have to have a vision in our business. You have to invest."

I must admit that I was having some difficulty following the visionary Georges Trappatin on his journey into the fourth dimension. In my head, the space-time continuum was merging with a kind of Andromeda cloud, where the cinema mogul's words seemed not to make any sense.

"Sensory seats?" I repeated with some difficulty, and filled my glass once again. "Sounds super. Can you fly in them, too?" For a moment, I imagined the audience at the multiplex cinema flying happily to the moon with their buckets of popcorn, and I chuckled slyly into my wineglass.

Georges Trappatin gave a surprised look, and then burst out

laughing. "Har-har-har, very good," he said jovially, pointing at me with his index finger. "I appreciate your humor, Monsieur Bonnard, I really do!"

Then he explained the incredible advantages of his new seating. Pearls before swine: I didn't understand a word. So I nodded from time to time and just let him babble on.

Georges Trappatin was known for his monologues. But after a while, even he noticed that the conversation was a little one-sided. "Ah! Here comes my food!" he said finally. "Well then, Monsieur Bonnard, be seeing you! I hope you'll invite me to the premiere in your little cinema. *Tender Thoughts of Paris* doesn't exactly sound like a blockbuster, does it? When I think of that story with the wheelchair . . . I was flabbergasted to see how the thing took off. *The Intouchables*—I would have bet my boots that it would be a flop. But then, I'm not Jesus, am I? Har-har-har." He grinned at me. "I'm no friend of Allan Wood films; there's too much blathering. But I wouldn't mind seeing that Avril from close-up. Quite a woman!" He made the appropriate gesture with his hands and flicked his tongue obscenely between his fat lips.

I gave him a hostile stare. All at once, I was convinced that I had the devil from *The Witches of Eastwick* standing in front of me. I had to warn Solène—it was obvious that this loathsome guy had her in his sights.

When Monsieur Trappatin, somewhat unnerved by my hostile stare, returned to his table, I swore that he would never step over the threshold of my cinema. Let him burn in hell!

After another glass of wine, I'd forgotten the devil in the shape of Monsieur Trappatin and begun to think of Mélanie, who always came to the Cinéma Paradis when she was looking for love. It looked as if she'd found love someplace else since then. Even Allan Wood had found his daughter. They'd all found what they were looking for. I was the only leftover.

Depressed, I sank forward, leaned my elbows on the table, took hold of my glass, and watched the red wine swaying in it. Suddenly, I saw Mélanie's hands, which I'd held in mine only a few weeks before, and pain washed over me like a huge wave. I put the glass down again, feeling miserable.

On Monday, the Cinéma Paradis would reopen, but Mélanie would not be coming again. She would never come again. It was as if the woman in the red coat had never existed. She might just as well have been dead.

"What a sad, sad story," I murmured gloomily, and my eyes became wet with self-pity. "Poor, poor Alain. It's a shame, old man, it's such a shame." In sympathy, I nodded a couple of times, no longer sure who the "old man" actually was—me, or another tragic figure who was also called Alain. In any case, it seemed to me best that I should go on drinking. "*A tes amours!*" I slurred. "To love!" The red wine swayed dangerously as I picked up my glass once more with a clumsy movement. But perhaps it was the ground that was swaying.

I waved the waiter over to me. "Tell me," I said, making an effort to speak clearly. "You noticed it, too? The ground moved. Think issan earquake?"

The waiter looked at me suspiciously. "No, monsieur, I'm sure you're just imagining it."

His ignorance made me mad. "What nonsense you're talking, monsieur! You don't just 'magine sothing like that. I feltit clearly. That was an earquake. You!" I pointed to him. "Don't try and puller wool over mize." Enraged, I stood up from my chair a couple of inches and then fell back again. A little tune interrupted what I was saying. The monotonous notes pierced my ears. "An switch 'at racket off. It shturbs me when I'm thinking."

The waiter was very patient. "I think your cell phone's ringing, monsieur," he said, and moved discreetly away from my table.

I fished the stupid thing out of a raincoat that was hanging over the chair beside me. Had I put it there? I couldn't remember. "Yesh?" I said with some effort. Speaking was quite demanding. "Whozzat shturbing me?"

"Alain?" said Robert. "What's up? Are you okay? You sound so strange. And—did you find Mélanie?"

"My friend," I said. "I'm fine, butchasking too many questions twonce. We foun Méla. But Méla znot Mélanie. Mélanie's dead, dinja know? Poor Alain. Ev'thing sucks for him. We're sitting here, drinking a glash tgether. Dyou want to come, too?"

"Good God, Alain!" My friend's voice sounded concerned, and I couldn't understand why. "You're completely drunk."

"Mnot drunk, jusht drinking," I explained emphatically, and felt the restaurant beginning to spin around me.

"Where are you?"

"Inlaffalette," I babbled, then keeled over and fell peacefully asleep on the table.

After an omelette and three double espressos, La Palette had stopped spinning. A trip to the toilet did the rest. Robert held me up and worked the flush.

"Better out than in," he said as I swilled my mouth out with water. I leaned on the washbasin and looked at my pale face, framed by disheveled dark hair. I'd definitely looked much better that morning.

"I need to go to bed," I said.

Robert nodded. "The first sensible thing I've heard you say all evening." He gave me an encouraging clap on the shoulder. "Get some sleep; then you'll really feel better. I'm sure it's not that bad."

I nodded without really being convinced. By then, I was sober enough not to share Robert's optimism. I felt anything but great. Still, what he said did me good, even if it was a bit banal. "Oh, well," I said, grinning bravely. "I suppose you're right."

"You'll see. In a couple of weeks, you'll be laughing about the whole thing. And then I'll introduce you to Melissa's friend. She's exactly your type. Dark blond and drop-dead gorgeous. She also likes going to the cinema. Just recently, she dragged me and Melissa to see a film about an old folks home in India. *The Best Exotic Marigold Hotel*," he said proudly. "A good film. I really liked it."

He was obviously doing everything he could to cheer me up. "Great," I said. "I know that film."

"And the main advantage is"—Robert pulled his eyelid down with his finger—"this girl is a real flesh and blood woman, not just a figment of your imagination in a red coat."

Robert was really good to me that evening. He paid my bill, and insisted on taking me right to my own front door.

As we left La Palette, I noticed a big beefy man leaning against a lamppost. He glanced quickly over at the entrance; then, in the best Marlboro Man fashion, he lit a cigarette and threw the match to the ground. Other people were lonely in this world, too.

As he left me that disastrous evening, Robert couldn't resist a parting shot: a quote from a film that he'd probably been saving for just such an occasion.

"Don't take it so hard, Alain, and call me if there are any

problems, okay? And if you have to drink, let's do it together. It's never been good to drink on your own."

I nodded. My friend was absolutely right for a change. I was still a bit sleepy, but at least I could stand up now. I leaned on the door frame and watched Robert heading for the stairs. He turned once more.

"What did that nice young Indian in *The Best Exotic Marigold Hotel* say? 'Everything will be all right in the end . . . if it's not all right then it's not yet the end.'" He gave me a meaningful wink, and I shut the door. What he'd said was very interesting. In India, where they believe in reincarnation, it had a very particular resonance. But here in the West, we just have to live with unhappy endings.

And yet Robert turned out to be right. We hadn't reached the end of the story, not by a long shot.

When my doorbell rang a few minutes later, I thought my friend had come back because he'd forgotten something. With a muttered curse, I got up and went to the door in my striped pajamas. On the way, I almost tripped over Orphée, whose curiosity always led her to hang around the front door whenever the doorbell rang. She leaped aside with a reproachful meow. I shooed her away and opened the door.

But it wasn't Robert. That day was obviously Astonished Face Day—and this time, it was my turn. Before me stood a man I'd never seen before in my life. He pushed his hat back a little, and that was when I recognized the Marlboro Man who'd been leaning on the lamppost outside La Palette.

"Sorry," he said in a broad American accent. "Are you Alain Bonnard?" He had a good-natured, weather-beaten face and small, watchful eyes.

I nodded in surprise. And before I had time to say anything, I felt his fist in my face. I fell straight down. The world was spinning around me again, but this time I was seeing little dancing stars. Strangely, I felt no pain, just a pleasant dizziness that prevented me from getting up.

The man with the hat looked down at me, cool as a cucumber. "Keep your hands off Solène, snail eater," he said.

I heard the door slam shut. And then I heard nothing more.

When I came around again, I was looking straight into two green eyes that were staring piercingly into mine. I felt a light pressure on my chest and blinked in the harsh light, confused. There was a continuous ringing in my ears, and the mattress was very hard—although strictly speaking, it wasn't a mattress. I was lying on my Berber carpet in the middle of the hall; on my chest sat Orphée, meowing fearfully. The ceiling light was shining in my face, and my head was aching like mad. I felt as if a truck had driven over my face, and the damned ringing in my ears just wouldn't stop.

I sat up with a groan and pulled myself up using the bureau. A look in the mirror confirmed my worst suspicions. The man in the mirror was finished with this world—and he really looked the part. Tentatively, I touched my left eye, which was bruised and swollen. Then I remembered the big man with the big punch who'd stood at my door the previous evening and called me a snail eater. And I don't even like snails! His fist in my face was the crowning conclusion to a day that had begun so hopefully and then, following the laws of classical tragedy, headed straight for its catastrophic ending. But at least I was still alive. Even though I'd gone deaf.

When the penetrating ringing in my ears stopped for a short

time and then began again, I realized that it was my telephone. Unusually, it was where it should be—on the charger on the bureau in the hall. I reached for the handset. It was probably Robert, calling to see how I was feeling. But that early on a Sunday morning, my friend was still asleep. It was Solène Avril's anxious voice that I heard on the line.

"Thank God I've reached you at last, Alain," she said with relief. "Why don't you answer your cell phone? I was trying to warn you."

I nodded, feeling, as so often in the recent past, that I had totally lost the plot.

"So?" I replied expectantly.

"Ted's in Paris, running amok. He somehow came across that article in *Le Parisien* and saw that picture of us—you know, the one in the place Vendôme. I tried to explain that we'd just been taking a walk, but he wasn't having any of it." Solène sighed. "He's going wild with jealousy. Anyway, he's out to get you. I don't know what he intends to do, Alain, but you must be careful, do you hear? He could just turn up at your door. I'm really worried."

I smiled. "You can stop worrying, Solène," I said. "He's already been here."

Twenty-two

....

The scallops were taking their time. We were sitting at a long table on the terrace of the Georges. The day had been unexpectedly warm, people were wearing their summer clothes, and over the restaurant, which was on the roof of the Centre Pompidou and was well known for its spectacular view of Paris, the indigo blue evening sky was unhurriedly darkening.

Unhurried also seemed to be the motto of the waitstaff. For half an hour, we had been trying in vain to attract the attention of the long-legged waitresses, who had obviously been trained more for a modeling career than for serving at table. They stalked past us with flowing hair and beautiful but impassive faces, totally ignoring us.

Solène smiled at me and raised her champagne glass. It was her birthday and she was determined not to let anything spoil her good mood. I tried to do the same.

In the past few sunny days of May, normality had once more taken over—in the Cinéma Paradis, where François had removed the CLOSED FOR FILMING sign from the door the previous Monday, and in my own life. Apart from the fact that the gigantic chandelier was still hanging in the auditorium and that the old cinema was still basking in the glory of the famous names who'd been there, there was nothing to remind us of the turbulent week when the film crew had turned everything upside down. The trailers had vanished from the street and the filming of *Tender Thoughts of Paris* was nearing its end. It would be only another four weeks until the last scenes that were to be shot in Paris would be in the can.

Allan Wood was beaming broadly. He was sitting diagonally opposite me with his arm around a young redhead with massive earrings hanging down her neck in a cascade of golden disks. It was Méla, his daughter, who was in the process of discovering the nicer side of the father her mother had so demonized.

I hadn't seen Allan Wood's daughter since that day—so black for me—in the rainy Marais. And though I was glad to grant him his happiness, my heart grew all the heavier as I thought of that wonderful moment when we were standing outside Méla's with our bouquets and I believed I had found Mélanie.

That evening was also the first time that I'd seen Carl Sussman since the filming. He had sat down next to Solène with a satisfied air and winked at me—as far as that was possible. The bearded cameraman's left eye—like mine—shone a beautiful blue. We grinned meaningfully at each other. Ted Parker had done a good job.

However, the Texan with the cowboy manners was not present at this congenial evening on the roof terrace of the

Georges, where half the film crew had gathered to drink to Solène Avril's health. In her anger, she had exiled her jealous lover to the Texas desert before he could do any more damage. To the great delight of Carl, who now never left her side.

And even handsome Howard Galloway, who was sitting farther down the table in an elegant gray Armani suit, must have been very relieved to hear that the belligerent American— who had apparently also turned up in the Hemingway Bar and, with the words "Let's settle this like men," challenged him to fisticuffs outside—had now been banished to the other side of the Atlantic Ocean.

"It's all over with Ted. *Çela suffit*," Solène had said to me when she invited me to her little birthday party. "You have to know when it's finished."

Even though the starters had not arrived, the mood at the table was exuberant. I toasted Solène, who was sitting opposite me with champagne-flushed cheeks. She was so lovely that evening in her sea blue gown, which seemed to reflect the color of her eyes. She was sitting there like a benevolent Scheherazade, telling one story after another and even allowing Carl to squeeze her hand from time to time. It was her birthday, and she was as happy as a little girl. Her high spirits carried us all along with them—even me, the most miserable of all.

I leaned back in my chair and let my gaze wander over the terrace with its atmospheric lighting. Three gigantic white tubes towering diagonally out of the floor a bit farther away transformed the restaurant into the deck of an ocean liner, sailing through the Paris night as if through an endless, sparkling sea. You forget from time to time, as you forget a beautiful hanging in the living room over the dinner table, but anyone who has ever sat up there on a spring evening knows once again why Paris is called the "City of Lights."

On my left was the spotlit cathedral of Notre Dame; I could see the sparkling Eiffel Tower in the distance. I saw the lights on the grand boulevards, where the cars were traveling up and down incessantly, as small as children's toys. I saw the bridges spanning the Seine like golden bows. I saw the laughing faces around me, and wished I could be lighthearted once more, experience the lightness I had sensed as I walked the streets of Paris by night, thinking myself the happiest person in the world.

Once again, I thought of the crumpled little letter that was now lying in the top drawer of my desk. How often I had taken it out and tenderly smoothed it flat in recent weeks.

Mélanie was not the adventurous type. That was what she had written to me. But wherever she was now, and whatever she was doing, she had given me the most adventurous weeks of my life. "We'll always have Paris," Humphrey Bogart said to Ingrid Bergman in *Casablanca*. And I would always have a happy evening that ended under an old chestnut tree. The girl in the red coat would remain the sweet but sore point in my biography: the promise that was never kept; the mystery that would always remain a mystery. And yet I regretted nothing. Someday it would be less painful. Someday my heart would be light again. I had only to let it happen.

I finished my champagne. Solène was right. You have to know when it's finished. Robert had arranged for us to have dinner with Melissa and her friend the following weekend. The friend was supposed to be exactly my type. We'd see.

Liz, who was sitting next to me, got me involved in conversation. After a while, I saw, to my astonishment, that half an hour had passed without my wallowing in my misery. And when the plates with the scallops were finally banged down on the table by a Claudia Schiffer look-alike, I got as annoyed as everyone else about the unfriendliness of the service, and like everyone else, I burst out laughing when Allan, in comic desperation, said that the lamb he'd chosen as his main course tasted somehow of ashes—and, in fact, the underside was black and charred—and Carl had to saw away so violently at his steak that the whole table rocked. "How are you supposed to eat steak with such a blunt knife?" he complained. "I might as well eat it with my fingers."

Solène waved to the blond waitress, who, after awhile, tottered over on her stilettos.

"*C'était?*" she asked, and without waiting for an answer, she began to clear our plates away.

Solène shook her head. In a couple of short sentences, she put the waitress straight, pointing out Allan's charred lamb and ordering a steak knife for Carl.

With a sigh of irritation, the blond would-be model with the coral red lips took the plate with the half-incinerated lamb, and then with a bored look at the steak, she said impertinently, "Excuse me, monsieur, that meat is soft as butter; you don't need a steak knife for it," and moved away from the table.

"Hey, wait a minute!" Carl shouted angrily after her. "Do you know who you're talking to? And this steak is *not* as soft as butter. Just take it away!" You could see that he was just about to leap up from his seat and throw plate and steak together after the ignorant creature who didn't give a damn that she had a world-famous star at her table.

Solène put her hand on his arm. "No, don't, Carl—it's such a lovely evening."

And so it was, even if the food was mediocre and the service catastrophic. We'd all drunk and laughed a lot, and in spite of everything, it was an unbelievable privilege to sit here floating over Paris by night.

The dessert was delicious—unexpectedly. After the raspberries and strawberries, the crème brûlée, and the pistachio macaroons had been served and eaten, I excused myself for a moment and strolled over to the edge of the terrace to smoke a cigarette. I leaned over the railing, flicked the ash downward, and looked at the sparkling city.

"Magical, isn't it?"

Even without turning, I knew it was Solène. She had quietly followed me and come to stand behind me. A waft of heliotrope filled the air and I could feel the warmth that emanated from her and her desire to share this quiet moment with me. So we stood silent for a while at the metal railing as if we were on board a ship, absorbing the view of the glittering city; it looked as if the sky with all its stars had crashed at our feet.

"Sometimes I long to be what I once was," said Solène suddenly.

"What were you?" I said, turning around to face her.

Her eyes were deep blue as she swept Paris with her gaze. "So unself-conscious. No purpose in life. Happy in a simple way. As a child, I was happy without wanting to be. I mean, I never thought about whether I was happy or whether I wanted to be happy; I just was."

"And today?"

She said nothing for a while. "Sometimes I am, but often I'm not. When you get older, there comes a time when you realize that what's called happiness consists only of individual lovely moments, those special times that you remember later on." She smiled pensively. "This is one of those moments. I feel overwhelmed by a sense of being at home."

I nodded silently. The view over the city gave rise to a kind of longing in me. It was as if there was, over the evening horizon, something that I was missing terribly without being able to define it exactly.

"And you, are you happy?" asked Solène.

"I suppose I was very close to it."

I didn't want it to sound so sad, I really didn't, but I suppose it must have, because Solène suddenly put both her arms around me and hugged me tight. "I'm so sorry, Alain," she said softly. "I wish you had found her. If only I could do something for you. I know it's not the same, but I'd gladly be there for you. I like you a lot."

We stood together for a moment, and then I gently freed myself from her embrace. "Thanks, Solène. I like you a lot, too." I sighed. "It's dumb, but we often have so little influence on the important things in life."

She smiled. "Sometimes we do."

We looked at each other for a moment, considering our options. I was leaning with my back against the iron railing, and all at once I had the feeling that someone was watching us. Irritated, I looked over at our table. But they were all chatting away and no one seemed to be missing us, not even Carl, who had slid over to Solène's place and was talking to Allan Wood's daughter.

I was strangely moved. Shaking my head, I said, "Come on, let's go back to the others," and just took a last searching look over Solène's shoulder.

And then I saw her. At the other end of the roof terrace, right beside the entrance, stood a young woman in a white summer dress with a bright flowery pattern. She was standing bolt upright and perfectly still, her unwavering gaze fixed on us. And the color of her hair was reminiscent of caramel.

Twenty-three

....

It was Mélanie. There could be no doubt of that. It took me less than three seconds to realize it. Our eyes met across the laughing, chattering guests, and all of a sudden it was just as if the sound had been turned off. Everything that took place after that happened unbelievably quickly, and yet I felt that I was stuck in a slow-motion film.

The woman in the white dress saw that I had noticed her. She turned away and hurried toward the exit. I said *"Mon Dieu!"* pushed an astonished Solène aside, and ran as fast as I could after the white figure that was disappearing at the far end of the terrace. I rounded tables, narrowly avoiding two waitresses, who stared at me in outrage; I bumped into an old lady, who squawked and yelled a curse after me; I knocked over a tray, raising my hand in apology—but heard the crash of breaking glass behind me; I got caught in the handles of a purse that had been left beside someone's chair and tripped, my shirt popping out of my pants; I staggered up and ran on, keeping my eyes fixed hypnotically on the exit.

"Mélanie!" I shouted when I'd finally fought my way through to the exit and saw the young woman in the flowered dress running down one of the escalators in its glass tube with her hair flowing behind her. "Mélanie, wait!" I waved wildly after her, but she didn't turn around. She was running away from me; it was inexplicable, and I wondered for a moment if she'd gone mad. Then I decided I didn't care. I had to stop her—at any price.

And so I charged down the Centre Pompidou's five floors of escalators, barging past other visitors. At every turn, I saw the figure in white below me; then I heard hasty steps echoing through the entrance hall as she headed for the exit.

On the square in front of the Beaubourg, a few people had gathered to watch a fire-eater. A bit farther back, a Gypsy was sitting on a folding stool. He was playing a mournful tango on his *bandoneón* and singing about some Maria or other. A few couples sauntered past me. I stopped for a moment and looked around. My heart was hammering in my throat. Mélanie was nowhere to be seen.

I cursed quietly, ran a bit farther, and looked in all directions. In the distance, a white figure was running along the rue Beaubourg toward the Rambuteau Métro station. That must be her! I thought.

I ran as fast as I could. I was catching up; there were only a hundred yards between us. I saw her disappear into the Métro station. Pulling out a ticket, I shot through the entrance and rushed down the steps.

A scruffy guy with a guitar was heading toward me. He made way for me in surprise. "Hey, hey!" he said.

"A woman!" I gasped. "In a white dress."

He gave an indifferent shrug of the shoulders. "That way, I think." He pointed vaguely toward one of the tunnels that led down to the platforms.

"Thanks!" I blurted, heading down into the depths of the Paris Métro. A warm, muggy odor, which seemed to come directly from the interior of the earth, smelling of garbage and gravel, hit me in the face. I rushed onto the platform, where there were only a few people waiting at this time of night. A punk couple with green hair were necking enthusiastically on one of the benches.

At the very moment, a hot blast of air announced the arrival of the next train, and I saw her. She was standing on the opposite platform among a group of other passengers under a giant poster advertising shampoo, and she was just looking at me.

"Mélanie! Wait! What's going on, damn it?" I shouted across to her, and a couple of people looked up before continuing to gaze vacantly into the distance. Loud quarrels between lovers were obviously an everyday occurrence on Métro platforms.

"Stay where you are, I'm coming right over!" I shouted, and then the train came in on my platform, separating us. I felt rage beginning to mingle with my desperation. What was wrong with this woman? Why was she reacting so strangely? Or did Mélanie have a doppelgänger who thought she was being pursued by a maniac? No matter, in a few seconds it would all be explained. I ran back up the steps to get to the other platform. As I reached the top, I felt a blast of warm air down the tunnel: The train was coming in on the other platform, too.

"No!" I shrieked, hurtling down the stairs. I jumped the last five steps and landed with one bound on the stone platform, where I fell over, losing a shoe. Never mind, I thought. I ran, hobbling on one stocking foot beside the train, looking in the direction where Mélanie had climbed into one of the rear coaches.

My heart was hammering; my throat was burning; I felt a stabbing pain in my left foot—and then I found her.

"Mélanie!"

It was too late. A shrill alert was ringing in my ears.

Unmoved, and beautifully synchronized, the Métro doors shut in my face.

"No!" I cried in wild desperation. "Stop!"

Through the glass I saw Mélanie and hammered on the window with my fist. I mindlessly kicked the door a couple of times. My face was bright red, my left eye was black, my hair was wild, and my shirt was hanging out of my pants. That's what people look like when they're totally out of control—combative types looking for a fight or running amok, shooting in all directions without rhyme or reason.

"*Mais, monsieur, je vous en prie!* What sort of behavior is that?" Some guy in a Lacoste pullover tried to put me straight.

"Ah, shut up, you dork!" I shouted, and he retreated behind a trash bin. The Métro hissed. My shoulders drooped, and I stood there staring at Mélanie, who had taken hold of the grab pole and was looking silently back at me. In her gaze there was a strange, fatalistic sadness that took all my spirit away. That's how you look at someone you're saying good-bye to forever. Someone you have to say good-bye to. I couldn't understand what was happening here. I couldn't understand what I'd done.

I was the idiot in a film whose script I didn't know. I stood on a platform in the Rambuteau Métro station, forced to watch the woman of my dreams disappearing.

With a final helpless gesture I put my hand to the window and looked imploringly at Mélanie. The train began to move and then, in the second before it finally left, Mélanie raised her hand and placed it against mine.

I slunk back home like a beaten dog. It was eleven thirty and I didn't feel capable of returning to the Georges and explaining my strange behavior. What could I have said anyway? I've finally found the woman I love again, but she's run away from me?

It was Mélanie; it definitely was. Was it? I was gradually beginning to doubt my own sanity. Perhaps I had just gone mad. Mad with love for a mysterious woman who had come closer to me than anyone ever had before and who was driving me to lunacy with her inexplicable behavior.

I hobbled unhappily over the pont des Arts—with one shoe and without any hope. Yes, it was hopeless! With every step, my mood became more disastrous.

The unexpected meeting on the roof terrace of the Georges had torn open the sweet wound that I had just managed to come to terms with. I was as sure as anyone in my confused state could be that it had been Mélanie looking over at me from the other side of the restaurant. It had been Mélanie who had run away from me like a frightened unicorn in a fairy tale, and it had been Mélanie on the other side of the Métro window.

I knew that face. I would have recognized it among a thousand others. I had touched it, traced its contours with my fingers. I had lost myself in those big brown eyes. I had kissed those soft lips again and again. Those lips had so often gifted me with that enchanting little smile—but this time they had remained serious, even reproachful. Even if she had seen someone else briefly hugging me—and that was all it had been—that was no reason to rush away like that.

In my turmoil, I asked myself one question after another, but I found no answers. My foot hurt, but that pain was nothing in comparison with the pain that clamped my heart like a band of iron. As I finally dragged myself along the rue de Seine, a thought struck me, one that took hold of me with increasing anxiety and was not without a certain logic.

Until now, the woman in the red coat had vanished without trace. There could have been a thousand reasons for that which had nothing to do with me. And as long as I didn't find Mélanie, I could at least pretend to myself that some stroke of fate had been the obstacle to our love. Even the idea that Mélanie had never returned to Paris would have been easier to bear than the shattering realization that evening had produced: The woman I'd been looking for was here in Paris. She was obviously alive. And even more obviously, she wanted nothing more to do with me.

A young woman in a white summer dress had run away from me, and whatever reasons she may have had for that, it had indubitably been Mélanie. I knew it from the moment I saw her in the distance on the roof of the Centre Pompidou. And even if I had had the slightest doubt in the beginning, that had finally turned to certainty on the Métro platform.

We had only been a few inches apart as she stood behind the train window, and I could see by her look that she also recognized me. What could possibly have caused a total stranger to look at me like that? What could have caused her to press her hand against the inside of the window—against my hand, with the kind of yearning gesture two people use to assure each other of their love before the train rolls out of the station?

I laughed bitterly. The whole thing made no sense. I was suddenly struck by the memory of those first few seconds of film history showing, in grainy black and white, the train drawing into the station; I thought of the painting of the train shrouded in steam that I had so admired long ago in the Jeu de Paume, and of the childish conclusions I had drawn from it about the meaning of Impressionism. French cinema is deeply impressionistic, Uncle Bernard had said.

At that time, I'd thought that I'd understood something. But the reality I was living in now was utterly surreal. And I understood nothing. I walked through the darkness as if through a parallel universe ruled by different laws and wondered if I'd ever wake up from it.

That night, I had a dream. It was one of those dreams you remember long after waking up, perhaps even for the rest of your life, as the worst thing you've ever dreamed.

There are those collective images of terror that lurk somewhere in our subconscious. They are mostly short sequences where we drown or fall from a great height, get lost, or are pursued by dark shapes and try to run away in panic but are unable to move. And then on the other hand, there are those nocturnal images that are linked to an individual's peculiarly personal fears and create a unique dark fantasy out of fragments of that person's experiences.

For example, I've dreamed that I'm walking through a cemetery and suddenly come across the gravestone of a loved one who is actually still alive. Or I'm standing in a room with nine doors. I want desperately to get out, but behind every door I open, there is an impenetrable wall of rubber. Or I'm in a hotel elevator. I want to go back to the fifth floor, because that's where the room is where my wife is waiting for me. But every time I stop at the fifth floor, I get out, only to find an unknown corridor. I can no longer find the place I'm trying to get to.

The many ways in which the greatest anxieties find their expression are as varied as the different lives that people lead. And although there were no knives in my dream, no dark shapes rushing toward me, threatening my life, the ending of this dream, which had begun in such a fairy-tale fashion, threw me into a state of deepest misery. In the end, I had lost everything. Even today I can still remember every detail, the strangely oppressive atmosphere, the state of incredible distraction that persisted long after I woke up.

And yet—as terrifying as the dream was—it was also the reason why I went back to the Cinéma Paradis the following day to search for something I had failed to see until then. A detail that finally proved to be the key to everything that seemed so inexplicable to me at the time.

I dreamed about Mélanie. It was New Year's Eve, and she was wearing her red coat. We were at a party and were strolling arm in arm through the halls of a big old building. There were Baroque mirrors everywhere on the walls; candles flickered; the rooms were thronged with people. The women wore dresses with puffed silk skirts and narrow waists; the men wore tight knee breeches, vests, and ruffled sleeves. It felt like being at a ball in the Palace of Versailles. And yet we were in Paris. You could see that when you looked out of the building's high windows at the illuminated city.

As the bells ring the New Year in, I go with Mélanie into one of the rooms where they have hung up a gigantic flat screen. It shows, one after the other, the places in the city where people are celebrating: the Arc de Triomphe, the Champs-Elysées, the Eiffel Tower, the glass pyramid in the Louvre grounds, the hill of Montmartre, the bridges and the boulevards, where the drivers are exuberantly hooting their horns.

We walk about a little longer; then I look for Mélanie, who has stopped somewhere. When I return to the room with the big flat screen, I see that they are showing pictures of the earth. The world is a blue sphere that seems to be floating beneath us. I am suddenly seized by inexplicable terror. I run to the high windows. There is nothing outside but darkness.

And then I understand: Paris has become a spaceship that is inexorably moving away from the earth. We are already light-years away. The people celebrating around me, laughing and dancing in their Rococo costumes, haven't noticed yet.

I wander through the halls, looking for Mélanie, looking for any familiar face at all. In one room, I see stands full of clothes, which I rummage through in feverish haste, pushing the hangers to one side. There are children's clothes on them, hanging in size order, and ladies' summer dresses, men's suits. I'm searching for a clue.

I go back into one of the endlessly long corridors and see a line of people. They're waiting for something. I walk along the line, hoping to find someone I recognize. Then finally I see my parents among the people waiting. Mélanie is there, too, and

Robert; even Madame Clément is standing in that line. I call to them in relief; I'm so happy to have found them. But one after the other, they turn to me with a look of incomprehension, as if I were a stranger.

"Papa, Maman!" I call. "It's me, Alain." Papa raises his eyebrows regretfully and shakes his head. Maman looks at me; her eyes are empty.

"Mélanie, where have you been all this time? I've been looking for you. . . ." But even Mélanie turns away, perplexed.

None of them seems to know me, none of them remembers me, not even Madame Clément, not even my friend Robert.

My panic grows; my desperation shoots right off the scale. Why are they all standing there as if they've never seen me before? I walk a bit farther and see a person near the front who seems familiar to me. It's Uncle Bernard. It is only now that it dawns on me that these people are standing at a box office. It looks like the box office in the Cinéma Paradis.

But Uncle Bernard is dead, I think. Nevertheless, I call out his name. He turns to me and smiles his peaceful, cheerful smile.

"Uncle Bernard!" I exclaim with relief.

"Who are you?" he asks with some surprise. "I don't know you."

I groan and curl up for a moment in despair. "But Uncle Bernard, it's me, Alain. Don't you remember? I used to come to the cinema every afternoon and we'd watch the films together. Méliès!" I call.

"Locomotives! Impressionist cinema! Cocteau, Truffaut, Chabrol, Sautet . . ." I name all the important directors who come into my head, in the hope of producing some reaction in his good-natured face, which at the moment is gazing at me as blankly as that of an Alzheimer's patient.

"Giuseppe Tornatore," I cry. "*Cinema Paradiso.* That was your favorite film. We watched it together. Don't you remember anything at all? Our cinema. The Cinéma Paradis." I produce this as if it were a magic spell that could open all doors.

All of a sudden, a look of recognition crosses Uncle Bernard's face. He narrows his eyes for a moment as he looks at me. Then his mouth curves into a hesitant smile, which slowly becomes much broader. "Yes," he says. "Yes, of course—I remember. My memory is a bit hazy. But you're Alain . . . my little Alain. . . . But that was all so long ago. . . . I was still alive then. . . ."

I cry with relief, and I'm crying because a dead man has recognized me. Perhaps I'm dead myself. I'm somewhere out in space, and I have no people anymore.

I try to make the tragedy of my situation clear, but Uncle Bernard just shakes his head, totally baffled.

But don't you understand?" I repeat emphatically. "I've lost everything. I've lost everything."

Uncle Bernard becomes blurred before my eyes. "You must go to the Cinéma Paradis, my boy. Go to the cinema. You'll find everything there . . . in the Cinéma Paradis. . . ."

His voice becomes quieter and begins to fade away. I stretch my arms out toward him before I fall and fall and fall. . . .

Twenty-four

....

Long after I woke up, that strange dream was still buzzing in my head. It stayed with me the whole morning, underscoring the disturbing events of the previous day with a dark minor key.

When I opened my eyes and the morning reached my ears with its many familiar little sounds, the first thing I did was to go to the window and look out into the courtyard to reassure myself that Paris had returned into the earth's atmosphere. I was relieved to establish that this was, in fact, the case, but the gloomy mood the images of the previous night's dream had inspired in me was not so easy to shake off. Indeed, I found I had little enough reason to celebrate as I tried to drive away the phantoms by making myself some coffee in my tiny, narrow kitchen.

I kept seeing Mélanie's pale face in front of me and the sad little smile with which she had traveled away into the Métro tunnel.

On my cell phone, which I'd switched off during the dinner at Georges, I found several messages. Three were from Solène, who had obviously tried to reach me immediately after my hurried exit from the restaurant. Her voice sounded increasingly concerned and—it struck me—even a little embarrassed. One call was from Allan Wood, who had immortalized himself on my voice mail with the question of whether the food had disagreed with me. My tax adviser warned that several documents needed for my return were missing, and my mother, who normally never called my cell phone, and didn't even have one because she'd heard that the waves cause cancer, wanted to tell me she was back from a trip to Canada and ask how I was. Compared with all the questions of the last few weeks, which I had had no answer to, this last was easy enough.

I was feeling bad, not to say miserable, and I hadn't the slightest desire to answer any of the messages. I just wanted peace, like Diogenes in his barrel, and even though I wasn't a philosopher, I had a deep-seated need to crawl off somewhere and be alone with my thoughts.

I sent Solène a text, giving a headache as my excuse.

Then Robert called, and I picked up the phone. Robert, with his scientific fatalism, was the only person I could bear to speak to at that moment. When I told him about my strange meeting with Mélanie and my wild pursuit—well worthy itself of being filmed—through the tunnels of the Paris subway, it silenced even him for a moment.

"Robert?" I asked. "Are you still there?"

"Yes." His voice sounded perplexed. "Unbelievable" was the next thing he said. "I can tell you one thing: The chick is

totally screwy. Probably some kind of psychopath with para-
noid delusions. That would explain everything."

"Just listen to yourself," I said. "Melanie's no psychopath!
No, no, there must be something else."

"What else? Most likely a man. Was there a man with her?"

"No, there was no one. She just looked at me and then ran
straight for the exit."

"Who knows," Robert pondered, "perhaps she's going with
some violent guy who's threatened her that something nasty
will happen if she ever meets you again. Perhaps she's just trying to protect you. Like that . . . Elena Green in the James Bond
film."

"Eva Green," I said sharply, correcting him. "Yes, of course,
that would be it. Silly that I didn't think of that myself!"

"What? I'm only trying to make myself useful." Robert
would not allow himself to be deflected. "Ha! I have it! It's her
twin sister!" He seemed to like the idea. "I once knew twin
sisters—you couldn't tell one from the other, both blond, both
freckled, both with fantastic figures. The whole time I was with
them, I thought I was drunk and seeing double." He clicked his
tongue. "That's it. Did you ever think she might have a twin
sister?"

"Yes, yes." I jammed the handset between my shoulder and
my ear and spread a chunk of baguette with butter and jelly. Of
course I'd thought of that. There was nothing I hadn't thought of
in the last few hours. "Of course that could be it. Theoretically.
But why should her twin sister, who doesn't even know me, run
away from me? That's absurd. I mean, I don't look so terrifying
that anyone should take to her heels to get away from me."

"That's probably true." Robert thought over my words, and I thought of my totally terrifying performance in the Métro station, shouting wildly and kicking the train door.

"To be honest, I'd hoped that the whole thing would have sorted itself out by now. And now this mysterious woman pops up again. It's enough to drive you crazy." Robert sighed.

"Yes," I said, sighing as well. "Tell me about it!"

Then we both said nothing.

"You've got to stop this, Alain," he said eventually. "It's all going nowhere. It's like with black holes: The more you feed them, the bigger they grow. The best thing to do would be to file it under 'Unsolved Mysteries of the Universe' and put your energy into more realistic projects."

I guessed what he was going to say next.

"You are coming to dinner on Friday? Anne-Sophie's looking forward to meeting you."

"Anne-Sophie?" I asked gloomily.

"Yes. Melissa's friend."

"Oh, yeah." I didn't sound all that euphoric. "I don't know if that makes much sense, Robert. I'm totally devastated."

"For goodness' sake, Alain, pull yourself together. Your self-pity is getting just too bad. What's really happened?"

"Enough," I said. "I have a sprained ankle and a black eye."

"A black eye?" I heard Robert's astonished laughter. "Have you been scrapping with someone?"

"No, someone's been scrapping with me," I growled. "Solène Avril's jealous boyfriend came to Paris and laid into all the men in her vicinity with his fists, including me."

"Wow!" said Robert. "You really do lead an exciting life. Famous actors and mysterious psychopaths, wild pursuits and brawls—Bruce Willis has nothing on you." He whistled admiringly through his teeth. "A black eye," he repeated, impressed. "Well, that promises to make for a good evening! Women find that sort of thing attractive."

"Please, Robert! I'm totally out of it. Let's just postpone the meal. I'm not in the mood to chat to any girls, no matter how nice they are. My heart is broken."

"Oh, for crying out loud, Alain, don't be so pathetic. You sound just like a soap opera. Hearts can't break."

With gritted teeth, I bore his laughter, and I had only one wish: that Robert should one day fall so hopelessly in love that he would feel, in the flesh as it were, what it was like when your heart breaks with a quiet *ping*. And then *I'd* be the one laughing.

"Go on, laugh," I said. "Wait till it gets you! You don't know what it was like to see her going away in the Métro like that . . . or just to see her again. I can't get the picture out of my head. I came home and couldn't sleep. She gave me the cold shoulder and I can't understand it. I just can't understand it. If I could at least understand it, everything would be easier."

"That's the awful thing about women," Robert said matter-of-factly. "There's no formula for it, no authoritative instructions. Even Stephen Hawking says so, and he's really a genius. He said that women are a complete mystery." Robert was in his element. "And then there is always all that sensitivity, all those emotions. Personally, I have no time for all that empathy garbage—that you should always try to understand people. What's the good of that? I mean, people misunderstand themselves half the time anyway. Yes, you touch someone, you reach out to others, but in your heart of hearts you're a stranger even to yourself. Ultimately, we're all trapped in our own skins. In what we believe to be the truth. That's why I like astrophysics so much. There is clarity in the universe. There are regular rules."

I thought of my dream. "I had a terrible nightmare," I said. "Paris was a spaceship, we were moving away from the earth at breakneck speed, and no one recognized me—not even you."

"Yes, yes," said Robert impatiently. "it's in the nature of dreams to be confusing and unpleasant. The brain's garbage-recycling system. You'd probably eaten too much."

I sighed. "Why are you my friend, Robert? I seem to have forgotten."

"Because opposite poles attract. And unlike you, I've got to go now—to introduce my students to Newton's laws. I'll pick you up this evening after the late performance and we'll go for a drink. No, no objection! And then we'll talk about Friday evening. There's no question of allowing you to just wallow in misery." With those words, he hung up.

I finished my coffee and put the cup in the sink. Orphée jumped up and meowed reproachfully around the faucet. I turned it on and watched the cat contentedly lapping up her water. That day, I would gladly have changed places with her.

My friend was one thing above all: strong-willed. So of course he came to the cinema, and of course I went for a drink with him that evening: no objection allowed. But Robert turned out to be wrong about one thing.

We didn't talk about whether I'd go to dinner with him that Friday to impress Anne-Sophie with my damaged eye. We didn't talk about Friday at all. We sat in the bistro and talked about men's names. Because in the meanwhile, I'd discovered something that added new fuel to an old story.

That Monday, it was Madame Clément's day off, and so I—after the main feature had run twice—was the one who had to go along all the rows after the last performance to clear up the auditorium and pick up all the things the audience had forgotten to take with them.

"Sit down a moment. I won't be long," I called to Robert, who was inspecting the new film posters in the foyer. We were alone in the cinema. François had left the projection booth in an unusual hurry after the last performance.

"*The English Patient*—what's that like?" Robert asked. He was looking at the stills from Anthony Minghella's film, which I had chosen for that Wednesday's performance in the *Les Amours au Paradis* series, and was eyeing up Ralph Fiennes and Kristin Scott Thomas.

"A literary film. A great, tragic love story—not your kind of thing," I mocked. "You'd do better sticking to *Basic Instinct*."

"What's wrong with that? It was really exciting, and that Sharon Stone was so sexy."

"Exactly," I said, disappearing with the vacuum cleaner into the brightly lit auditorium while Robert retreated into my office and lounged around on the swivel chair.

Vacuuming a cinema—perhaps simply vacuum cleaning—has something contemplative about it. While you're doing it, you can follow your own thoughts, and as long as the machine is switched on, there's no chance of anyone disturbing you.

I didn't hear my cell phone ringing; I didn't hear Robert making several phone calls and giving several loud, flattered laughs. I cleaned the rows with uniform movements, looked out for handkerchiefs and coins, enveloped by the monotonous hum of the machine.

I thought of the time I'd sat in the front row many years before, holding hands with the little girl with the braids. In the fifth row, I thought of the first time I'd been allowed to put a reel of film in the projector under the watchful eye of my uncle, and how, when I took it out, I'd forgotten to hold it firmly in both hands, so half the film unwound in seconds like a paper streamer. In row twelve, I thought how I'd reencountered my dead uncle Bernard for the first time in my peculiar dream the night before. I saw his kindly smile, and his final words seemed to blend in with the noise of the vacuum cleaner: *You must go to the Cinéma Paradis, my boy. Go to the cinema. You'll find everything there . . . in the Cinéma Paradis. . . .*

It may sound strange—and I'm not actually the spiritual type—but in the loneliness of the cinema and my heart, I suddenly asked myself if there could be such a thing as messages from the other side. Had my dead uncle sent me a message, or was it just my own subconscious trying to make me aware of something?

I was in the Cinéma Paradis, but apart from a scarf in row three and a lipstick in row fifteen, I had found nothing of note.

When I arrived in the seventeenth row, I switched off the vacuum cleaner. It was worth a try. Mélanie had always sat in row seventeen. That had aroused my curiosity even at the time, when I was still thinking about what might be a fitting story for the girl in the red coat.

I went back to my office and looked for a flashlight.

"Are you done?" Robert, who was still telephoning, looked up as I entered with a determined expression.

"Nearly," I said, and went back into the auditorium with a quaking heart. I walked slowly along row seventeen.

I bent down, felt in every crack with my hand, shone the light into all the gaps. I found two bits of chewing gum stuck under seats and a ballpoint pen that had fallen between two seats. I looked at all the scratches and notches on the wooden backs of the seats in the row in front. I put my head under every seat. I don't know exactly what I was looking for, but no one had ever examined the burgundy seating as closely before. I was absolutely sure that I would find something.

And I did find something.

When Robert came into the auditorium a quarter of an hour later, I was still sitting, lost in thought, my heart thumping, in front of the next-to-last seat in row seventeen. I was running my finger in amazement over two initials that you couldn't see at first glance because they were darkened, having probably been scratched into the wood a long time before. It had obviously been two lovers who had wanted to immortalize their love. You could hardly make out the heart that surrounded the two letters with the plus sign between them in the middle, but the letters were quite visible: M. + V.

I suddenly remembered the enigmatic words that Mélanie had said to me on our first date in La Palette. I still feel how much those words moved me, and that I'd automatically linked them to my cinema, my wonderful choice of films, or even—in a moment of audacity—to myself.

"Whenever I'm looking for love, I go to the Cinéma Paradis," Mélanie had said. And now I knew why.

Twenty-five
....

"Okay," said Robert, his blue eyes sparkling. "It's all crystal clear. *M* stands for Mélanie. You're absolutely right: It can't be a coincidence." I nodded excitedly. Robert and I agreed at last. We'd gone to Chez Papa, a pleasant jazz club almost hidden away behind the Deux Magots in the rue Saint-Benoît. After the discovery I had made in row seventeen, I was really in need of a glass of red wine, or even two. The pianist tinkled away quietly in the background, accompanied by a bassist plucking languidly at his strings.

"But who is V.?" I said.

"Well, if we start from the premise that M. isn't a lesbian, it can only be a guy."

"Not just any guy. That's her boyfriend. Perhaps the man who cheated on her with her colleague. The one with the jade earring."

Robert shook his head. "No, no, just think a moment. You don't have to be Sherlock Holmes to see that the initials are more than a year old. It must be something that happened quite a while ago." He took his battered old Moleskine out of his jacket pocket and opened it. "So," he said. Men's names beginning with *V* . . . there aren't all that many: Valentin, Virgile, Victor, Vincent—can you think of any more?"

"Vianney, Vivien, Valère, Vito, Vasco . . . It doesn't have to be a French name, does it?"

"Not necessarily." Robert had written all the names down carefully, one beneath the other. "What else? Vadim, Varus, Vasilij . . ."

"Vladimir," I added, and my lips curled as I suddenly thought of the crazy old Russian woman in the building on the rue de Bourgogne whose bell I'd mistakenly rung.

"What are you grinning at?"

"Oh, I was just thinking of Dimitri."

"Dimitri? Who's Dimitri?" Robert asked.

"Oh," I said, trying frantically to suppress a laugh. "Doesn't matter." I gave a dismissive wave of the hand. "Let's say . . . an old acquaintance." I burst out laughing.

"It seems to me that you don't have the seriousness we require." Robert looked at me with irritation. I think he felt his authority was being undermined. "What are you doing, Alain? Stop fooling around. We're only looking for people whose name begins with a *V*."

"Yes, I know. Sorry." I pulled myself together.

Robert took a sip of wine and passed the little book with the names over to me. "So . . . and now concentrate. Do you recognize any of these names? Did Mélanie mention any of these names when you were talking to her?"

I looked at the list and muttered the names under my breath

several times. Then I tried to remember everything Mélanie had told me. But if she had actually mentioned a man's name, it wasn't one that begins with a *V.* "Sorry, but none of these names says anything to me." I was disappointed.

"Think again. I'm sure that this V. is important. When we know who V. is, all the rest will become clear."

"Shoot," I said with annoyance. "Aren't there any other names that begin with *V*?

"Well, yes . . ." Robert raised his eyebrows and put on a mysterious expression. "I can think of one more."

"Well?" I held my breath.

"Vercingetorix?"

It was twenty past eleven when we finally parted. I would never have dreamed that just before midnight I would once more be sitting in a taxi, heading for somewhere that was not totally unfamiliar to me.

"If you think of anything else . . . you can always call me," Robert had said as he handed me the list with the names. He was speaking like a detective in an early-evening TV series— and that's probably what he felt like. He was having so much fun with our inquiries in the V. case that he'd totally lost sight of his own main project—the forthcoming dinner with Melissa and Anne-Sophie.

I walked down the rue Saint-Benoît and turned right into the rue Jacob. My foot was still hurting, but I was so lost in thought that I hardly noticed it. Even if we hadn't really gotten very far in the search for names, I had a good feeling: We'd at least gotten on the track of the mystery.

The reason why Mélanie had come to my cinema and always sat in the same row was nostalgia. That suited her very well.

How long ago had it been when two lovers had tried to immortalize their love in that row, in the deceptive certainty that their feelings would last forever? Had they often visited the Cinéma Paradis, or perhaps just once? Had they sat cuddling closely in row seventeen, watching *Cyrano de Bergerac,* Mélanie's favorite film, and the best film there has ever been for people in love? I felt a little stab of jealousy. I would have liked to have been the one who had held hands with Mélanie while watching the amorous correspondence between Cyrano and the lovely Roxanne.

With a sigh, I stopped at Ladurée's store window and glanced indifferently at the pretty dusky pink-and-lime-green boxes full of macaroons and other delicacies. If I had been going out with Mélanie, one evening, just for the hell of it, I would have brought her a box of raspberry macaroons because their delicate red reminded me of the color of her lips. I would have showered her with attentions just to see her smile. The previous evening, her smile had had something heartrending about it—almost as if she had had to let me leave, rather than her leaving me. What was the mystery that was keeping us apart? What was this obstacle to our love? Did it have something to do with the past? Did it have something to do with the Cinéma Paradis? Once again, I saw the two initials in front of me. What had happened to M. and V.? What had become of their love?

Thinking of the way Mélanie had spoken of the men in her life on our one and only evening together, it couldn't have been anything good. "I have a talent for falling in love with the wrong men," she had said. "In the end, there is always another woman."

Had the mysterious V. been a married man who had deceived her? Had another woman come between them? Or had there been a tragic, fatal accident that left the loving M. behind all alone? Was it possible that there was some similarity or some connection between me and V.? Was that why she'd been prepared to take up with me? Had she really been prepared to do so at all?

I didn't know. There was so much I didn't know. But at that moment, I felt so close to Mélanie. I looked at the reflection of my face in the window and almost expected to see Mélanie's face appearing behind mine.

Strangely enough, I'd had the same feeling I'd had that evening as I stood on the roof terrace of the Georges, looking out over Paris as you'd look out on an ocean. A woman had quietly come up behind me, and yet I had been aware of the slight, almost imperceptible movement. It was Solène, and I'd sensed it immediately. But this time, there was no woman to stand silently behind me; the window remained empty.

I was about to move on, when I heard steps approaching hurriedly. A woman in a hat ran up the street carrying a heavy shoulder bag and waved to a taxi that was just traveling up the rue Bonaparte toward the boulevard Saint-Germain. It came to a halt outside Ladurée. The woman opened the back door of the taxi and thankfully threw in her bag. Then, before she got in, I heard her say breathlessly, *"Avenue Victor Hugo, vite!"*

The taxi drove off and I continued on my way, idly musing on the fact that the writer Victor Hugo also had a first name beginning with a *V.* It could just be that I already had a special antenna tuned to men's names beginning with *V*; it could be that I particularly liked the name Victor. At any rate, a vague memory popped out of the depths of my subconscious. Should the name Victor mean anything to me? It meant nothing.

And yet . . .

Shaking my head, I continued for a few paces. And then I stopped stock-still and smacked my forehead. A lightning vision came to me: a quiet square, the lighting of a match, an exchange of confidences by night outside a jeweler's window.

There was, in fact, someone who had mentioned the name Victor only a few weeks before. Someone who, strangely enough, knew the Cinéma Paradis of old and had returned after many years, searching for what it had once been. In my mind's eye, I saw a truly beautiful woman with blond hair.

But it wasn't Mélanie.

Twenty-six

....

The carpet muffled sound completely. On impulse, I had turned on my heel in the middle of the street, run back to the taxi stand outside the Brasserie Lipp, and driven here. My thoughts whirled around like brightly colored leaves in fall, and yet, now that I was standing outside the door of her suite, there was a breathless calm in my head. It was just before midnight, and I only had one hope: that she would be there.

I knocked on the door, first softly and then more loudly. Only then did I notice the little bell push, but before I could press it, the door slowly opened. In bare feet, wearing a flowing silver-gray satin nightdress, Solène was standing there, looking at me in astonishment.

"Alain!" was all she said, and a light blush colored her bright face.

"May I come in?"

"Yes, yes, of course." She opened the door a bit wider and I went in. Under other circumstances, I might have paid more attention to the extravagant decor—the costly furniture upholstered with expensive yellow material scattered with roses, the heavy gold-braided drapes, the marble fireplace with two candelabra and a clock that looked as if they'd come straight from Versailles—but at that moment I was only interested in the woman who was staying there. She walked in silently in front of me and pointed to a chair. I sat down, my heart pounding.

"I'm sorry for disturbing you so late at night," I began.

"You don't have to apologize, Alain. I never go to bed before one."

Solène fell into a picturesque pose in the chair next to mine, resting her blond mane on the high back of the chair and smiling enigmatically.

"I love being disturbed at night. Is your headache better?"

I breathed in deeply. "Listen, Solène, I have to talk to you. It's important."

"Yes, I thought so." She fiddled with a strand of hair. She sat there, lovely and mysterious as a Lorelei, and seemed to have all the time in the world. "So, what do you want to tell me, Alain? Out with it. I won't bite."

"Yesterday evening on the terrace, you said you'd like to do something for me."

"Yes?" She let the strand of hair slide out of her hand and looked attentively at me.

"Well, I think you could really help me."

"Anything that's in my power."

"So," I said, trying to get my thoughts into some kind of order. "Everything is so incredibly confusing. . . . Where should

I begin?" I thought for a moment. "I didn't have a headache yesterday evening—I mean, that wasn't the reason I . . . I ran away in such a rush. . . ."

Solène nodded. "I know." She tipped her head to one side and looked at me. "I've known that for a long time, you dummy. I could see it in your face—how confused you were. You don't have to explain anything to me; I'm just glad that you came. Just running off like that . . ." She laughed softly. "But I understand you only too well. Sometimes you just run away from your own feelings—at least at first. . . ." She leaned over toward me, and her gentle, meaningful look irritated me.

I sat up straight. "Solène," I said. "I wasn't running away *from* anything or anyone. Yesterday evening, I saw Mélanie. I followed her, but she actually ran away from me, jumped into the Métro and vanished. It was obvious that she didn't want to speak to me. . . ."

"Méla?" Now it was Solène's turn to look confused.

"No, not Méla. Mélanie, the woman in the red coat. The woman I've been searching for the whole time. She was standing at the far end of the roof terrace and staring over at us. I'm sure she recognized me. And then she was off, as if she'd seen the devil himself."

For a brief moment, Solène's face crumpled, but then she regained control of herself. "And what do you want from me now, Alain?"

I took a deep breath, and then the words just tumbled from my lips. "I was in the Cinéma Paradis this evening," I said. "And there, in row seventeen—that was the row she preferred—I found something interesting. A heart with two letters, scratched into the back of the seat in front. It was almost impossible to

make out the heart, but you could see the letters *M* and *V*."
Solène followed what I was saying, wide-eyed.

"*M*—that stands for Mélanie, it can't be anything else," I
continued excitedly. "And *V* for a man's name. But Mélanie
never mentioned a name beginning with *V.* On the other hand,
you did. And you know the Cinéma Paradis from your childhood. It took me a while, but then it came back to me: You
wanted to get away from Paris at that time, and there was that
student from San Francisco. Your boyfriend, if I understood
rightly. Victor. His name was Victor."

My chest was very constricted and I had to catch my breath.
"None of this is just chance, Solène. And now I'd like you to
tell me just one thing: Who is Victor? What happened at that
time? What happened between Mélanie and Victor, who was
your boyfriend? What is the connection between Mélanie and
you?"

Solène had gone pale. Her eyes fluttered uneasily. Then she
stood up and, without a word, went over to her dressing table.
She picked something up. It was a picture in a narrow silver
frame. She held it out to me and I took it.

The picture, and old black-and-white photograph, showed
two little girls in thick winter coats standing on a bridge in Paris,
holding hands and laughing. The bigger one had her bright
blond hair tied up in a gigantic white bow and stood with one of
her bootees forward in a coquettish pose. The smaller one had
dark blond braids and her big brown eyes radiated a charming
shyness.

I looked in disbelief at the happy children's faces, in which
you could see everything that would develop into the women
they'd later become. Some sensitive corner of my memory held

a trace of a laugh, an impetuous, heartwarming 'Ha-ha-ha,' which, without being aware of it, I had recognized in another woman—in the woman who was standing in front of me now, so distraught and looking so guilty.

"But . . ." I said softly. "That's not possible."

Solène gave a barely perceptible nod. "Yes, it is," she said. "Mélanie is my sister."

Twenty-seven

There are some things that are said to you that you never forget as long as you live, Solène had said, and I could see how a deeply felt sorrow darkened the blue of her eyes. The words she would never forget had been said by her sister.

"The only thing that's important is that you get what you want; you don't care about anything else," Mélanie had said, full of hatred. "I never want to see you again, do you hear? Get out of my sight!"

That night in the luxury suite in the Ritz, I took a journey back in time that led directly to the hearts of two wounded sisters who had been inseparable as children.

Before Solène began telling me her story—and it was to last into the early hours of the morning—she asked me for an exact description. "I want to be completely sure," she said, and I did as she asked, although for me there was no doubt that the younger of the two girls in the photograph was Mélanie.

When I mentioned the golden ring with the roses, Solène

nodded in dismay. "Oh my God," she murmured. "Yes, that's Maman's ring." She looked at me in anguish, and I nodded.

"Mélanie said at the time that her mother was dead and that the ring was her only memento of her," I added. "She didn't say anything about her father."

"Mélanie loved Maman most of all. She never really got on with Papa. In our family, I was Daddy's darling. I was the tomboy, the adventurous one, the girl who made everyone laugh and hung out with the boys in the neighborhood. Mélanie was the quiet one. She lived in her own little world. She was fanciful and highly strung. When Maman once came home an hour later than expected, she found Mélanie hiding, totally distraught, in the wardrobe. She'd hidden in there, convinced that something had happened to Maman. She had a lively imagination and invented stories that she wrote in an exercise book that she hid jealously under her mattress and wouldn't let anyone see."

Solène smiled. "Although we were so different, we really loved each other. Sometimes Mélanie would slip into my bed at night, and then I'd stroke her back until she fell asleep. My first experiences with boys were with the boys from the local lycée, and my little sister would stand behind the door, secretly watching us kissing. Sometimes, not often, we'd go to the Cinéma Paradis. Papa worked for the post office, but he never advanced very far, and we had very little money for amusements of that kind. We both loved movies—Mélanie even more than I. I saw the cinema as an opportunity to meet boys in secret, but for my sister those afternoons in the cinema were something immensely precious. She lost herself completely in the films, simply dreamed herself away."

Then Solène interrupted her story. "That sounds as if we

were unhappy, but that's not true. We had a lovely childhood. We felt completely secure. My parents often had money problems, but they never quarreled—or only rarely. You could always sense the deep affection they had for each other. 'I'm always glad when your mother comes in the door,' Papa once said to me. He suffered because he couldn't offer Maman anything more than that dark ground-floor apartment, where in winter we sometimes only heated the living room and the kitchen to save money. But in her quiet, friendly way, Maman was contented. The only luxury she allowed herself was buying flowers. There were always flowers on our kitchen table: sunflowers, roses, gladioli, forget-me-nots, lilac—she particularly liked lilac. Everything was good."

She broke off for a moment and put the picture of the two girls carefully back on the dressing table.

"But then—I'm not quite sure exactly when it happened—I began to feel cramped at home. I went away a lot, had boyfriends who lived in upmarket homes and could afford to be generous. I became dissatisfied. I would have liked to study singing, but instead I did an apprenticeship. Mélanie had just turned seventeen and was still at school. I was twenty, and swore that I was not going to waste my life in a gentlemen's outfitters on the boulevard Raspail. I wanted to conquer the world."

"And then? What happened then?" I asked, and answered my own question. "Then along came Victor, the exchange student, and you fell head over heels in love with him."

"Then along came Victor, the exchange student, and my little sister fell head over heels in love with that good-looking fair-haired young man with the twinkling eyes. His lodgings were a few doors away. Mélanie met him one Sunday at a movie in the Cinéma Paradis. I had better things to do that day. The family of a friend of mine had invited me to spend the summer in their cottage at the seaside, and of course I couldn't refuse that. And while I was turning the heads of the young men of Deauville, Mélanie struck up that fateful friendship in Paris." Solène ran her fingers through her hair and gave a sad little laugh.

"Victor just chanced to be sitting next to her in the cinema. They looked at each other, and it was love at first sight, as they say. My shy sister, who had never been in love before, who, like Princess Turandot, had rejected all her suitors—between you and me, there weren't very many—gave her heart away without hesitation. They became inseparable, and Mélanie was deliriously happy. She idolized Victor, and whenever she mentioned him, her eyes took on a soft glow, they gleamed like candles. It was touching to watch them. I believe she would have gone to the end of the world with Victor."

"And then?" I asked breathlessly.

"And then came the wicked sister," replied Solène drily. It was meant to sound indifferent, but you could see she was having difficulty going on. She got up from her chair. went over to the minibar, and poured herself a scotch. "I think I need a drink. How about you?"

I shook my head.

Solène slowly took a couple of sips from the cut-glass tumbler and then leaned on the dressing table.

"When I came back at the end of the summer, Mélanie introduced me to her boyfriend. He was really sweet, a regular sunny boy from California, and I must admit I was surprised that Mélanie had landed such an attractive guy."

She took another sip of her scotch.

"Yeah, well . . . The rest is a very short story. We went to a little café in Saint-Germain, and I told them all about my vacation and my seaside experiences in my usual lively way. I laughed and joked; I flirted a little with my sister's boyfriend. I can't say that I had any particular aim in view. I was just being myself, do you see?"

I nodded without a word. I could imagine the situation very clearly.

"And then it happened, as it always happened when Mélanie and I went somewhere together. I attracted all the attention, and my little sister paled beside me like a little moon and gradually fell totally silent."

"Oh my God," I said. I could guess what was coming next. "She's like a sun—everyone wants to be close to her" was how Allan Wood had described Solène.

"After a while, Victor had eyes only for me. No matter how enchanted he had been by Mélanie, he was now smitten with her big sister, who seemed to be much more suited to him both in character and in age. He waylaid me on the way to the boulevard Raspail—he'd waited secretly for the opportunity to be with me—and he kissed me behind my sister's back. 'Come on, just one kiss,' he said every time I laughingly turned him down. 'No one will see. And you have such a lovely mouth, no one could resist it.' And then later he said, 'Come to California with me. The sun shines there all year round, and we'll have a wonderful life together.' He was very good-looking and had a wonderfully easy manner, which I began to like more and more. Then came the time when I stopped saying no." Solène sighed and gazed into her glass.

"Perhaps I might have been capable of putting a stop to the whole thing, but in those days I didn't really understand. After all, I said to myself, I can't help it if a man falls in love with me, even if he is my sister's man. Who knows if Victor would have stayed with Mélanie if I'd behaved differently? But I was young and thoughtless, and the prospect of going to America with Victor made me cast all my reservations to the winds."

She looked at me and raised her hands in an apologetic gesture. "Good grief, who ever stays with their first love?" She shook her head. "I just hadn't understood how serious it all was for Mélanie. She was only seventeen, after all." Solène bit her lower lip.

"One day, she walked in on us. It was awful, the most terrible experience of my life." Solène faltered for a moment before going on. "For some minutes, she just stood in the doorway, completely pale, and neither of us dared speak a word. And then all of a sudden she just burst out screaming. She was totally hysterical. 'My God, Solène, how could you do this to me? You're my sister! You're my *sister!*' she kept on screaming. 'You could have had anyone. Why did you have to take Victor away from me, why?' And then she said the words that I still hear sometimes even today, and her dear, gentle voice was filled with hatred. 'The only thing that's important is that you get what you want; you don't care about anything else,' she said. 'I never want to see you again, do you hear? Get out of my sight!' "

"My God, that's awful!" I murmured.

"Yes, it was awful," said Solène. "In the weeks that followed,

Mélanie wouldn't speak a single word to me; not when my parents tried to make peace between us; not when, for the last time before my flight to San Francisco, I went into her room and tried to say good-bye to her. She just sat at her desk and wouldn't even turn around. It was as if she'd been turned to stone. I'd betrayed her; I'd hurt her deeply. She couldn't forgive me."

I put my hand to my mouth and looked in anguish at the blond woman leaning on the dressing table, fighting to maintain her composure.

"And later? Did you have any contact later on?" I finally asked.

Solène nodded. "We saw each other on one single occasion—at our parents' funeral. But that was not very pleasant." She put her glass down.

"When was that?"

"About three years after I went to California. By then, I was getting on in my career, I'd had my first big parts, success seemed to be falling into my lap, and I was so happy that I could give my parents that trip to the Côte d'Azur. I told you about that during our walk around the place Vendôme. Do you remember?" I nodded. How could I ever forget that walk?

"And then my parents had the accident on the way to Saint-Tropez. They both died instantaneously. My mother's sister was kind enough to let me know. The bodies had already been brought home. I flew to Paris. When Mélanie saw me at the funeral, she went completely wild. She screamed at me that I'd first taken her man away from her, and now her parents. I should just go away, because all I ever did was destroy everything."

"Oh my God, that's totally absurd!" I exclaimed in shock. "That wasn't your fault."

Solène wiped a tear from her cheek and gave me a hurt look. "And all I'd wanted to do was to give my parents their hearts' desire."

"There's no need to reproach yourself, Solène," I assured her. "At least not where your parents are concerned. My goodness, that was just a tragic accident. No one can help that kind of thing."

Solène nodded, taking out her handkerchief.

"That's what Aunt Lucie said, as well. She called me and said Mélanie had had a nervous breakdown. And that she was sure she hadn't meant those harsh words. Later, I heard that Mélanie had moved to somewhere near Le Pouldu, where our aunt lived. She obviously couldn't stand living in Paris anymore. She'd been living with our parents when the accident happened."

"And then?"

Solène shrugged her shoulders helplessly. "Nothing. I've heard nothing from Mélanie ever again. I've tried to respect her wishes. But I've never stopped missing her."

Twenty-eight

....

Solène came toward me and fell into her chair, exhausted. You could see what turmoil she was in.

"The affair with Victor isn't exactly the most glorious chapter in my life. I don't really like talking about it," she said, burying her face in her hands. Then she looked up again. "I wish I could undo it, but unfortunately that's impossible. How often I've cursed the day I took up with Victor. All I would have had to do was say no. It would have been so simple." She sat up and folded her hands. "Believe me, Alain, if I could turn back the clock, I would."

"What became of Victor then?" I asked.

"I don't know. Shortly after we arrived in San Francisco, I lost sight of him. And then I moved on myself." She stroked the arm of the chair with her fingers. "For me, it wasn't such a big deal—I just felt attracted to him."

"Like to me?" I asked.

Solène's face turned a delicate shade of pink. "Yes . . . perhaps. I do like you; I liked you from the start. What can I do?" She gave me a bright look despite her weepy eyes and tried to lighten the heavy atmosphere that had fallen over the room like a raven's wing. "You must surely have noticed? But this time, I suppose I have no chance."

She smiled, and I smiled, too. Then I became serious.

"I like you, too, Solène, a lot, in fact. I told you so yesterday evening on the terrace. That was a wonderful moment. I'm as unlikely to forget it as you are."

"And it's precisely that moment that may possibly turn out to be your nemesis."

I nodded and rubbed my forehead.

"Mélanie loves me and I love her," I replied unhappily. "I really love her, more than anything in the world. And the idea that she believes that the worst moment of her life was repeating itself is tearing my heart apart." I looked at Solène. "Why didn't you tell me sooner that she was your sister?"

Solène looked at me helplessly. "The idea never occurred to me, Alain. Why should it? That time on the place Vendôme, you told me you had fallen in love with a woman, but you never mentioned her name. Then there were the paparazzi and all the newspaper stories, and the woman in the red coat disappeared. But I knew nothing about that at first, and at the beginning even you didn't see any connection between our arrival and Mélanie's disappearance. Then Allan told me later on that you were looking for his daughter, Méla—and that was the first time I heard the name Mélanie. And yes, I admit that when Méla turned out to be the wrong Mélanie, I had some doubts for a moment. But the last I'd heard of my sister was that she was living in Brittany. Why should I have assumed that my sister was your Mélanie? It seemed totally unlikely to me. I mean, what an idiotic coincidence! I return to Paris after ten years and my sister has just fallen in love with a man that I could also like." She smiled wistfully. Then she reached for my hand.

"Believe me, Alain, I had no clue. And if I did, it was only a wisp of a clue. I certainly didn't want to pull the wool over your eyes. It was only when you told me about the two letters and that she always sat in that row when she went to the Cinéma Paradis that it dawned on me that it was Mélanie. You've just got to believe me." Her voice sounded despondent.

"It's all right, Solène," I said. "Of course I believe you. It's just tough luck that your paths crossed in the Cinéma Paradis. For the second time. But at least the whole thing makes sense to me now."

For a long time, we sat there in silence. I sat back in my chair, and my gaze fell on the golden scrolls on the clock on the mantelpiece. It was ten past four. I was incredibly tired, and yet not tired at all, and as I fell into a strange state of lethargy of the kind you probably feel when you've passed the point of no return, I ran through the whole story once again, with all its strange twists and turns, all its coincidences, some of which ultimately were not coincidences.

Cleverer men than I have tried to answer the question of what is fate and what is chance. Was it chance or fate that the sight of a striking young woman in a red coat touched my heart so deeply that I fell in love with her? Was it fate or chance that her sister was standing outside the Cinéma Paradis just one day later?

It was certainly not chance that I took a walk around the place Vendôme with Solène and was moved enough to take her in my arms when she told me about her parents' death, but it was certainly fateful, because it led to an embarrassing paparazzi photo in a newspaper that by chance fell into the hands of a young woman who had previously been struck by fate. A young woman in love who, far from Paris, was staying with her aunt in a place called Le Pouldu and was now convinced that the worst moment of her life was repeating itself.

On the other hand, something I had thought to be a coincidence at first, two things simply happening at the same time without any deeper meaning, had not been the case. Solène Avril had come to Paris and Mélanie had not turned up for our date. I hadn't seen any connection. Yet Mélanie had deliberately pulled out, and I now knew the reason why.

I didn't know if it was chance or fate that led to Mélanie standing there on the terrace of the Georges at the exact moment that Solène put her arms around me, but in any case, this innocent and yet not totally unintentional embrace was, for her, renewed proof that a man she loved had once more fallen for the charms of her sister. Upset and deeply disappointed, she had run off, and then given me an enigmatic and—it now became clear to me—resigned smile as, in a spontaneous gesture, she held her hand up to the window of the train.

Solène was the first to recover the power of speech. "We must find her, Alain," she said. "Nothing is lost yet. We must find Mélanie and explain everything to her."

I nodded slowly. Only now was my mind, overwhelmed as it was by impressions and images, beginning to see that there was now hope once more, that the chances of reaching the goal I desired so much had never been so good.

"At least I have a name at last—that will make things much easier." With a smile, I remembered playing the detective on the rue de Bourgogne. Now that it was out of the question that Mélanie had another man, it seemed all the stranger that she had disappeared into the building with the chestnut tree. In any case, the name Avril had not appeared on any of the name-plates.

"Mélanie Avril," I said, trying the name out. "That sounds so delightfully light. It makes you think of a spring day in Paris. The rain is bouncing from the cobbles, and then the heavens clear again, the sun is reflected in the puddles, and people are all in a good mood. . . ."

"Oh, Alain, you are truly hopeless. Mélanie's name isn't Avril. It's Fontaine. Just like mine. Solène Avril is my stage name."

"Oh," I said sheepishly. And then added a not very eloquent "Oh, I see!" I should really have realized that Avril was a stage name; everyone knows that lots of actors take on a catchy name.

Solène smiled. "Yes, my dear. That's the way it is in show business. My first name isn't Solène, either. . . . It's all made up."

"And what's your real name?"

"Marie. But that was far too unspectacular for me. And little Marie from the ground-floor flat in Saint-Germain no longer existed, anyway. So I just reinvented myself." She grinned. "I hope I haven't destroyed all your illusions now."

"Not at all." I waved dismissively. "Fontaine's a very nice surname, too."

And I meant what I said. I really did like the name. The

only problem I had with the new surname was that hundreds of Parisians were named Fontaine. It was one of the commonest French surnames, even if, regrettably, no one in the building on the rue de Bourgogne had been named Fontaine. Even my resourceful friend Robert would have had to put all the students in his faculty to work to comb through the Paris phone book. That is, *if* Mélanie Fontaine was actually in a phone book. Perhaps, like so many people today, she only had a cell phone. Although I found it easier to imagine her with an old black Bakelite telephone to her ear than a smartphone. Searching for a Mélanie Fontaine was not exactly going to be a piece of cake.

Solène seemed to have read my thoughts. "Don't worry, Alain," she said. "If necessary, I'll find her through my aunt. Mélanie was there, as you said, just a little while ago. I'm sure Aunt Lucie will have her address." She wrinkled her forehead. "Although Aunt Lucie did remarry after my uncle died. I hope the name will come back to me." She sighed in comic desperation. "Don't be afraid—I'll get hold of it somehow, even if I have to get on a train and go to Le Pouldu. Perhaps I should do that anyway. My family's not that big, after all."

Solène, whose name was actually Marie, was quite animated by the thought of finding Mélanie. "I'll find her, you'll see," she said several times.

"Thanks, Solène." For me, she would always be Solène.

When I left her in the early hours of the morning, she hugged me tight. "It's done me good to talk about it . . . after all these years." She looked me directly in the eye. "Do you know, Alain, I don't believe it was just a stupid coincidence that we met. I came to Paris to shoot the film. But I really came because I was homesick. I thought so often about the early days and my sister as I walked along the familiar old streets and alleys of Saint-Germain, and I wondered what she was doing. I went past our old home and looked to see what the name on the ground-floor flat was. I went to my parents' grave and told them how much I miss her. How much I miss Mélanie, I mean. And now I have the chance to make up for all the trouble I caused back then. This time, I'm not going to destroy anything." She shook her head determinedly. "This time, I'm going to make sure that my sister gets the man she loves. And who loves her," she added.

I found that very touching.

"And now, off you go." She gave me a little kiss on the lips. "But in my next life, I can't guarantee anything."

"In your next life, I'm sure you'll have a brother."

"Exactly," she said, her eyes sparkling. "One like you."

At the end of the long hotel corridor, I turned around once more. Solène was still standing there, watching me go. She was smiling, and the glow of the ceiling light caught her blond hair, making it gleam.

A few moments later, I walked out onto the place Vendôme. Paris was waking up.

Twenty-nine

....

All that love waits for is opportunity, Cervantes once said. All I was waiting for was the opportunity to take the woman I loved in my arms, and I was not very good at it. Waiting, I mean. Who likes waiting? I've never met anyone who does.

I spent the next few days in a state of happy and excited turmoil, which reminded me of the impatience you feel as a child just before Christmas, walking past the living room door, hoping to catch a glimpse of your presents. I began counting the hours. I've very rarely looked at my watch quite so often.

So far, I hadn't heard anything from Solène except for a cryptic phone call—interrupted by loud crackles on the line— telling me it wasn't easy but she was staying on the ball. She was shooting a picnic scene in the Bois de Boulogne and the signal wasn't very good.

In order to have something to do, I'd leafed through the Paris phone book under the letter *F*. The result was, as I might have expected, depressing. It began to look as if Solène would really have to go to Le Pouldu to find her aunt Lucie.

Robert found the whole story sensational. "What a story," he said. "She's a great girl, that Solène—I'd really like to meet her. Don't forget, Alain, you owe me a favor." My friend was also firmly convinced that he'd provided the decisive clue because he'd had the idea of writing the list of men's names beginning with *V*.

"You see," he said. "All you have to do is proceed systematically and you find the solution. Keep me in the loop. The suspense is killing me." And it was killing me, as well. When I wasn't working in the cinema, I walked through the Jardin du Luxembourg to calm down. I sat around in cafés, looking dreamily out the window. I lay motionless on the sofa at home, staring fixedly in the air until Orphée leaped up on me, meowing reproachfully. I spent every free minute picturing my reunion with Mélanie. Where it would be, how it would be, what she would say, what I would say—I fantasized the most magical and sublime dialogues. Those days, I would have been the perfect scriptwriter for a romantic movie. There was only one question I didn't ask myself: Would our meeting take place at all?

The late show at the Cinéma Paradis was *Design for Living*—an Ernst Lubitsch comedy based on the popular two men and one woman scenario, and as I put up the old posters with Miriam Hopkins, Gary Cooper, and Fredric March, I thought that if the film were ever to be remade, Solène Avril would be the ideal casting choice for the blond bombshell played by Miriam Hopkins: a woman unable to decide between two men, both in love with her, and both actually good friends, who ends up deciding to take both. She would surely have liked the famous last line: "It's a gentlemen's agreement." As a rule, gentlemen's agreements between men and women are not kept. I smiled. In our case, the design for living had worked out differently, but as with the old Lubitsch comedy, I was sure that everyone would be reconciled. I was hoping for a happy ending.

I decided that I'd ring Solène again that evening to ask her if there were any news. Then I took out my cell phone to see if I happened to have missed a message. But of course I hadn't.

I hadn't divulged the details of the crazy story of two very different sisters and the unwitting owner of a little art cinema to Madame Clément and François, but I had not been able to conceal my lovesick state and my constantly changing moods from them during the past couple of weeks. Euphoric infatuation, proud excitement, complete helplessness, and deepest depression were now followed by a phase of irritable nervousness.

In his laid-back way, François contented himself by raising his dark eyebrows as, for the fifth time that day, I came into the projection booth, hummed, and fussed around the cans of film and finally knocked over his cup of coffee.

Madame Clément was not that patient. "What on earth is the matter with you, Monsieur Bonnard? I can't stand it. Have you got ants in your pants or what?" she said in her blunt way as I kept tidying the program flyers over and over again, looking frequently at the display of my cell phone as I did so. "If you're just going to get in the way, why don't you go off and have a drink somewhere?"

"Don't be impertinent, Madame Clément," I said. "I can stand where I like in my own cinema."

"Of course you can, Monsieur Bonnard." Madame Clément nodded resolutely. "But not in my way, please!" With a sigh, I decided to follow her advice.

As the cinema began to fill up for the six o'clock performance of *Little White Lies,* I went out into the street, lit a cigarette, took a couple of steps with my head down, and bumped into a couple who were heading for the entrance of the Cinéma Paradis arm in arm.

"*Oh, pardon,*" I muttered, and looked up.

A woman with curly dark hair and a businessman—this time without his briefcase, and clearly having lost a considerable amount of weight—wished me good evening.

"*Bonsoir,*" I replied, nodding in confusion because the two of them looked so unashamedly happy. The dark-haired woman stopped and tugged her companion by the sleeve. "Shouldn't we tell him, Jean?" she asked, and turned to me without waiting for an answer.

"You're Monsieur Bonnard, the owner of the Paradis, aren't you?" she asked.

I nodded.

"We wanted to thank you." She beamed at me.

"Oh, yes," I said. "What for?"

"For your cinema. The Cinéma Paradis is to blame for our falling in love."

A blind man would have noticed that they were in love.

"My goodness!" I said. "Well, I'll be . . . . I mean . . . that's just wonderful!" I smiled. "That's the nicest thing that can happen to you in a cinema."

They both nodded happily.

"We couldn't get tickets that evening because the cinema

was sold out. . . . We'd both really been looking forward to the film and then . . . no tickets."

The businessman blinked behind his glasses. "She was disappointed. I was disappointed. What were we going to do with the evening now?"

"And then he invited me for a coffee and we discovered that we'd both been coming to the Paradis for a long time. Although I hadn't really noticed Jean before." She laughed, and I thought of how she'd always come to the afternoon performance alone with her little daughter.

"That's how we got to know each other. Jean was very unhappy because his girlfriend had left him. And I was also in a crisis because I'd discovered that my husband had been cheating on me with another woman. We sat there and talked and talked and . . . well, now we're together. And all because of cinema tickets we couldn't get. Isn't that an incredible coincidence?" She laughed, as if she still couldn't believe it.

I nodded. Life was full of incredible coincidences. Who should know that better than I?

In the café near the cinema, an old acquaintance was waiting for me. That is, he wasn't actually waiting for me, but, as he so often did, he had gone there to drink a glass of wine before the late show, and he looked up briefly as I entered.

It was the professor, and we exchanged nods before I went and sat at one of the little round tables. I had no real idea what I should order—my coffee consumption had gone through the roof in the last few days, or even weeks. If I went on like this, I was soon going to have a stomach ulcer.

"*Vous voulez?*" The waiter wiped the table energetically, brushing off a few crumbs.

Nothing better occurred to me. In crisis situations, there is nothing like a coffee.

"*Un café au lait, s'il vous plaît,*" I said. When the big white cup of hot coffee was standing in front of me, I took my cell phone out of my pocket. It was eight o'clock and gradually getting dark. I hoped that Allan Wood had finally stopped shooting his picnic scenes in the Bois de Boulogne and that I would be able to reach Solène.

She answered straightaway, but there was no real news. Solène had asked around again in their old neighborhood, but among the people who still remembered the Fontaine family, none was able to say where Mélanie had gone to live after her return from Brittany. Solène had rejected the idea of trying to contact all the Fontaines in Paris. "We can always still do that," she said. "But at the moment, that would waste too much time. Fortunately, we do have other options."

"*One* option?" I objected.

"But one that has every prospect of success. I'm doing all I can, Alain. Don't you think that I want to see my sister again as soon as possible? But we'll probably have to be patient until the weekend; I don't think I can get away before then."

I groaned. "But that's another three whole days!"

"I'll go to Le Pouldu this weekend," said Solène. "Don't worry, as soon as I've found my aunt, we'll find Mélanie, too. It's just a question of time now."

I sighed deeply and drummed on the pale marble tabletop with my fingers. I would really have liked a smoke.

"All this waiting around is driving me crazy. I have a really funny feeling, Solène. We're so close now. I just hope nothing goes wrong at the last moment. Your aunt could fall off a ladder and break her neck. Or Mélanie could be on a cruise and meet some stupid millionaire, and then I'd be out of the running for good and all."

Solène laughed. "You watch too many movies, Alain. Everything's going to be all right."

"Yeah, yeah," I said. "I've heard that so many times. I hate all this optimism. You're just like my friend Robert."

"Robert? Who's that?"

"An astrophysicist who loves women and never lets anything spoil his good mood," I growled, having to admit that that was true. I'd never known Robert to be in a bad mood. "He'll keep on saying that everything will be all right when he takes a parachute jump and his canopy doesn't open!"

"But that sounds wonderful," said Solène. "I hope you'll introduce me to him sometime."

"All in good time," I said. "At the moment, we've still got to find Mélanie."

As I put the cell phone down beside my cup, I caught the professor's gaze. I nodded an apology. When you use a cell phone, you end up bothering the whole world with your private business, as if you were sitting in your armchair at home.

"Are you trying to find someone?" The look in his clear blue eyes was full of sympathy. "Excuse my just talking to you like this, but I couldn't help hearing your conversation."

He gave me a friendly smile. And I suddenly had déjà vu. There had been a previous occasion when I'd just chanced to be sitting in this little café with the professor. Then he had wished me good luck. That had been several weeks earlier, when I'd spoken to Mélanie for the first time.

I shrugged and nodded. In the intimate atmosphere of the

café, the professor suddenly seemed like a dear and trusted old friend. "Yes," I said with a sigh. "But that's a very long story."

The professor put down his paper and looked at me attentively. "One of the few advantages of old age is having a lot of time. If you like, I'd be glad to listen."

I looked into the wise eyes of this old man whom I didn't actually know and thought that my story would find a good listener in him. So I began to tell my tale, and the professor leaned toward me, put his hand to his ear, and listened carefully to what I said.

"You actually know her," I said, interrupting myself at one point. "It's that young woman in the red coat, the one I had a date with the other week. You saw her in the cinema that evening, in the foyer, remember?" I sighed. "My goodness, I don't know how often I went to that house in the rue de Bourgogne because I was sure she lived there. I had walked her home, after all, right into the courtyard, where there's an old chestnut tree. But she wasn't there, and none of the people who live in the building had seen her. I was beginning to despair of my own sanity."

I took a sip of my coffee, and saw the professor raise his eyebrows in astonishment. "But she *was* in the rue de Bourgogne," he said slowly. "I've seen her there myself." He nodded, and at first I could hardly believe my ears. "I know the building with the chestnut tree," the professor continued. "It's opposite a stationer's shop, isn't it?"

"Yes!" I exclaimed, feeling the adrenaline filling every fiber of my being. "Yes! So it is. . . . But how . . ." I faltered.

"Once a week I visit an old friend in the rue de Bourgogne. We've known each other since our university days, and he's since gone almost completely blind. His name is Jacob Montabon.

And sometime at the end of March—I believe it was just before your rendezvous—I met the young woman on the stairs, and we exchanged a few words. She told me that she was staying in her friend's apartment for a week to look after her cat. She was really delightful."

And that was when the pieces of the jigsaw puzzle finally began to fit together to make the whole picture. I thought of the big black cat with green eyes that had jumped down from the chestnut tree into the courtyard that evening, and I almost gave a yell of triumph. I thought of the apartment door on the second floor behind which I'd heard the angry meowing of a cat. I thought of a cat that would only ever drink out of flower vases. Mélanie's friend's pet. The friend who worked in the bar of a grand hotel. I thought of the nagging voice of Monsieur Nakamura assuring me that his neighbor was never there in the evenings, and that when she did come back late at night, she always thoughtlessly let the door slam.

It was the night owl! The night owl was Mélanie's friend who could never go to the cinema with her on Wednesdays because she was working. And her name was . . . Once again I could see Monsieur Nakamura in front of me.

"Leblanc!" I blurted. "Her friend's name is Leblanc."

The professor thought for a moment. "Yes, I do believe that's what she said—Leblanc. Linda Leblanc."

I leaped up and hugged the professor. Then I rushed to the door.

"Hey! Monsieur Bonnard. You've left your cell phone behind," he shouted after me. But by then, I was already out on the street.

Thirty

....

"Wait here—I'll be right back!" I shouted to the taxi driver as we stopped outside the building in the rue de Bourgogne. I jumped out and pressed the bell next to the nameplate engraved with the name Leblanc like a madman. No one answered. I'd already thought that would happen, but I wanted to be absolutely sure.

I tore the rear door of the car open and fell into the backseat. "Let's go," I shouted. "To the Ritz, please. *Vite, vite!* Get a move on!"

The taxi driver, a dark-skinned Senegalese who didn't seem to understand the word *quickly*, looked at me with his big, wide brown eyes and smiled broadly. "Why people in Paris always so damn hurry?" he said hoarsely, changing calmly into second gear. "You not miss appointment, but miss everything else in life." He rolled his eyes meaningfully. "In my home is proverb: 'Only who walk slow see important thing.'" Nodding with self-satisfaction, he crawled along the rue de Bourgogne.

It was always the same. Whenever you got into a taxi in Paris, you ended up either with a political radical who would hold forth morosely about the state of the *grande nation* and the uselessness of all politicians while underlining his views by banging the steering wheel or you would get an amateur philosopher. Our man from Senegal was obviously one of the second type. "But couldn't we go a bit faster?" I urged. "It's really very important." I put my hand meaningfully to my heart.

The Senegalese turned around to me and grinned. "Okay, boss," he said. "You say. I drive tack-tack."

I wasn't really sure if "tack-tack" was a kind of war cry or the Senegalese version of "zigzag," but in any case, a few minutes later we were hurtling at breakneck speed through the narrow one-way streets of the government quarter toward the pont de la Concorde in order to get to the right bank of the Seine. I leaned back and watched the obelisks flashing past until the driver, his hand hard down on the horn, jumped a light that was just turning red.

A pedestrian jumped aside in terror, and for a moment I saw his enraged face appear in the car window and then vanish again. "Old people think street belong them," my driver said, unimpressed. "We still nearly had green." Traveling at the same speed, he turned to me again, and the car lurched and skidded dangerously. "At home, proverb say: 'Old man should stay in hut, or lion eat him.'"

"Our proverb says: 'You should always look where you're driving!'" I said in terror.

"Ah. Ha-ha. You good man. That damn funny." He laughed loudly, as if I'd made a joke, but at least he was now looking at the road ahead again.

We continued along the rue Royale, all its lanes jammed with traffic, and then we finally turned into the somewhat quieter rue Saint-Honoré. I sighed with relief and sank back in my seat again.

Linda Leblanc, one of the few people who could definitely reveal where Mélanie was living at the moment, worked in the bar of an old grand hotel in Paris. And unlike Fontaine, the surname Leblanc was relatively uncommon.

Of course, the hotel could also have been the Meurice, Fouquet's, or the Plaza Athénée, but as things stood, I figured I might just as well try my luck in the Ritz first of all. At least I already knew the Hemingway Bar.

A few minutes later, my taxi stopped on the place Vendôme. The driver looked at his watch and nodded with satisfaction. "Was good fast, yes?"

I gave him the most generous tip I'd ever given in my life.

There wasn't much going on in the Hemingway Bar at this time, not yet anyway. I stood in the entrance for a moment and looked around. Behind the bar, the bartender stood rattling his shaker enthusiastically before pouring its pink-hued contents into a cocktail glass and decorating the rim with a skewer of fruit.

Two waitresses were leaning on the bar. One of them tripped lightly over to me as I sat down underneath a photograph of Hemingway at his typewriter in his home in Cuba. I recognized her again immediately. It was the young woman with the dark chignon that Allan had said moved like a ballet dancer.

She gave me a professional smile. "*Bonsoir, monsieur.* What can I get you?"

I leaned forward to read her name tag. Melinda Leblanc. Linda. *Bingo!*

Thanks, Melinda. I heard Allan Wood's voice and my head began to buzz.

"Monsieur?" Melinda gave me a questioning look. "What would you like me to get you?"

I leaned forward over the table, rested my chin in both hands, and looked up at her. "How about an address?"

Thirty-one

....

After I had introduced myself to an astonished Melinda Leblanc as Alain Bonnard, her smile vanished. "Oh," she said. "You're him!" Her voice sounded anything but enthusiastic.

"Yes," I said with some irritation. "I'm him. You are Mélanie Fontaine's friend, aren't you?" She gave a barely perceptible nod. "Thank God," I said with relief. "Listen, you have to give me Mélanie's address. I've been searching for her for weeks."

Linda eyed me coolly. "I don't have to do anything at all. I don't think Mélanie is particularly interested in seeing you again—after all you've done to her."

"No!" I hissed. "I mean . . . for God's sake, I know what you're getting at, but it's all just a terrible misunderstanding. I haven't done anything at all. Please help me!"

"Well, well," she replied grimly, "a misunderstanding. Mélanie's version sounded somewhat different."

"Then listen to my version," I pleaded. "Please! Give me ten minutes, and I'll explain everything. I simply have to talk to

Mélanie. I . . . Good grief, don't you understand? I love your friend."

Love is always a good argument. Linda looked at me searchingly for a few seconds as if trying to decide whether her response would be favorable or not. Then she went over to the bar, exchanged a few words with the bartender, and signaled for me to follow her.

It took a great deal of persuasiveness on my part to convince the woman with the dark chignon that my intentions were good and to coax the address out of her—that address which was so important to me—together with a promise not to warn her friend in advance under any circumstances.

The fifteen-minute conversation—both quiet and excited—we had on a sofa only a few yards from the Hemingway Bar revealed that the name Alain Bonnard was far from music to the ears of Linda Leblanc. Admittedly, Mélanie had concealed from her friend the fact that the actress Solène Avril was her sister, but she had told Linda that she had fallen hopelessly in love with the owner of the Cinéma Paradis, who, in the most outrageous manner, had taken up with another woman only a few days after their first date.

"Mélanie had been going on about it to me for weeks. She kept talking about this incredibly nice cinema owner whom she didn't dare talk to. I was so glad when the jerk finally got around to chatting her up—oops, sorry!"

"That's okay," I said. "Carry on."

The day after my date with Mélanie, Linda had returned to her apartment in the rue de Bourgogne, where her friend was waiting for her with an ecstatically happy cat, breakfast, and great news.

I clearly remembered how indecisive Mélanie had looked outside the front door, the hesitation that made me hope for a moment that she was going to ask me to go inside with her. But it hadn't been her apartment. And the next day, her friend was coming back from her vacation. So Mélanie had said good-bye to me with unspoken regret. And I had lost all trace of her.

"Then when she got back from Le Pouldu a week later, she was devastated," Linda continued. "It was all over; the cinema owner had found another woman. At least that's what she said. How could I have guessed that all her unhappiness was based on a stupid newspaper article? And some traumatic experience she'd had as a girl. She presented it as if it were a proven fact that she'd been deceived. Anyway, she just sat on my sofa, sobbing that she'd never ever set foot in that damn cinema again."

Linda shook her head in bewilderment. "I tried to talk to her, suggested that she should try to sort the matter out directly with you. But she just kept on saying that she knew how it would all end. It had already happened to her once before. She was totally out of it, and so I thought it was best not to keep on at her about it. I had not the slightest clue that Solène Avril's her sister. I didn't even know that she had a sister at all! Mélanie doesn't like talking about the past."

Linda looked at me with a shrug of the shoulders. She could, of course, distinctly remember Solène Avril coming into the Hemingway Bar with Allan Wood. She even thought she could vaguely remember me.

It was only later that she'd read in the papers that Allan Wood was shooting some scenes from his new film in the Cinéma Paradis. But like all of us, she'd been unaware of the connections and assumed that the cheating cinema owner Alain

Bonnard, whose cinema was enjoying all that press attention, was sleeping with a different woman.

"My goodness, how complicated it all is," she said as, at the end of our conversation, she gave me an address in the eighth arrondissement, not far from the pont Alexandre III. "Mélanie loves that bridge so much that she sometimes walks to work just so she can stop and look over the parapet for a moment. Did you know that?"

I nodded. "Yes—on our very first date, she told me about the pont Alexandre."

Linda smiled. "What I mean to say, Mélanie is a very exceptional girl. Very strong-willed. And she's so vulnerable. You must promise me that you're going to make her happy."

"There's nothing I'd like better," I said. "If I can only get to see her."

"You might actually have run into her when you were making your inquiries in the rue de Bourgogne, because she works in a little antiques store in the rue de Grenelle. It's called A la Recherche du Temps Perdu. Perhaps you passed it sometime?"

I put the note away with a smile.

They say that Paris is always a good accomplice when it comes to making romantic dreams come true. My first impulse was to go to Mélanie that very second, to ring her doorbell and surprise her. I was already standing on the place Vendôme, waving for a taxi, when I suddenly felt uncertain. Was it really such a good idea just to drop in on Mélanie without warning in the middle of the night? Who knew if she'd even open the door to me. Perhaps she would simply refuse to believe me if I just turned up at her place and told her through the intercom that I had nothing to do with her sister. After all, she had seen me in the Georges with Solène.

I gnawed at my knuckles and thought. Just don't lose your nerve now, Alain, I urged myself. Don't do anything rash. I had Mélanie's address; that was the most important thing. Any further steps should be carefully considered. Perhaps it would be better to go and see her the next day at the antiques store, better prepared and armed with a huge bouquet of flowers. At that moment, although it was no longer important, I remembered the name of the owner. It was Papin. Papin, not Lapin, as I'd thought at the time. I laughed hysterically.

The taxi driver had rolled down his window and was looking curiously at me. "*Alors, monsieur*—what's up? Are you getting in?"

"I've changed my mind," I said. What I needed now was not a taxi, but advice from an ally.

It was only when I went to call Solène that I noticed that my cell phone was no longer in my jacket pocket. I'd probably left it in the café. That was annoying, but not disastrous. I looked up at the windows of the grand hotel. I'd manage without a telephone. Luckily, I was, for once, in the right place.

"Alain! You again!" exclaimed Solène in surprise as she opened the door of the Imperial Suite. "We mustn't let these nighttime visits become a bad habit!"

She smiled and stood aside, and I went in.

"You won't believe it," I said. "I know where Mélanie lives."

························

Thirty-two

The following day was the longest day of my life. But in my memory, the bittersweet anguish of waiting and my anxiety—partly arising from a small remnant of doubt—is already beginning to fade. That's how people are. When something ends well, they forget all the rest. And I'm no exception.

Solène had been right about everything, and I was glad I'd followed her advice, even if I found it difficult at first. After all, it was I who had found out where Mélanie lived. But it was not to be me who went to the little antiques store in the rue de Grenelle just before the lunch break the next day.

Solène had implored me to let her go first. "It's only when all the old stories have been gotten out of the way that we can start anew," she had said as we sat on the sofa in her suite, plotting like a pair of conspirators.

So Solène was to be given the first chance to hash things out with her sister. She would explain everything to her, and then that was where I would come in. We'd agreed that Solène would call me when she'd spoken to her sister. I'd remembered just in time that I no longer had my cell phone, and so I gave Solène the number of my landline.

Early that morning, I'd left my apartment to buy flowers for Mélanie. My heart hammered as I chose twenty sweet-smelling, delicate pink tea roses and bore them happily home. I put them in water and then sat down on the sofa with my telephone to wait for Solène's call.

I realized, of course, that it could take quite some time for the sisters to talk everything over. Between men, a thing like that would be dealt with relatively quickly with a few brief words and a handshake, but women are obsessed with details and always have to discuss everything very minutely. I tried to read the papers a bit, but I quickly saw that what was going on in the world in general was not of the slightest interest to me.

Noon came, the afternoon dragged on, and the telephone was silent. I made myself one coffee after another. My heart was beating irregularly. Orphée sniffed at the roses.

At four thirty, I checked the phone to make sure it was actually working. At five o'clock, I was seized by an unutterable sadness. All of a sudden, I was sure that the meeting of the two sisters had ended in an unimaginably dramatic scene, and that there was no hope for me, either.

At five thirty, I leaped up from the sofa and prowled up and down in the living room. No one needed that long to talk things over, not even two women.

"Damn it! Damn it! Damn it!" I shouted, and Orphée shot under the armchair, peering out fearfully from beneath it. I cursed Solène's idiotic idea, I cursed myself for not going straight to the rue de Grenelle that morning, and finally, in an attack of hopeless despair, I snatched the roses out of their vase. "Oh, what's the point? It's all finished," I said, and stuck them headfirst in the wastebasket.

Then the phone rang.

"Alain?" Solène's voice sounded tearful.

"Yes?" I said huskily. "Why didn't you call? What's going on?" I ran my fingers nervously through my hair. "Have you seen her, or what?"

Solène sniffed down the line and then burst out in tears. "Oh, Alain," she wept.

Oh, Alain! That was all. Good grief, I sometimes hate women! I'd been agonizing on the sofa for hours in a state of extreme tension, I was close to having a heart attack, and all this woman could say was, "Oh, Alain!"

What had happened? Had they not been reconciled? Had Mélanie's old hatred been too strong? Had Solène arrived too late? Had Mélanie perhaps jumped off the bridge by then? Or had she held one of those old pistols to her brow and pulled the trigger?

I forced myself to remain calm. "Solène," I said firmly. "Tell me what happened."

"Oh, Alain," she sobbed again. "It was so awful. I'm totally wiped out. Mélanie has just gone home and I'm on my way back to the hotel." She breathed in with a sob. "It's our nerves, you know. We shouted at each other so loudly. We wept. But finally we made up. Everything's all right again." She made a sound somewhere between laughing and crying. "I just can't stop crying, Alain. . . ."

She went on sobbing, while I sank to the floor beside the wastebasket in relief.

I was never to find out what had passed between the two sisters in those unimaginably long hours before they finally made their peace after ten long years with a tearful embrace. Only one thing mattered to me: Mélanie wanted to see me. That evening at nine o'clock, she'd be waiting for me on the terrace of the Café de l'Esplanade.

Thirty-three
....

There are wishing places in life; places where you wish for something, places where you find yourself, places that leave nothing to be desired. I may be biased—that's certainly the case—but for me, the pont Alexandre III is just such a place. Paris has many bridges, some of them very famous. But that old bridge with its wonderful candelabra, with the four tall pillars on which gilded horses seem to be flying in the air, with all its dolphins and cherubs and sea gods dancing playfully beneath the stone parapet seems to me to be different from any other bridge that I know.

If you live and work in Saint-Germain, you very rarely go there. Of course I'd driven over the pont Alexandre, but I'd never taken the trouble to stop and get out. And I had never crossed the old bridge on foot—not until that day when I was to see Mélanie again.

After Solène's call, I had carefully taken the roses out of the wastebasket and put them back in the vase again. I knew the

Café de l'Esplanade. It was not far from the pont Alexandre, on the corner of the rue de Grenelle and the rue Fabert, and when the weather's good, you can sit there well into the evening, looking out over a splendid view.

It was six o'clock. Still three hours to go till my meeting with Mélanie. That was definitely too long. I couldn't think straight, and I wandered about in the apartment, my restlessness growing every minute. I went into the bathroom and looked searchingly in the mirror. The bruises around my left eye were fading. I went back into the living room, sat on the sofa, and closed my eyes for a moment. A short while later, I leaped up again and put on a fresh shirt for the second time that day. I shaved again, put on aftershave, combed my hair, looked for my brown suede shoes, and, just to be on the safe side, put my jacket on again.

As I got ready, more nervously and carefully than I ever had done in my life, I imagined Mélanie doing the same somewhere on the other side of the Seine. Orphée sat on the bureau in the hall, attentively watching all of my movements. She seemed to sense that something was different than usual. Her calmness made me even more nervous.

And then I had an idea that seemed to suit my impatient mood very well. Why should I stay in the apartment any longer anyway? It was a beautifully mild evening, and I would just go and intercept Mélanie on the way. I was sure that she'd walk to the Café de l'Esplanade over her favorite bridge. How lovely it would be if I was there on the bridge waiting for her.

I took the roses out of the water. Two of the opulent pink blooms were a bit crumpled, but the rest had survived being crammed in the wastebasket.

"Wish me luck, Orphée," I said as I stood at the door. Orphée sat enthroned on the bureau and looked at me out of her green eyes without moving.

I pulled the door shut behind me and went on my way.

Thirty-four

....

It was a quarter to eight when I walked onto the pont Alexandre III. The first thing I saw was a bride in a full white dress, leaning on the parapet as she snuggled up to her brand-new husband. They were standing on the left side of the wide sidewalk, smiling into a photographer's camera. Brides are like chimney sweeps: You're always glad to see them because you think luck will be on your side. But it wasn't just that.

When I stopped about halfway across the bridge and leaned over the stone parapet, I was suddenly surrounded by a sense of magic I had seldom felt in my life before. The air was soft and golden, and the view out over the river filled every fiber of my being with an exhilarating sense of vastness and beauty. On the left bank, the cars streamed tirelessly along the Avenue de New York; on the right bank of the Seine, where the glass roofs of the Grand Palais and the Petit Palais stood out against the sky, there was no traffic. You could see the linden trees, which in a few weeks would spread their sweet perfume. A couple of stone steps led directly down to the quiet riverbank, where a few people were taking a walk and the houseboats were bobbing up and down in the water. Beneath me, a *bateau-mouche* was gliding almost silently down the river; farther away, the broad arches of the pont des Invalides spanned the river, and in the distance the Eiffel Tower seemed quite small.

After all the excitement of the last few weeks, I was engulfed by a wonderful, sublime sense of perfect calm. I took a deep breath, and a single sentence filled my whole mind: Now everything will be all right. The sky began to change color and the whole of Paris was transformed into a magic lavender-colored place that seemed to be hovering a few yards above the ground.

At the very moment the lamps came on, seeming to shine on the bridge like little white moons, I saw her. An hour too early, she was coming along the bridge in a summery dress, and she seemed to be in no hurry. She was wearing red ballet flats, had draped a little cardigan over her shoulders, and with every step the hem of her dress fluttered around her legs. She was walking on the side where I was leaning on the parapet, but she was so lost in her own thoughts that she noticed me only when she was standing almost directly in front of me. "Alain!" she said. Surprise produced a dear little smile on her face, and she tucked her hair behind her ear in that little gesture I knew so well. "What are you doing here so early?"

"Waiting for you," I said huskily. All the fine words I'd intended to say when we met were forgotten; the roses lying on the parapet behind me were forgotten. I saw her eyes, which were red from crying, and her cheeks, which were suffused with a delicate blush. I saw her trembling lips, and my heart was almost torn apart with joy and excitement and relief and happiness. "You're the only one I'm waiting for!"

In the twinkling of an eye, we were in each other's arms, crying, laughing. Our lips met without the need for words. We kissed, and the seconds became years, and the years became a piece of eternity. We kissed beneath an old lantern that hung over us like a moon among moons. We were kissing on one of the loveliest bridges in Paris, which at that moment belonged to us alone. We flew up into the sky, higher and higher, and Paris became a star among the stars.

We went on standing there for a long time, overwhelmed with happiness, two time travelers who had finally reached their desired destination, looking at the reflection of the lights in the river. We leaned on the parapet and our fingers entwined as they had done that first time.

"Why didn't you just come to the Cinéma Paradis at the time?" I asked softly. "You only had to trust me."

"I was afraid," she said, and her dark eyes shimmered. "I was so afraid of losing you that I preferred to give you up for lost of my own accord."

I took her back in my arms. "Oh, Mélanie . . ." I said softly, burying my face in her hair, which smelled of vanilla and orange blossom. I held her very tight, trying to contain the wave of tenderness that washed over me. "You'll never lose me. I promise you that," I said. "You'll never get rid of me. You'll see."

She nodded and laughed and wiped a tear from her cheek. And then she said exactly what I'd been thinking as I stood on the bridge. "Now everything will be all right."

There was a shuffling sound behind us. We turned around and, to our amazement, saw the old man slouching across the bridge in his slippers. He was bent over as he walked and every now and again thrust his fist into the air.

"Everything here's a total rip-off!" he gasped angrily. "A total rip-off!"

We looked at each other and laughed.

When we walked over the pont Alexandre arm in arm a moment later to get to the other bank of the Seine and the Café de l'Esplanade, it was eight thirty.

At the spot where we'd just been kissing, a forgotten bouquet of roses lay on a stone parapet, evidence that even wise old men can occasionally be wrong.

"We'd actually arranged to meet half an hour from now," I said. "Why were you on the bridge so early?"

"I just wanted to be here." Mélanie shrugged in embarrassment. "I know it sounds a bit odd, but at quarter to eight I suddenly had the feeling that I absolutely must go to the pont Alexandre. I thought I could just as well wait on the bridge until we met in the café. And then suddenly you were there, too." She looked at me and shook her head, laughing. "I suppose we both just had the same idea!"

"Yes," I said, and smiled, too. "Looks like it!" We reached the end of the bridge, and Robert's words came back to me. He'd been right: Life isn't a movie where two people meet and then lose each other, only to meet by chance a few weeks later at the Trevi Fountain because they've both simultaneously had the idea of throwing a coin into the fountain and making a wish.

But sometimes, inexplicably, it is.

Epilogue

....

A year later, the premiere of *Tender Thoughts of Paris* was held in the Cinéma Paradis. The movie became one of the most successful Allan Wood had ever made.

In the months in between, a lot had happened.

First of all, I'd gotten my cell phone back. The professor had taken it to the cinema for me the next evening, but fortunately I wasn't there. I was at Mélanie's, and we had forgotten the world around us.

When the filming was over, Allan Wood had flown to New York with his daughter, Méla, to show her his favorite places and then to go fishing in the Hamptons—his latest passion.

Solène had bought herself a massive apartment near the Eiffel Tower—in order to have, as she said with a twinkle in her eye, a little pied-à-terre in Paris. Mélanie and Solène met up whenever Solène was in the city, and that happened quite often. Sometimes the two sisters also came to the Cinéma Paradis to see an old movie, but Mélanie never sat in row seventeen again.

Madame Clément had gotten herself a little dog. And François had recently found a girlfriend. She often sat beside him in the projection booth, waiting patiently until the show ended.

Monsieur and Madame Petit's marriage announcement was stuck up on the big bulletin board in my office. They were the two fortunate people who'd fallen in love because there were no more tickets for them.

Melissa had passed her exams summa cum laude and had gone to Cambridge for a postgraduate year.

Robert, somewhat nonplussed, had remained behind, but he soon found his feet again, and a month later he introduced me to a classy dark-haired beauty called Laurence.

The greatest thing, though, was that my apartment had been occupied by a woman for four weeks. Melanie had moved in with me, and the place was full of boxes that had not yet been unpacked. It didn't bother me. To wake up in the morning with her lovely face as the first thing I saw made my happiness complete.

All the puzzles had been solved, all the questions had been answered. There was only one thing that kept running through my mind: Who was the old man in the slippers? I'd been to the building in the rue de Bourgogne several times with Mélanie, the building with the old chestnut tree in the courtyard. Her friend Linda had invited us to a meal. Linda's skill as a cook was limited, to say the least, but, on the other hand, she did make wonderful cocktails. I was never to see the old man in the slippers again. Some things remain a mystery forever.

On the evening of the premiere, crowds flocked to the Cinéma Paradis. I saw several well-known faces. Solène Avril was there, of course, because my cinema was more or less her local,

and she was the incontestable star of the show. Howard Galloway was lying in his hotel with a virus, feeling at odds with the
world. Allan Wood had flown over, as had several members of
the film crew—I even saw Carl, who looked totally different,
because he'd shaved off his beard and was now running around
with a Hemingway mustache. The journalists were already
waiting for the stars in the auditorium, and Robert was waiting
for me to introduce him to Solène at last. All my friends and
acquaintances were there—there were a few more than there had
been a year before.

Linda had taken the evening off and was visiting the Cinéma
Paradis for the first time, the professor and the Petits were there,
and I even found the wrong Mélanie from the building in the
rue de Bourgogne in the foyer.

They all wanted to see *Tender Thoughts of Paris,* and I was
also particularly looking forward to it, but seeing all the familiar
faces smiling at me kept me thinking of my own story.

Suddenly, Robert was at my side. "Now introduce her to
me at last," he said. "I've specially come on my own."

I sighed. "You're evil, Robert, you know that?"

I took him by the sleeve and led him into my office, where
Solène, together with Mélanie, Allan Wood, and Carl Sussman,
was drinking coffee and waiting for the film to begin. "We've
even reserved a table in the Brasserie Lipp for afterward," she
said. Solène was superstitious. No toasts until after the show—
anything else would bring bad luck.

"Solène, here's someone who really wants to meet you." I
pushed my friend in through the door. "This is Robert, the in-
corrigible optimist. . . . I've already told you about him."

Solène looked at my blond, suntanned friend with his

sparkling eyes, and you could see that she liked him. "Ah, Robert!" she said. "*Enchanté, enchanté!* Why has Alain hidden you away from me for so long? You're a chemist, aren't you?"

"An astrophysicist," Robert replied with a grin as he absorbed the sight of this radiant woman.

"An astrophysicist—that's so great!" said Solène, and anyone who didn't know her would have thought that she had been wild about astrophysics all her life. "You must tell me more later on—I love astrophysics!"

And then we went into the auditorium and the show began.

Of course, theater is not the same as the cinema. On the screen, there isn't the same sense of immediacy that you get from a stage, and the audience doesn't have the same opportunity to express enthusiasm or displeasure in a way that makes the actors or directors feel it directly. Anyone is free to leave the cinema if they don't like the film, but public reaction is confined to sold-out houses or empty auditoriums. But anyone who has ever been to a movie premiere, especially if the actors were there, knows that it's a really unique experience. Cinema also has one incontrovertible advantage compared with the theater; nowhere on any stage in the world is the illusion more perfect, identification closer, and reality more strongly suspended than in a dark cinema looking at a screen. In the theater, people laugh; less frequently, they cry. But the cinema, with its films, is the place where really great emotions are evoked, the place where everything that goes on beyond the dark velvet curtains has, for a while, no meaning at all. It's the place where dreams become reality.

Tender Thoughts of Paris was that kind of film. It was a bittersweet comedy that hit people where they were most vulnerable: in the heart.

When the last lines had been spoken and the music accompanying the credits had died away, there was, just for a moment, an unusual silence in the auditorium. You could have heard a pin drop. Then applause flooded through the rows of seats. I was sitting beside Mélanie, who had a crumpled handkerchief in her hand and clapped like everyone else. At that moment, I was just one spectator among all the others.

When the director and his star appeared before the audience, they chanted their "Bra-vo! Bra-vo! Bra-vo!" for several minutes—that wonderful sign of the greatest appreciation, which is the same in all languages.

Then I went up front, too. The journalists asked their questions. Photos were taken. Allan Wood said a few words. Solène was delightful, as always. The audience laughed and clapped.

Finally, Solène raised her hand with a smile. "This film is something very special for me, and filming in Paris, most of all in this cinema, is something I will never forget," she began. "Because I have—as a result of some very strange coincidences that would be too complicated to explain here—rediscovered someone who means a lot to me: my sister."

She stretched out her hands and Mélanie rose hesitantly from her seat. "She doesn't like the limelight," said Solène with a twinkle in her eye, "but this evening she has to make an exception. After all, we were here together as children, watching films."

Amid applause from the audience, Mélanie came up to the front. Her cheeks were bright red and she gave an embarrassed smile as Solène hugged her. Seeing the two so dissimilar sisters together like that was something that left no one unmoved.

"How can you beat that?" Allan Wood sighed, beaming behind his glasses.

One after another, those in the audience got up from their seats, clapping frenetically. Then I stepped forward, answered a few questions, and said a few words of thanks. The first spectators were already turning to go when there was one more interruption.

"What is your favorite film, Monsieur Bonnard?" shouted one of the journalists.

"My favorite film?" I repeated, and thought for a moment. All of a sudden, silence fell across the whole auditorium. Mélanie was standing beside me, and I took her hand. She looked at me, and in her eyes I saw all my happiness, my whole world. "You'll never see my favorite film on any screen in the world," I replied with a smile. "Not even here in the Cinéma Paradis."

Les Amours au Paradis

THE TWENTY-FIVE LOVE STORIES FROM THE CINÉMA PARADIS

Breathless (A Bout de Souffle)
Before Sunrise
Camille Claudel
Casablanca
César and Rosalie (César et Rosalie)
Cinema Paradiso
Cyrano de Bergerac
The Green Ray (Le Rayon Vert)
The English Patient
The Things of Life (Les Choses de la Vie)
The Girl on the Bridge (La Fille sur le Pont)
The Last Métro (Le Dernier Métro)
The Lovers on the Bridge (Les Amants du Pont-Neuf)
The Unbearable Lightness of Being
An American in Paris
A Good Year
Breakfast at Tiffany's

Goethe!
Children of Paradise (Les Enfants du Paradis)
Orpheus (Orphée)
Design for Living
Pride and Prejudice
Something's Gotta Give
A Room with a View
Hunting and Gathering (Ensemble, c'est tout)

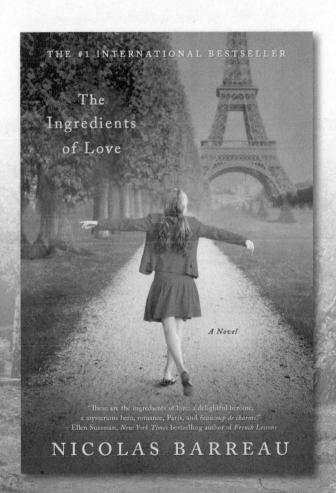